SUSAN COMBS

Susan Combs, a fourth generation rancher and former trial attorney, lives in Texas with her husband and three children. She says juggling writing, a four hundred mile drive to her ranch, and a family has meant her life is very chaotic. She hopes someday to share her experiences in cleaning out cattle troughs, leaping for the top fence of a corral when shipping cattle, and getting stranded miles from the nearest habitation.

A PERFECT MATCH

Susan Combs

A KISMET™ Romance

METEOR PUBLISHING CORPORATION
Bensalem, Pennsylvania

KISMET™ is a trademark of Meteor Publishing Corporation

Copyright © 1990 Susan Combs
Cover Art copyright © 1990 Alan Reingold

First Printing December 1990.

ISBN: 1-878702-22-X

Printed in the United States of America

ONE

Ross Harding slumped behind the steering wheel of the rental car, and reminded himself how much he hated baby-sitting. Checking his watch, he saw that it was barely five-thirty, time for the first wave of New Yorkers to pour out of their underground holes like rats fleeing floodwaters.

The early October breeze curled in through the open window and ruffled his hair, carrying with it sharp scents of roasting chestnuts, automobile exhaust, and something else unique to Manhattan—a blend of pulsating excitement, money, and power.

He yawned, feeling his jaw pop with strain. When Walker had told him about this job so soon after his last one, Ross had balked. Walker had given his infamous shark's smile, saying only that Ross and the woman were going to be together while "matters were sorted out." Ross had a feeling he knew what that meant.

The muscles in Ross's tall frame protested when he shifted in the tight space. The invariable aftermath of months of tension was a deep, bone-crushing exhaustion. He should be used to it after all these years, but the pendulum swings from high peaks of activity to valleys of desk work seemed more pronounced.

At thirty-six the game was catching up with him. Muttering an oath, he sat up and focused again on the scene outside the car.

The West Side street was quiet, lined with narrow apartment buildings, jammed next to each other. At intervals along the pavement, hardy trees surrounded by concrete struggled to stay alive. A few women were coming back from last minute grocery shopping, dragging their metal carts behind them.

Six o'clock. He decided Emily Brown wasn't going to

5

come straight home from work, when he saw a blue van come down the block. Well-honed instincts flared to life. The van cruised slowly by and Ross yawned deliberately, looking bored. His face could frighten women and young babies, he thought wryly, but there wasn't any harm in trying the harmless routine.

The slight decrease in the van's speed as it continued by his window caused his eyes to narrow. Maybe Walker was right. He'd asked Ross to make the quick trip to New York from Washington to see if someone had a dangerous interest in Emily Brown.

The van turned the corner. Momentarily distracted, Ross almost missed the slight figure limping along the far side of the street.

He reviewed Walker's description of the woman, and decided she was his quarry—Emily Brown, senior cryptanalyst for the New York section of the National Security Agency. Ross's brow furrowed. No limp had been mentioned. His frown deepened when he saw the bloody scrapes on her leg and noted her halting progress.

A shapeless dress and flat beige sandals presented an uninspiring picture as did dark brown hair pulled back carelessly in a knot. Her head was away from him, hiding her face.

After she disappeared through the door of the brownstone, he waited for the lights in her fourth floor apartment to come on. He looked at the window again. It was lighted. Walker had asked him to check her out, be sure she arrived home safely, then report back the next morning in Washington.

Ross started the car and pulled out into the street. He'd returned two days before from three months in the Middle East where he'd worked with a cadre of American-backed rebels. Undoubtedly, Walker would give him good reasons in his own time for the abrupt recall. Ross turned his head, checking for traffic, and headed south on Central Park West, then turned east on Seventy-Second.

The traffic across town was heavy and Ross felt exhaustion slice through him. He'd been awake now over thirty hours and a good bit of that had been spent in a car or an airplane. He fought another face-splitting yawn.

At a stoplight, Ross gazed idly out the window at the traffic at the intersection and stiffened. A blue van was two lanes over on his right. A casual glance away and back was confirmation. It was the same van.

Ross cursed himself. He'd driven away from her apartment without checking to see if he had a tail. He damned his inattentiveness while he slowly eased the automatic transmission into low. He calculated his options. The light changed and Ross accelerated swiftly, the bumper of his car dangerously close to that of the car in front. He shot through a tight gap between two cars, and swerved left onto a one-way street, going the wrong way. His pulse thudded. He'd managed to lose the van.

His brain was accustomed to making rapid fire calculations about terrain, escape routes, and presence of enemy personnel in remote locations. But he wasn't used to employing his skills in major metropolitan areas occupied by friendlies, and it threw him temporarily off balance as he accelerated up First Avenue, before turning onto another side street.

Ross slowed, a sick feeling roaring through his stomach like an express train from hell. He'd come perilously close to hitting a pedestrian. Perspiration dotted his forehead and his shirt stuck to his back. Walker could damn well find another bodyguard. He needed time off, he told himself. Right now he was hovering on the ragged edge of reliability, and luck was a notoriously fickle ally.

Continually checking the side and rear mirrors, he made it to his hotel fifteen minutes later. When Ross walked into his cheerless room, his jaw was set. He'd return to Washington and set Walker straight. Shoving his still unopened suitcase aside, he threw himself down on the rumpled bedspread. Shifting through nine time zones in two days had thrown his body out of whack and he was exhausted. Slowly, tense muscles relaxed. As his body settled deeper into the mattress, the hand gripping his gun inched open, and he slid into sleep.

*   *   *

Emily stepped out of the shower, pushing her wet hair behind her ears. The tiny bathroom was thickly fogged with steam from the cheap fiberglass shower she'd persuaded the landlord to let her install. Tying her robe about her, she walked down the long narrow hall into the living room and sat in the easy chair by the window.

Emily's expression was wry as she considered her surroundings. The building had possessed a quiet charm when she'd first seen it and signed a long lease. The early charm had faded, however, into grime, verging on squalor. Her own apartment thus far had resisted the worst incursion, but not the hallway outside her door.

She grimaced as she rubbed her drying hair, the damp strands curling around her neck. So far, it hadn't seemed worth the effort to look for another place, but she hadn't ruled it out.

Leaning her still damp head against the chair, she stared outside at the fading sky, her habitual sense of isolation closing around her. Loneliness had dogged her footsteps during her childhood on the West Texas ranch where she and her brother had grown up. The familiar ache had not abated during her years at M.I.T.—her youth and brilliance only reinforced her uniqueness. Emily sighed as she remembered the long days in college and graduate school. Occasionally she thought she'd never find anyone who could see past the intellect to the lonely woman beneath.

Perhaps she'd armored herself too well over the years to make it easy for anyone to make the effort.

The breeze rippled the curtains again as daylight faded. Along with a single street lamp in the middle of the block, lights from the buildings illuminated the outside.

A dog barked, a deep-throated sound. Drawn by curiosity, Emily got up, walked over to the window, and looked out. She froze as her gaze fell on the vehicle parked below her window. Emily had noticed the van three days before.

When she'd started work at the agency, she'd been warned there were risks. Emily enjoyed risk taking. Usually. But for the first time since she'd come to New York, she felt uneasy.

She pulled back slowly from the window, her entire

body tense as her slim fingers reached over to the table lamp, to click off the light. Telling herself she was finally experiencing a New Yorker's paranoia, she repressed a shiver.

When she'd moved in she'd been amused by the elaborate series of locks on the door which her landlord had pointed to with pride. There were two chains, a dead bolt, and a police lock. Until now, it had seemed unnecessary. Emily hesitated, out of view from the street. Maybe there was a divorce on the block and an irate husband was trying to get the scoop on the soon-to-be ex-wife. The surveillance was probably harmless. She walked slowly down the hall to her small bedroom and pulled back the bedspread.

Still, as she shifted restlessly under the covers, she decided maybe it wasn't so stupid to be securely bolted in from the world.

The city of Washington lay spread out below the window of the large, anonymous government building.

"Why me?" Ross asked, turning to face Walker.

"Why you what?"

"Why send me to babysit when I'd just spent twenty hours in a series of airplanes? Why didn't you find somebody who's had more than four hours of sleep a night for the last month?"

Ross's gray eyes stared at the silent man behind the desk.

"Because I need you."

"Sure. If there's some gain for the agency, you label the job important. Never mind the body count!" He ticked off on his fingers. "Remember Afghanistan? Or the little matter in South Africa?" He deliberately didn't mention East Germany five years before. The cold war had been cold, but he'd still been burned.

Walker's face remained calm, a gleam of mild amusement the only sign that he and the man facing him were involved in a familiar ritual. "But I never forget you while you're in the field."

"How well I know," came the dry response. "You still

haven't answered my question. Find some off-duty flatfoot to take the job. I need a vacation." He hadn't told Walker about his carelessness in New York. His fingers raked through his hair impatiently. "You don't have to have me in particular. I'm not available."

That was the last-ditch catchphrase for anyone who worked for Walker. It meant they were opting out, their reasons personal. Ross had never used it in the ten years since he'd left his special Army combat unit for Walker's more exotic turf.

Walker tilted back in the chair, his heavy frame causing it to creak, while he carefully lit his pipe. Small puffs of smoke appeared as the match flared. He was a master at pipe lighting, turning it into a negotiating tool Henry Kissinger would have envied. On occasion Ross had seen the procedure take ten minutes.

The pipe was removed with a last suck and Walker said, "Did you say 'not available?' "

Ross was tired of playing games. "Come on, Walker, give me a good reason why you want me in particular."

Both men knew the earlier phrase had been partially withdrawn.

"N.S.A. intercepted a message from a Canadian source that is potentially troublesome," Walker said.

"Why are we involved? N.S.A. has its own operatives."

"Three reasons. First, our existence as an agency depends on being available when requested. We've been asked to step in by N.S.A. since there's some fear their security has been compromised. A second reason, equally compelling, is that we have a problem within our own agency, namely a mole, directly connected to the N.S.A. situation. Lastly, this concerns our Canadian friend."

Ross didn't move. A powerful undercurrent entered the room and Walker's look sharpened. Ross, Walker, and one other person knew about the man, code-named Alain, who'd infiltrated the separatist movement in Quebec. Even Ross didn't know his real identity.

Ross unlocked his frozen muscles, walked slowly to the

nearest chair and sat down. "What about him?" His face was impassive.

"He's sent us a message about our Miss Muffet in New York. Seems there may be a big bad spider coming down to sit beside her."

"Then stash her somewhere. I could have gotten her out last night. Why did I have to come back here?"

"I needed to talk to you face-to-face since I couldn't be absolutely sure the phones were secure." Walker paused. "That's why I sent you. I had to have somebody I could trust, somebody I knew wasn't involved in this mess." Walker's face remained uncharacteristically solemn. "I wasn't sure I was right to be so cautious. Now I'm afraid I may not have taken enough precautions."

Ross nodded, his thoughts elsewhere, unaware of the extraordinary fact that Walker had almost apologized.

Backpedalling quickly, Ross said, "What's so important about her that the Canadians would be interested? You told me she's a cryptanalyst. She hasn't broken a new Canadian code, has she?"

"Not exactly, although she's getting close. Alain believes the message Miss Muffet intercepted described a plot to unseat several pro-unity leaders . . . perhaps using violence." He puffed on his pipe. "This is one of those times when a neighbor's problems become ours. It's well known that various top officials have been trying desperately for several years to hold Canada together in the face of the growing separatist movement. The failed referendum on the new constitution to grant broadened recognition of the French is the latest effort in the twenty year dilemma. Don't forget, a splinter group kidnapped and killed one of the local cabinet ministers in nineteen seventy over this very issue."

Ross felt a chill. "How does the woman fit it?"

"The danger to her comes from the fact she either told someone what she'd started to decode, or the Canadian agent in her organization learned she deciphered the message."

Ross considered the information. If Alain was right, Emily Brown was definitely in trouble. "Wait a minute," he said. "If the message isn't completely decoded, that means it was sent by a sophisticated method. I wouldn't have thought that splinter group would have had either the money or the talent to take that on."

Walker's face was impassive. "As far as talent goes, we may have done the training ourselves. Alain indicated he thought the pro-separatist group planted someone in N.S.A.'s crypto section back in nineteen eighty when the earlier secession movement failed. I can imagine plenty of scenarios in which a pro-secession group would be interested in finding out what the national Canadian government was doing and used the U.S. as spy. Using the U.S. information system wouldn't be a bad backup to whatever infiltration they're already doing in Canada. At any rate, they've had plenty of time to acquire all the necessary skills since then."

Ross rubbed his hand across his eyes. "It's been bad enough locating moles from countries with totally different languages and cultures, but it's impossible to tell an American from a Canadian."

"Yes, they forget to carry the correct identification cards," Walker said dryly.

"But what about funding for their operation? It still takes expensive, state-of-the-art electronics."

"There may be a nasty twist," Walker said, gripping his pipe firmly between his teeth. "My counterpart in Toronto informed me he suspects our Libyan friend is providing a hefty bankroll."

"Makes sense," Ross commented with a grimace. "If they can cause any kind of upheaval on the North American continent, so much the better. Besides, fanaticism often finds a common ground."

"And they don't care where the money comes from."

"Does she know exactly what she was looking at in the message?"

The older man shrugged. "I don't think so. It'll be your job to find out what she remembers . . . while you keep her alive."

"How old is she?"

Satisfaction gleamed briefly in Walker's eyes. "Twenty-eight." Walker waited while Ross paced. "Well, are you in or out?" Walker never pressed, but the stakes this time were high.

Ross stopped in his tracks, turning to face him. "I'll do it but I'd better get a double, hell, make it a triple dose of vacation when I get back. Does she know she's in danger?"

"Double it is," said Walker smugly, unworried about further bargaining. "And she knows nothing . . . yet. I thought you might take her to one of the safe houses out of state while we get our underground burrower out of the way."

"That's the real problem, isn't it?" Ross said. "The fact someone knows about her work means we've got a rotten apple at her agency, and you suspect there's one in ours, too." The implications were appalling. "Makes you wonder what else is being planned if they've gone to this trouble."

Walker leaned forward in his chair to tap the plug of pipe tobacco into the ashtray. "That's right. And we have to find him or her or them before other leaks take place. With regard to the woman, you make all the arrangements—you know the usual places. She shouldn't be a problem. She's calm and even-tempered to work with. At least that's what her dossier says. A piece of cake."

"Piece of cake or not, she's limping, or at least she was when I saw her walk down the street to her apartment."

"Limping?" Concern crossed Walker's face.

"Probably just tripped over her own feet. Unless there's something else going on already."

"I see." Walker was silent a moment, reflecting. "I'll stay by a phone but I can't promise how secure it will be. Be careful."

"I will." Ross nodded and exited.

The next morning, Emily got out of bed slowly. Her leg ached, it was stiff and sore. But she was lucky to be alive. A man had stumbled into her at the subway station yesterday. Remembered horror washed over her. If she hadn't grabbed hold of one of the stanchions, she would have fallen off the platform directly under the wheels of the incoming train. Just thinking about it again caused her heart to pound. The man hadn't looked back or apologized. That had made her blindly furious.

Emily vowed to watch every step she took for the next few days. She was about to close the door of the apartment as she left for work when a deep voice came from behind her.

"Miss Brown? I'd like to talk to you."

Emily whirled, and swallowed a scream, her purse slipping from her shoulder. The man grabbed at the strap and handed her handbag to her with a small smile.

She backed away. He was tall, with broad shoulders and powerful arms, apparent even in the trenchcoat he was wearing over slacks and a casual striped shirt.

"I'm Ross Harding. I need to talk to you," he repeated as he handed her his identity card. Emily peered at it in the dim light, and he noted her caution. "Call your boss at work if you'd like. He was contacted last night about my coming. He'll vouch for me. Shall we go inside?" He waited, his body angled carelessly away from her in a non-threatening stance.

Emily frowned. "I'll call first." She shut the door in his face. Minutes later she opened it again. "Come in."

Ross followed her into the apartment. Emily caught a glimpse of a quirked eyebrow as he surveyed the variety of locks swinging from the back of her door.

"Native New Yorker?"

"These were here before I moved in."

"Right," he agreed blandly.

But his disbelieving look irritated her.

"This way," she said shortly. He stepped past her and moved in the direction she'd indicated. He looked even bigger in the cramped space than he had outside her apartment, his shoulders practically brushing the painted walls of the hall.

"All right, what is it? My boss said he didn't know why you wanted to talk to me."

"I didn't tell him."

Emily took a chair and motioned him to the couch

across from her, assessing the man who'd just sat down. He looked like the type that bit first and barked later.

Ross sat where she directed returning her survey with unreadable eyes. "Miss Brown, there's been a certain amount of interest in your activities in the last week by persons my agency might call unfriendly. Do you remember the message from Montreal that showed up unexpectedly last week?"

"Yes," Emily said slowly. "Normally all traffic from Canada comes in clear, but this was definitely encrypted. Although the name 'Rocket' was used, it didn't fit with the rest of the text."

"You were correct. Evidently there's a possible plot to unseat several pro-unity Canadian leaders and the word Rocket relates to that. Somehow the message was accidentally transmitted to the U.S. You're in danger until we can find out who leaked the information that you read it. Since there's the possibility that you know more than you think about the message itself, I've been assigned to debrief you after I've taken you to a safe house."

She sat silently for a moment analyzing the implications of his words then said calmly, "Fine." Her eyes remained steady.

The lady, Ross realized, was tough. Her initial shock when he'd surprised her in the hall had been quickly hidden. And she hadn't apologized for slamming the door on him.

Apologies weren't her style, he decided. Neither was feminine hysterics. Instead, Ross detected a hint of arrogance and self-assurance in her calm, relaxed pose, along with an odd damn-you-to-hell look in eyes he'd discovered were a dark blue.

"I suggest you treat this seriously." Ross' tone was deliberately harsh, testing for effect.

Emily's look widened slightly before narrowing on his face. "Oh, Mr. Harding, I am taking this seriously. I just hope you are. After all, it's my hide that's in danger of being nailed to the wall, not yours," she said sharply.

Ross fought to keep his face blank. He hadn't expected this cool acceptance of risk. Miss Emily Brown was turning out to be quite a surprise. He wasn't at all sure it was pleasant.

He cleared his throat. "By the way, if we run into problems, we may have to pose as man and wife to make our being together believable. It's hackneyed but effective."

"I can handle that." She shrugged. "How long will this take?"

"Three or four days. I suggest you call in sick to your office. We need to move quickly."

"No problem," she said with another cavalier shrug. "I'll take care of that and pack." She got up quickly and left the room.

Ross stared after her a moment before turning to look out the window. A piece of cake Walker had said. Ross snorted derisively. Emily Brown gave a surface impression of docility, but he sensed an iron will underneath. And something suspiciously close to anger.

Ross checked his watch. Animal instincts urged him to take her and get the hell out of the city. The prickling of his senses warned him he and the woman didn't have much time. He hadn't seen the van that morning but undoubtedly more than one vehicle was involved in surveillance. He'd have to keep his eyes open.

She reappeared in the living room a few minutes later, suitcase in hand. "I'm ready."

"Did you call your office?"

"Of course." She looked at him with disfavor. Did he think she was an idiot?

He gave her stare for stare. She'd changed clothes and had put on a pair of tennis shoes, a faded shirt, and well-washed jeans that fit her slim legs snugly. A suede jacket was slung over her arm. Her shoulder length hair was caught in some kind of a slide and it gleamed over her shoulders in a fall of russet brown. She looked totally at ease in her casual garb.

She held up her case. "This should be adequate for virtually anything. We're not likely to run into severe weather—unless we drive into the mountains?"

Ross shook his head as he heaved himself out of the

soft, low chair. "Nope. We're only a few hours from a place I know."

The morning rush hour traffic was behind them by the time they stopped on the western edge of New Jersey. Ross drove without speaking, his hands resting lightly on the steering wheel of the compact he'd rented. He hadn't spotted a tail yet but his nerves were still jangling.

Emily finally broke the silence. "Do you think you'll be able to protect me from the unknown bad guys?"

A bleak look appeared briefly on his face. "Don't worry. I'll take care of you." His voice was hard and the bleakness vanished.

"Fine. Then I'll take your advice."

He turned to look at her. "What advice?"

"Not to worry."

Ross gave a short laugh. "If you can manage that, you'll be different from most civilians."

"That's not particularly surprising. I am different from other 'civilians,' " she said matter-of-factly.

Ross didn't respond and Emily turned back to look at him. His attention was on the road, and she could stare at him at her leisure. He had a compelling face, dark brows, and hair with a slight curl combed carelessly back from a broad forehead. The purity of strong bones covered tautly with tanned skin was marred by a puckered scar high on his right cheek.

The flickering smiles he'd given her had been doled out sparingly. A brief warmth was offset by the calculating intelligence in his cold gray eyes. When he'd mentioned risks, something had surfaced in the depths of his eyes, a threatening quality which was quickly masked, disappearing under an impassivity that mocked her efforts to probe beneath its surface. When he spoke, he chopped off his words, as if he were afraid of giving something away. His voice had a faint rasp that lingered in her mind. Normally she listened to what people had to say, analyzed it, and then continued whatever she was doing. He wasn't so easily dismissed.

Manhattan was far behind them, and they were now moving through western New Jersey. The foliage had turned and the crisp November air burnished the leaves to russets, bronzes, and warm yellows. Blurs of color slid over the hood of the car, and up the windshield, slipping away before her unseeing gaze. Thoughts churned in her mind, but she wasn't afraid. She'd mastered physical fear years before. The only question was whether she could get along with the hard, silent man at the wheel.

"So you're different?" His voice broke the silence.

Emily shrugged. "I am, if not worrying is out of the ordinary. You seem reasonably competent, and I'm no dunce." She gave him a quick look. Unless he thought someone with a Ph.D. from M.I.T. was automatically deficient in common sense. "Basically I'm trusting you to take care of the physical hazards that arise, while I help with strategy."

Ross's face held an odd expression. "You'll help with strategy?"

"Don't sell me short, Mr. Harding. That would be a mistake," she said smoothly.

Silence filled the car. A throbbing silence.

"Really?" His one word response was barely audible.

"Really."

Not another word was spoken, by Emily's calculations, for ninety-three minutes. She was in a half waking state lulled by the movements of the car when he finally spoke.

"What happened to your leg?"

"I fell when someone bumped me at the subway station."

Ross didn't move but it was as if a very powerful force flexed, filling the car with palpable menace.

"Did you get a good look at him?"

"Yes." Emily proceeded to give in minute detail a description of the man, missing the look of incredulity on Ross's face.

"You're sure of all this?"

His voice sounded strange, and Emily felt a tingle in her nerves. "Yes. Why? Do you know who he is?"

"No. It's just that your description was very detailed. That's unusual. Most people don't pay sufficient attention to their surroundings. I suspect we both have a lot to learn about each other.''

''You do, at any rate,'' Emily returned without missing a beat.

TWO

She had more nerve than was good for her, Ross decided, quelling the impulse to give vent to an unexpected bubble of amusement. As quickly as the humor arose, it melted away, under the realization of their situation.

The itch between Ross's shoulder blades wouldn't go away. He automatically checked his rearview mirror again. He didn't see an obvious tail, but the obscure got you every time. Frequently in the past, only his instincts and reflexes had saved his skin. Ross frowned, remembering his slip-up with the van. Now he wasn't sure he still had the skills that had once been second nature.

He hit the accelerator hard to pass an eighteen-wheeler, then tucked the rental car in front of it.

With interest Ross noted Emily's foot stomp the floorboard before she sat up straight, her eyes trained on the road. He wouldn't have pegged her as a nervous rider.

"Where are we going?" she asked after a short silence.

"Out of state."

"Exactly where?"

"Not too far."

She rolled her eyes. "How long will it take to get there?"

"We'll be there before dinner," he said, conscious of her hand, as her slim fingers beat a staccato rhythm on one leg.

"What's with you? Don't you want to talk right now?"

"No."

She hissed in exasperation. "Are you capable of speaking in anything besides monosyllables?"

"Certainly."

A strange expression crossed his face as he spoke and

Emily wasn't sure whether it indicated amusement or irritation. "If that's your best, I don't think much of it. I presume you're a spy. Right?" When he didn't answer, she continued. "You must be," she said, "or you'd have denied it, since we all know silence is assent. Let's see," she said, "that means you have to be strong and silent. Or do I have that wrong?" she added sweetly. "Perhaps it's just your personal style."

"Lady, style doesn't have anything to do with my job. I've been told to be your babysitter while we take care of your problem. That's what I'm going to do but it doesn't require fraternization."

"I'm impressed," she said mockingly. "A nice long word which doesn't tell me a thing. Back at the apartment you said we might have to pose as man and wife. What's that if not fraternization?"

"Business."

"I see." She turned halfway in her seat to face him, her blue eyes thoughtful. "So you're not willing to while away our travel time by sharing personal confidences?"

He shot her a look full of incredulity. "You've got to be kidding."

"I must have been." Her tone was dry.

"Don't take this wrong, but we're not required to like each other."

"Who was talking about liking?" she asked in honest surprise. "I tried to make conversation, ask about the things I certainly should be entitled to know, like where we're going, and it's worse than getting blood out of a stone."

"Sorry, but I need to pay attention to what I'm doing."

He was maddeningly uninformative, Emily thought, when he didn't have to be. She considered her options.

Tell him to take a flying leap and go it on her own. The only thing was, he probably wouldn't take kindly to the suggestion.

Or she could kill two birds with one stone. Polish the rough edges off the hunk of granite sitting next to her while finding out who was after her. And maybe, just maybe, get a shot at turning the tables on the guys with the black hats.

"Feel like lunch?" His voice broke a long silence.

"That would certainly be pleasant. Especially since I've decided that subsisting on food for thought isn't very nutritious." She smiled at his narrow-eyed look. "You've been so informative that I've been just consumed with excitement, reviewing the morsels of information you've shared."

"How about a humburger, instead?" His mouth twitched just for a moment then he gestured to a fast food restaurant at the side of the road.

"Whatever you say." Emily's nose wrinkled in mild distaste. She hadn't counted on a cardboard burger and fries. "After all, you're running this . . . caper. Is caper the correct word?"

Silence.

Until finally, he said, "That term usually refers to B-movie bank heists."

"Is there a special phrase for our type of mission?" she asked mockingly.

Ross's hands tightened on the wheel as he reviewed which seven letter expletive in Czech, Russian, or German would serve him best. He scrapped them and said tersely, "Safety mission."

He pulled into the parking lot of the fast food restaurant and got out without answering. He slammed the door and walked toward the restaurant, stopping at the door.

Emily exited slowly, and strolled toward him, noting the impatience evident on his face. "Are we really going to eat here?"

He held the door open. "If you don't trust the food, don't eat. I intend to. I'm hungry."

"Undoubtedly you have a cast-iron stomach. Something a blowtorch couldn't touch," she commented as she walked past him, hearing with satisfaction his indrawn breath.

"Lady, you're something else," he muttered under his breath.

"I hope so. And of course, since I'm your responsibility, I'm counting on you to be sure I'm properly cared for. I have been designated your responsibility, haven't I?''

A shadow passed across his face and vanished. ''Yeah. You're my responsibility. Sit down.''

Emily took mercy on him and ordered. The hamburger, fries, and milk shake were actually delicious and she ate rapidly, touching her lips with the napkin to remove the last of the catsup she'd energetically slathered on the bun.

''Trying to make sure you can get it down with your delicate palate?'' he asked, staring at the red sauce covering her food.

''Right. Catsup is the great leveler. Absolutely anything can be eaten if it's coated enough.''

After that, he ate in silence, except to ask her if she wanted anything else.

''No, thank you, Mr. Harding.'' Her tone was polite but laced with a hint of deliberate mockery.

His jaw twitched but he didn't reply.

It occurred to her that she was being awfully unfair. Emily Brown of N.S.A. never would have done this kind of prodding and poking of a fellow worker. On the other hand, she was fed up with her carefully constructed image, the protective coloration she'd assumed when it became apparent she had to dress to fit others' preconceived expectations. Besides, he deserved a little goading for the way he'd shut her out.

She turned and gazed at Ross. Her deliberately provocative behavior had produced no effect she could see. She was figuratively chunking rocks at something that looked and acted like mineral but still breathed animal. She snorted and Ross eyed her.

''You all right?''

Her smile was all innocence. ''Just fine.''

He shot her a look full of misgivings, but refused to respond. Ushering her back out to the car, he carefully checked the area before pulling onto the highway. When she remained silent beside him, Ross hoped he'd gotten his message across.

He frowned. Civilians were all cast in the same mold.

They didn't realize danger was present even in innocence, that harm lurked in peace, and death could follow humor.

How could anyone tell who the friendlies were? Black was black and white was white. Trying to see gray complicated everything. Philosophically, it was a hell of a way to think, but it made staying alive easier.

He glanced over at Emily again. She was still ignoring him and he repressed a faint sigh. Aware of a change in Emily's position, he turned his head. She was curled up beside him, her knees bent and her head back against the seat. Her hands lay curved loosely in her lap. She looked almost like a kid without makeup. Freckles dotted her straight nose. Her mouth was soft and full, the lips slightly parted. Ross looked away.

The last time he'd begun seeing details about a woman, she hadn't been around long enough for him to notice more. Since then he'd preferred to deal with professionals. It was easier to handle when you saw them later, life wiped from their faces. There were still regrets, but not as bitter.

For the umpteenth time, Ross wished Walker had chosen someone else to watch over the woman beside him.

She awoke without moving a muscle, suddenly aware the car was slowing. She sat up and looked out the window. Stifling a yawn, she rubbed her eyes.

"Where are we?" she asked in a voice husky from sleep.

"About four miles away. We'll be at the house in ten minutes."

When she shifted in her seat, he felt her staring at him.

"What kind of danger am I really in?"

"We're not sure. A mole we've been trying to catch knows you've read the message. He has to remove you if he thinks you could identify him."

"I see," she said slowly. "Remove is such a nice, neutral word. Not like kill, murder, or wipe out. I presume we are talking about murder?" Emily felt anger welling up in her and fought to keep her voice steady.

"Yes." Ross let out a slow breath.

"Must be nice having your job. Wrap up dirty deeds

in clean phrases. I think I prefer what I do," she said. "I uncover things, expose them to the light, not hide them in ridiculous verbiage when the result is bloody and final."

Ross's hands tightened on the wheel, the pressure turning his knuckles white as her words sank in. The awful truth was that she was correct. He felt a familiar sense of foreboding grip him and deliberately pushed it away. Fear clouded the mind and right now he needed all his wits about him.

He let a moment lapse and then said, "Speaking of your job, did you finish the decoding on the message?"

"No, but that's not unusual. Sometimes all you've uncovered is the first layer of meaning. There's often a second or third. And with this one, the normal rules don't apply."

"If you want to talk about it now, I'm available."

"Thanks, but not just yet."

He nodded, telling himself she wasn't rebuffing him. He hadn't intended to make the offer anyway. A few minutes later, he lifted his foot from the accelerator, letting the car drift until he spotted the turn-off.

Ross turned down a country road, his senses on full alert. Years of living by his instincts had made him rely on his nerves, and they were jumpy as hell.

"If anything odd happens when we get to the house, call my boss, Walker, in Washington—if you get away. Let me give you his direct number."

There wasn't any point in commenting on his throw-away line, "if you get away." She was going to make damned sure she did.

He repeated the string of numbers. "Write it down."

"I memorized it."

"Figures," he muttered, his gaze sweeping the area before him.

Emily ignored him, only the faint exhalation of her breath indicating she'd heard.

Approaching a narrow lane overgrown with trees whose foliage was just turning the bright colors of autumn, Ross slowed to a crawl. He reached over and flicked open the door of the glove compartment and withdrew a black automatic.

"Stay in the car while I check out the house." He could see the white farmhouse at the end of the drive. A small porch jutted out to the east under a low roof. He couldn't detect any signs of occupancy but his muscles tightened in anticipation. The whole setup stank—the farmhouse looked deserted but didn't feel like it.

He stopped a hundred yards away at a perpendicular angle to the dwelling so he could move the car quickly if need be, leaving the keys in the ignition. "I'll be back." Ross got out slowly. His big body moved gracefully and carefully as he walked up the road, his hand with the gun held away from his body.

As he disappeared around the corner, Emily rolled down the window. After a moment, she could hear the birds suddenly begin to sing. There was a smell of woodsmoke in the air and the quiet rustle of leaves, moved by slight puffs of wind. Peace lay over the landscape, but Emily shivered, nerves jangling.

Five minutes passed while she sat tensely waiting. When he still hadn't reappeared, her worry increased. How long could it take to walk around a house?

Moved by sudden anxiety, she got out of the car quietly and had started forward when three sharp, familiar cracks echoed in the stillness. Emily froze. Then she heard sounds of crashing through underbrush and saw a flash of color as a man darted through the foliage. Ross came running towards her from around the corner of the building.

"Get into the car," he yelled.

Emily whirled and jumped inside. Ross threw himself behind the wheel. With one smooth motion he started the car, shut the door, and accelerated down the drive.

"I thought I told you to stay put."

"I was worried." Emily held on to the armrest as he swerved around a corner and accelerated.

"Don't be. Just do what I say." He hadn't bothered to look at her after his first comprehensive glance.

"What happened? I saw someone running after I heard a couple of shots."

"Yeah. Two guys were waiting. I winged one but the other got away."

Emily felt a surge of adrenaline as she kept her eyes riveted on the mirror. "Why were they there?"

"They were the welcome wagon. What do you think?"

He jerked the wheel to avoid a tree stump and the car bounced over the rutted track until the pavement showed in front of them.

"You're assuming they were waiting for us rather than someone else," she persisted. "I thought only your boss knew where we were going."

"Someone must have overheard."

"Aren't your offices swept or debugged periodically?" Emily asked as they continued to speed down the road. She noted he never let his attention lag, his gaze flicking from mirror to the road in front, his hands controlling the wheel with little effort as he moved around cars that blocked his lane.

"Yes, but no system's foolproof against leaks. This makes things a little harder from here on in, since we can't expect any help from Washington."

"Is that all bad? The fewer people who know our plans, the better, I'd think."

The light turned red at the next intersection and they stopped. Emily felt her heart rate slow for the first time since they'd left the house.

"We'll have to see," he replied.

Something had been bothering her about the whole setup. "Why would they just start firing? If they were after me, wouldn't it have been smarter to wait until we went into the house?"

"Just shows you can't get good help these days." The guys he'd winged had been a kid, early twenties and trigger happy. The other wasn't much older but had better reflexes. At least the opposition hadn't had time to get real professionals on their trail. Yet.

"Get out the map, will you? It's in the glove compartment."

Emily found the map, and unfolded it. "What do you need?"

"How far is it from here to the airport in Baltimore?"

She looked down and did a quick mental calculation. "About eighty-five miles. The Philadelphia airport would be closer."

"Yes, but they'd expect us that way."

"We could always backtrack to New York."

"Too many people."

She turned her head, looking at him in exasperation. "What's wrong with that? We could disappear in a big crowd."

"The answer is no." He couldn't risk involving any more civilians. "We need a place no one would suspect that's easy to defend."

"Do you have a particular destination in mind?"

"A house near Pittsburgh. It belongs to a former fellow employee who said I could use it when I wanted. He retired a couple of years ago from the agency and spends the winter in Florida. Heading to Baltimore, then doubling back should throw anyone off the track." At least he hoped so.

"Who else knows about the place?"

"Just me." Unless Chuck Collins had decided to make the same offer to another old buddy.

Traffic was thinning out as the first spate of commuters left the roads. Ross planned to drive into the airport complex, circle through the rental car section and then out again.

Ross slowed down to let a van in from an access road then jammed on the brakes suddenly.

"I don't believe this." He swore and jerked the wheel to the left.

"What is it?"

"There's a yellow Ford behind us two cars back. I remember seeing it at the restaurant."

"Why hadn't we noticed it before?"

"They must have used a team, one car in front, playing leapfrog with another car in back. That can be effective but takes a lot of manpower. I wouldn't have expected that level of talent, considering the jerks I ran into.''

''Maybe they didn't think you'd be foolish enough to just waltz in there.'' Feeling anxiety nibble at her composure, Emily couldn't help her dry voice.

She twisted her head, but couldn't see the car Ross had told her about. But there was a dark blue Volvo. The two men were staring back at her. She turned to Ross.

''There's a car over there, with two men in it. They could be helping the other ones.''

Ross didn't look, his attention on the road. ''They're not.''

''How can you be so sure?''

''Because if you take another look, you'll see that they're pulling off to the side. They've got a flat.''

''Why were they staring at us?''

The granite softened. ''Possibly because I was driving like a maniac which sometimes attracts attention. Or they might have simply thought you were cute.''

As soon as the word registered, Emily turned. ''Cute? Now just a darned minute . . .''

''You really get down and dirty don't you, Miss Muffet?'' he said, then realized his slip.

''Muffet?''

''Walker's code name for you.'' He waited, his shoulders tense.

''One from nursery rhymes? Why? To emphasize the fact you guys don't have any use for civilians so you sneer at us?''

Her tone had been completely pleasant. He wished she'd been angry. A muscle jumped in his cheek. The silence lengthened.

''So what do we do now?'' she asked, deciding she'd jabbed hard enough.

''You tell me.'' He wove in and out of traffic, his eyes moving ceaselessly from the road to the mirror and back.

''All right. I will.''

He laughed.

''What's so funny?'' she demanded.

''Nothing. Absolutely nothing.''

"Well, I was going to suggest," she said coldly, "that you let me out at the airport. I'll make reservations for London, or somewhere in Europe. On the assumption that we're being followed, I expect someone will come inside and hear me ask for an overseas flight. In the meantime, you ditch the car, and get another one. I don't care how." She waved her hand grandly. "Then we'll meet and go from there."

"Just like that."

"Just like that."

"And how do you propose we get out of the airport without being seen?"

"Can't you take care of anything?" The effect of her words was galvanizing.

He pulled into the access road at the next exit which had just appeared and floored the accelerator around the band before slamming on the brakes in a cleared space off the road. Emily felt her head jerk forward and held onto her purse tightly.

Ross's face was grim. "You probably think this is some kind of lark, where you'll throw a bodylock like a Bruce Lee clone and the bad guys will disappear." He took in a deep breath. God save me from well-intentioned, naive government employees. "This isn't TV. This isn't the movies. This is real." His eyes bored into hers. "Got it? Because, lady, if you don't, I'm going to be shopping for a body bag. And it won't be for me."

Emily didn't move a muscle. Her face was a little pale but that could have been due to the light. It was dusk and the sky had turned a metallic gray with rapidly darkening edges.

"Message received. Do you think my plan is a bad one?"

He plowed his fingers through his hair. "No. The idea's fine, but your attitude stinks."

"You've told me that." She didn't hide her irritation.

"All right, but remember we're talking about safety. Mine. Yours." His forefinger jabbed the air for emphasis. "I have to be in charge. One ship, one captain."

"Which branch of the service are we in?"

He shook his head wearily. "The stakes here are enormous. You're at risk, and frankly I don't relish being in your zone of danger simply because you won't pay attention. If you spent less time on oneupmanship, we'd both be better off."

"Now that you've gotten that off your mind, what about my plan?" Emily felt a suspicious lump in her throat. Ross's anger, palpable from its strength, was wearing her down. Worse, he was right.

He rubbed a big hand over his face. "It sounds fine."

"Let me off at the Pan American entrance. There are bound to be flights this evening for London or Paris. I'll meet you outside the . . ." she thought a minute ". . . Delta door."

"You have ten minutes," he warned. "Don't be late."

She nodded and he punched the car into drive and headed for the ramps leading to the departure zone. He pulled in to the curb.

Emily exited without looking back, hurrying inside the terminal before walking swiftly towards the Pan American counter. The line was long, moving sluggishly in marked lanes, and she guessed it might take her over the ten minute deadline to buy a ticket. Her eyes quickly registered department flights and their destination.

Moving forward, she stumbled and fell against a well dressed man near the front of the line. His arm came out to help her.

Emily's face turned teary. "Oh, I'm so sorry. I just . . . I'm trying to make the London flight and my husband doesn't even know I'm coming."

The man looked down at her. "I beg your pardon?"

"I'm two months pregnant and my husband is an airman stationed in London. It's vital that I make this flight." Her hand gestured at the wall board. She bit her lip anxiously. "Would you mind terribly if I just slipped in line ahead of you?" The man seemed on the verge of refusing and she clutched her middle, sagging against him, almost knocking him off balance.

"All right." He looked harassed and she smiled gratefully.

"Thank you so much." She waited until her turn came, then bought the tickets using her American Express card. She left the area briskly and the man whose place she'd taken stared after her, then shrugged and moved to the counter.

Emily hurried to the Delta section of the terminal and located the exit doors immediately across from it. She was about to walk out when she heard the sound of running footsteps.

A tall, grayhaired man wearing a trenchcoat was jogging down the carpeted hallway towards her. When he saw her he changed direction, but not before Emily had seen his look flicker her way.

Emily hesitated then walked swiftly back in the direction she'd come from. Peering around a column, she saw the man was gone and ran to an outside door. Ross was nowhere in sight. She muttered a colorful word under her breath. As if commanded, a black limousine slid to a smooth stop beside her and the driver's window on her side rolled down.

"Want a ride, lady?" Ross was inside, a chauffeur's cap perched on his dark hair.

"Absolutely, Henry." She slid in quickly beside him.

"You're supposed to sit in the back," he said.

"I didn't think you'd appreciate the grande dame treatment," she replied, unruffled. Her hand stroked the soft leather. "Where did you pick this up?"

"A friend offered it to me."

Emily laughed. "I'll bet. With the help of a little friendly force undoubtedly."

"Yeah. You might say that." Ross moved the big car out into the traffic. "Did you see anything?"

"Some guy was running down the hall and I dodged him. But he got a good look at me. I don't think he saw me leave."

"He did if he wore a trenchcoat, and was about six feet tall."

"Oh."

"Right. He's getting into a taxi. We'll leave him behind."

Ross drove the big car expertly and soon they were out of the airport.

Emily tucked her hair behind her ear and relaxed, concentrating on the recent events. Either coincidence had reached new levels, or something was definitely amiss.

She and Ross left New York and were followed. They reached the safe house and were met by the bad guys. And this was after they'd supposedly taken every precaution. Then she was spotted at the airport. There was only one conclusion.

"You realize, don't you, that the rental car had to have a kind of homing transmitter alerting someone to our location?"

"I wondered when you'd figure it out." He dodged through a filling station. "Switching cars will take care of that."

Emily decided she wouldn't get mad at his oblique compliment. After all, light was beginning to dawn in his brain that she had something to offer in the way of teamwork. She looked at him assessingly as he drove. He wasn't bad looking, just tough. And tough wasn't bad. Just hard to deal with.

"How did the car get bugged?" she asked a moment later.

"Probably when I came inside to get you at your apartment. This operation is hot enough to warrant major effort."

"I see," she said softly.

"We better not plan on trying for my buddy's house. I've got a feeling that may not be as safe as I'd hoped." Ross cursed under his breath as a motorcyclist veered sharply into his lane, then wobbled into a sidestreet, causing Ross to brake sharply.

Her gaze wandered over him, and stopped at his hands. Powerful, long fingered, they looked capable of wringing a man's neck. Or stroking a woman to passion.

Emily's thoughts ground to a screeching halt at the mental image she'd evoked. Even though he'd used her name, he had sounded as though the word "Emily" had been squeezed out. It had probably galled him to be even that intimate, she told herself. Intimate. The word conjured up visions she ruthlessly repressed.

"How do you like enchiladas?" Emily asked.

THREE

"I don't. Are you out of your mind?" Ross shook his head in bemusement, then jerked the wheel to avoid a pole.

"Okay. A lot of people think they're too gooey, with all that cheese. What about burritos? Or tacos?"

"What in the hell are you talking about?" He practically snarled the words, his face taut with irritation.

"I just thought since we're going to Texas, it would be nice to find out if you liked Mexican food."

"We're going to Texas?" he repeated, convinced he'd misheard.

"Absolutely. You gave me the specifications for our next move. We have to be in a safe place," she ticked it off on her fingers, "that the agency doesn't know about and it has to be a location we can defend. I have it."

Ross cleared his throat. "Where?"

"West Texas."

"That covers a lot of territory. Where in West Texas?"

"My folks have a hunting shack that's used only during deer season later this month. No one will be there for several weeks."

"It won't work."

"Why not?"

Emily's mouth took on a stubborn slant. He sighed in exasperation. "Because you're too closely connected to it."

She smiled forgivingly. "If that's all that's worrying you, don't. My parents bought it forty years ago under a hunting partnership name. No one in my family has used it for nearly that long. The regular hunters who have the lease pay the butane bill themselves. Therefore the chances of its ownership being known are slim. And," she added the *coup de grace,* "it's approximately sixty miles from my parents' ranch, and I haven't been there in years. No one would ever tie me to it. Have a better idea?"

"Not at the moment. But if the link between you and the shack is so tenuous, how did you remember it?"

"Because my father told me six months ago he was planning on letting the hunters make improvements. My brother and I will own it some day and he wanted to be sure we didn't mind."

"How far is it from the nearest city?" He checked the rearview mirror. Thus far, no one had showed up on their tail.

"About a hundred miles to El Paso, two hundred to Midland. El Paso would be logical, so we should fly to Midland instead."

Ross pulled through a parking lot and turned the car in the direction they had come.

Emily's head whipped around in surprise. "Where are we going?"

"Back to the airport to catch a plane to Texas."

"You mean you agree?" Her respect for him went up a notch. He hadn't wasted time in useless arguing.

"Yeah. We don't have a lot of other choices at this point. I hope to hell you're right about this shack or house or whatever. My instructions don't include putting you in a firefight."

"Thanks," she said dryly. "My plans don't include that either. How long do you think we'll need to be out of sight?"

"Hard to tell. Probably a couple of days. The welcoming committee at the safe house changes the schedule."

"That's fine with me."

"This ranch you mentioned. Were you raised there?"

"Yes."

"Did you like it?"

"Sure. What kid wouldn't? Lots of room, incredible freedom and responsibility from an early age."

"So why did you leave Texas in the first place?" Ross asked.

Emily turned to stare at him in mild inquiry then shrugged. "Because M.I.T.'s in Massachusetts."

"Is that where you wanted to go to college?"

"Almost as much as they wanted me," she said matter-of-factly.

Ross somehow wasn't surprised. "Did you go to high school near your ranch?"

She gave a short laugh. "Not exactly. We were forty miles from the nearest town. My mother taught me and my brother at home."

"Did you like it? I mean, wouldn't you have preferred to be with other kids?" Ross didn't know what he expected but certainly not to hear she'd had such a sheltered childhood.

"No. I'd attended elementary school and discovered I didn't exactly fit in with the local children."

"Why not?"

"I was too smart. Worse, I liked the wrong things. Math. Science. The other kids were into horse and livestock shows, raising pets. I was, too, but not exclusively. I couldn't seem to turn off my mind. The kind of brain I have is a freak of nature."

The words shocked Ross momentarily. His hands tightened on the wheel. "How old were you when you went to M.I.T.?"

"Fifteen."

Oh great. At least, she hadn't said twelve. "And I bet you did well there, didn't you?"

"Sure. There wasn't much else to do besides study. Everyone did. Weekends, nights, crack of dawn, you name it. Somebody was always cramming."

She shrugged again in a way Ross was beginning to recognize as characteristic when she was uncomfortable.

"Did you enjoy the pressure?"

"Naturally. That was why I went."

"What about friends?"

"What about them? Look, the environment there is very competitive. It's full of people who work ferociously hard. Who had time to socialize? Besides, the social life of a fifteen year old kid is a lot different from that of an eighteen year old. I couldn't drink beer, the other girls thought I was weird, and the guys found me a bit . . .''

"Intimidating?" he offered.

"You could say that." She didn't add that they'd also found her too simple, too backward, and so they'd left her alone.

He was unwillingly fascinated with the life she'd revealed. "What did you do besides study?"

"What is this? Twenty questions? I didn't do one solitary thing besides study." She sighed in exasperation. "I had to do something to justify the money my parents spent on me. What did it matter if I was a loner?"

Ross's heart twisted.

"Don't misunderstand. I loved it there. I mean, it was great. For the first time in my life, I was really challenged."

He shot her a look. In her attempt to make him understand, she was animated, color climbing into her cheeks, her eyes such a dark, intense blue he felt his mouth dry.

"What did you do after graduation? Go straight to work?"

"No. I decided I might as well stay for my doctorate."

"In what?"

"Computer science."

"And that was when some guy in a nice suit approached you about working for the government. Right?"

"Yes." Of course. Ross had seen them before. Extraordinarily bright kids coming from lonely backgrounds, lured by the government into jobs where their peculiar talents could be used. Emily had probably jumped at the offer. He felt a pang of unexpected sympathy for her before he thrust the unwelcome thought away.

"What was the point of this interrogation?" she asked abruptly. "I distinctly remember someone telling me earlier that there was to be no fraternization. Using a fifty-cent word didn't hide the fact that you wanted nothing to do with me."

"That wasn't what I meant at all," Ross said, feeling the urge to squirm under her stare. "I just meant that . . ."

"You didn't want to be friendly."

He sighed. "No. I simply wanted to make it clear that I need to be objective . . . so I can protect you better. The questions I was asking were simply to get more background," he lied smoothly. "After all, I'm supposed to be debriefing you."

"Oh." She shot him a look he didn't see, a blend of skepticism and faint hopefulness.

She'd bought it, he decided a moment later. How in the hell was he going to hide the fact that he found her interesting and attractive, enough so he'd been driven to probe into her life?

He looked over at Emily's averted profile, her attention elsewhere. He couldn't explain how she seemed to have shed some sort of camouflage since he'd first seen her on the street and come out looking crisper, younger, and prettier. His gaze trailed over her body from her long, slender legs to the gentle swell of her breasts then to delicate skin of her throat. He looked away.

Sending him to guard Emily Brown was turning into a king-size mistake. He needed to see her as an asset to be guarded, not a woman made of flesh and blood all too easily torn apart by a bullet ripping its way through her slim body. Their enforced togetherness would breed familiarity, liking, and intimacy.

Intimacy. Ross scowled. He had to remember how it could all too easily turn out.

For a few moments, neither spoke.

Then Emily said, "I thought you were worried about being seen. Isn't it risky to return to the airport in the same vehicle?"

"Yes. But we're going to get rid of the limousine."

"More than one car theft a day is my limit."

"Just leave it to me."

He'd probably been a car thief in another life the way he swapped cars. "What are you going to do?"

"Don't worry. You can be my silent accomplice, watching from the safety of this car."

"Which is already stolen."

"Borrowed."

"Somehow I don't think changing the word makes a difference."

"You mean to a judge." His tone was understanding. "You won't get more than a five-to-ten stretch."

"Wonderful. I hope they have good libraries there. At least I could catch up on my reading."

"I'm sure that could be arranged."

"Are you serious?"

"What do you think?" he parried. "Being on a government assignment doesn't give us total immunity. It's just one of the risks you have to take. I've faced longer sentences."

Emily felt her face tighten involuntarily. Ross smiled then, a totally male smile full of irony, and Emily's pulse thumped.

"You were kidding." She bit her lip as his smile widened. She leaned against the door staring at him, her face thoughtful.

"I certainly hope so."

Emily snorted in response.

Ross slid the car into a slot at a supermarket and got out without waiting to see if she was following. He could hear her feet pounding after him. He stopped abruptly and turned. "I'll apologize if you want me to."

"You will?" she said in surprise. "For what?"

"Because I was being unprofessional."

"When?"

"I shouldn't have teased you."

"That's unprofessional?"

A light breeze lifted the gleaming, silky strands of hair from her forehead as she stared up into his face, her dark blue eyes oddly serious. The silence between them lengthened, then became charged as he returned her look, his expression unsmilingly intent.

"In this case it is." Ross saw the pulse beating under the white skin of her throat.

"I see." She didn't.

He could have sworn a flash of hurt traveled over her face before it was dispelled by a mask of indifference.

His gaze dipped to her mouth. Emily felt an odd tingle and reached for her rapidly vanishing composure.

"Are we here to commit a felony?" She looked away, around the huge parking lot.

"Nope. Talking about food made me hungry." Ross checked his watch. "It's almost seven. We'll pick up something to eat before we return to a life of crime."

It was dark outside. Emily realized with a slight sense of shock that usually at this hour she'd be sitting comfortably in her apartment in New York, dinner ready on the table.

They bought the makings of a picnic, then Ross drove to a shopping mall and pulled over into a space in front of a phone booth. He opened the door and was halfway out, digging into his pocket, when Emily spoke.

"Who are you calling?"

"My boss."

"I thought we agreed his telephone wasn't safe."

"It isn't. But I can at least let him know you're alive. I'll give him a false trail while I find out what's going on."

"And Walker will understand what you're doing?"

"Of course."

Walker answered on the first ring. "Where are you?"

Ross tensed. When Ross was in the field, Walker used two set phrases to indicate the line was clear. He'd said neither.

"In New Jersey," Ross lied evenly, "but I'm heading north."

"Fine. Take care of yourself and the prize package. By the way, things got a little hot in Miss Muffet's kitchen tonight. Seems her oven exploded. The apartment was demolished although nothing else in the building was damaged."

Ross felt a sudden cold nausea, his imagination all too vividly showing what might have happened to Emily if she'd been there. He swallowed hard. "Timed?"

"For dinner. Be careful," Walker added unnecessarily.

"I will." Ross hesitated then hung up, his mind struggling to push away the horrifying images his experience had conjured.

He went back to the car, opened the door, got in, and began opening the sack of food although his hunger had vanished.

"You leave your oven on this morning before you left the apartment?" he asked as he assembled a sandwich.

"No. Why?" She turned to look at him. The lights from the parking lot threw shadows on his face obscuring his expression.

"No particular reason."

She stared at him, an unwelcome suspicion crossing her mind. "I don't believe you."

"About what?"

"That you had no particular reason for asking. What did Walker tell you?" When Ross remained silent, Emily said, "Come on, Ross. I'm entitled to know."

"Your apartment exploded about two hours ago, at dinner time. If you didn't leave your oven on, it means someone fixed you a warm welcome."

His flippancy didn't conceal the harshness in his voice. Emily was stunned. "Was anyone hurt? How about the other tenants?"

"Everyone is okay. The blast was narrowly focused. If you had turned on a burner, or the oven to cook dinner, you would have been in the direct path of the explosion."

Silence fell as Emily stared unseeingly out the car window. "At least I won't take anything for granted anymore."

Her jaw firmed and he saw again the steely control he'd sensed in her apartment.

"And I'll do my best to make certain it doesn't happen again." As though she were consciously throwing off a weight, she produced a small smile. Gesturing toward the uneaten sandwich still in Ross's hand, she asked, "You going to hold that all night?"

He looked at it, aware he had to eat or throw it away. Within minutes he had downed most of the sandwich and a bag of chips.

Emily watched while she nibbled on a piece of cheese.

"You always eat like this?" she inquired, striving for a lighter note.

His eyebrows went up. "Sure."

"You'll get fat." She didn't believe it. From what she'd seen, there wasn't an ounce of fat anywhere on his body.

"I'm storing up reserves of energy, for when I need it."

"Since when do sour cream and onion potato chips do that?"

"You might be surprised," he said, holding the bag out to her. "I'll bet you've never even tried these."

"You'd be right. They're bad for you."

He shrugged, unconcerned. "That was one of the worst things about being overseas. I would dream about junk food. Greasy potato chips. French fries. You name it, I wanted it."

Emily had to laugh.

Minutes later the crackle of the paper bag indicated he'd ferreted out the last morsel. "I'm ready. Back in a minute with our new transportation."

He was wrong. It was closer to five minutes before he returned and they switched vehicles.

Emily's nose wrinkled in distaste. The car was fifteen years old if a day, the fabric of the seats was torn and it drove in fits and starts, black smoke belching out the back, while a large pair of dice swung giddily from the mirror. It bore all the earmarks of a teenager's dream and a parent's nightmare.

Emily sighed. "I thought we were supposed to be inconspicuous."

Ross, who was attempting to get the most out of the car, didn't answer.

She repeated, "I said, I thought . . ."

"I heard you. This was easy to steal."

Emily knew there was more to it than that. She'd seen him hesitate beside a nice sedan with a baby seat in the back then pass it up. The airport came into view and Emily's muscles tightened.

Ross picked up on her mood change and it affected him

as well. Which was a bad sign. He was letting her get to him. More disturbing, he liked her.

He pulled into the parking lot and motioned brusquely for her to get out. "We're more visible as a couple so we'll go in separately. I'll get the tickets this time while you make yourself scarce in the ladies' room. Meet me at the cocktail lounge near the entrance to the gates in exactly fifteen minutes." With that, he walked swiftly out of sight.

After marching into the ladies' room, she surveyed herself dispassionately, then began to comb her hair, reviewing the behavior of the man who'd just left her.

All day he'd confined his conversation to terse replies, or even briefer questions. His probing into her life had surprised her until he'd admitted he was gathering background. Yet vestiges of humor had leaked out—and been ruthlessly quelled. But there had also been a faint kindness underlying the toughness. Perhaps their time together would be bearable. An inner voice chimed in that she was kidding herself if she thought it would only be bearable, given how attractive she found him. She pursed her lips consideringly.

He was attractive, she admitted, but not for her. Too hard, too tough, too . . . *male*. But at least she trusted him.

Her time was up and she walked slowly to the entrance of the cocktail lounge. Ross was at a corner table, a beer in front of him on a small round napkin. Emily slid into the seat beside him.

"We leave on a flight in about an hour for Dallas, then we connect before midnight with another to Midland. Want a drink?"

"White wine, please."

The waitress took the order and left.

"I want to get something straight," Emily said quietly. "Whether you think it's important or not, I'd like you to know I trust you. Completely."

He looked briefly stunned. "Thank you."

"Are you sure?" she asked.

"What do you mean?" He folded his arms.

"It really bothers you that I said it. Is the fact I trust you an additional burden you don't want? Because I'm not trying to add to your worries. I was actually hoping it would make you feel better, to know I do rely on you."

Puzzled that he hadn't yet responded, she was shocked when his hand came out and he shoved her abruptly to the floor. She had opened her mouth to complain when she realized he was gone.

Instead, he'd disappeared around the corner of the bar into the hallway without a backward glance. The quick glimpse she'd had of his expression caused her heart to pound furiously.

He'd looked ready to kill.

She rose cautiously from a crouching position, willing her breathing to slow. While the patrons of the small lounge stared, she groped her way back to her chair before placing her napkin precisely in her lap. She was not going to panic, she told herself.

Ross sauntered in a moment later. "Let's go." He took her by the arm and pulled when she didn't move. "Now!"

"Okay, okay, but what's the matter?"

"We were on the verge of being spotted by someone I thought I'd seen earlier. Come on, let's move to a more inconspicuous place."

"Where's that?"

"You'll see." He scanned the hallway and, holding her elbow in an unshakable grip, propelled her away from the crowds near the entry.

"Are you sure we're safe at the airport?" she asked, restraining the urge to tell him to slow down.

He kept up a brisk pace. "I think so. The man went out the front door to a taxi. But it pays to be cautious."

It had turned dark outside the airport and the large windows along the corridor showed airplanes parked on the ramp, or taxiing along the ground, strobes flashing in erratic patterns. A gentle mist had started to fall, softening and blurring the lights.

"Here." Ross pushed her into a chair at the end of a long deserted hall, taking the seat next to her. "You think anyone else is hanging around the airport?"

"I don't know but there's no point in taking unnecessary chances. We've been lucky so far. All it takes is one mistake. You don't get a reprieve."

"I'm prepared," she said quietly.

"Like hell you are." Ross's muscles tensed as he heard the slow, even steps of someone walking toward them. He'd been careful to select a commuter airline waiting area with no flight scheduled for two hours. Turning his head slowly, he saw the uniformed figure of a janitor and was about to relax when the man's head lifted, and he stared directly at Ross and Emily. With a swift motion, Ross pulled Emily to him and kissed her.

At the touch of his mouth on hers, Emily gasped in shock, instinctively trying to pull away. She felt his mouth lift slowly. With pulses hammering, she asked breathlessly, "What are you doing?"

"Keeping you safe," he growled huskily, and lowered his head.

Her lips parted and the slight brush of his tongue sent a bolt of fire through her. Her heart sped up and she trembled, dimly aware of receding footsteps.

Ross's arms tightened, cradling her against his lean body. She melted against him, all rational thought gone as she sank into his embrace. Warmth flooded her. The outside world disappeared and she met him kiss for kiss, gasp for gasp, her hands threading through his dark hair as she gave herself up to the dark storm that threatened to engulf her.

She thought she heard him mutter something as his mouth left hers then she felt him nibble on her ear gently proceeding to administer slow, heated kisses along the slope of her throat. She moaned, and his mouth lifted abruptly.

Ross put her away from him firmly and saw that his fingers were trembling on her shoulders. What in the hell am I thinking of?

Emily opened her eyes and he saw they were dazed, her pupils expanded so the blue irises were almost obscured. For a moment he laid his palm against her cheek, and ran his thumb slowly across her still parted lips. He lifted his hand and sat back.

"I'm sorry," he said, inhaling sharply. Without another word, he turned away. So much for good intentions, he thought bitterly. Something about the woman got to him, causing him to react uncharacteristically. He cursed himself and Walker both.

A headache pounded its way slowly up from his neck through the back of his skull and settled in behind his eyes. He wiped his face free of expression as he stared at the opposite wall.

Emily fought the sting of tears. She'd been clutching Ross as if he were the only stable thing in her universe until he'd pushed her away, making it clear the kiss was of no importance. At least he'd made a mockery of her earlier notions about the ability of her body to respond to a man's touch.

Her senior year at M.I.T. she'd spent one entirely forgettable evening with a fellow student. The coupling had hardly been earth-shattering, more of an experiment she conducted to be sure her body was functioning in all respects. She hadn't been sure at the time what all the fuss was about. Now she was.

There was absolutely no doubt that every part of her body was in first class working order. Her skin felt sensitized and her breasts still ached. Emily licked suddenly dry lips.

Steeling herself to look at him she felt sharp disappointment. Ross looked controlled and contained, and she bit her lip in frustration. Yet she'd been convinced the electricity had flowed both ways. There had been a deep hunger in his touch and she'd reacted instantly to it.

Their mouths had fused hotly, desperately, a feverish urgency in his touch. Yet now he looked as though he'd never pulled her so tightly to him that she'd felt his body imprinted on hers, as though his heart hadn't raced against her breast.

"How much longer until the plane leaves?" she asked, clearing her throat.

"About thirty minutes. We can go to the gate soon."

His tone made it clear he didn't want to talk and Emily controlled a flinch.

Neither spoke again, except through body language. Emily crossed her knees and arms. Ross deliberately stretched out his legs in front of him in a casual, relaxed position and shut his eyes, lowering his chin to his chest.

Opening his eyes a short while later, he checked his watch, grunted, and sat up. He felt like hell and the headache had found new pathways to torture in his brain.

"Time to go." He stood.

Without a word, Emily grabbed her purse and followed. They filed onto the plane after carefully checking the surrounding area. By the time they finished the light meal provided by the airline, Emily was tired and shut her eyes. Ross read a magazine and not a word was exchanged until they approached Dallas-Fort Worth Airport.

There Ross shepherded her off the airplane and over to the gate for the next flight. There was just enough time. They landed at Midland shortly before midnight.

"I'll drive to the cabin since I'm more familiar with the route," Emily said as they left the automobile rental counter.

Ross shrugged. He was tired and didn't feel like arguing. He'd watched Emily on the plane while she'd slept, his churning thoughts leaving him restless and tense.

"Are you sure you don't need a map?" he asked, fatigue roughening his voice.

"No. I'm fine. The interstate goes directly to El Paso. I'll keep on it and as I get near the shack, I'll peel off. Why don't you take a nap? It's about two hundred miles."

Ross did a quick calculation. It was now after midnight and he expected they would be in before four in the morning. He nodded and settled close to the door, his shoulders slumping against the cool window. The desert temperature dropped rapidly and it had been crisp outside the airport.

Emily took note that Ross had closed his eyes. Moments later she heard his even breathing. Shifting to a more comfortable position, she settled down to drive, a small smile on her face. She'd always loved cars, the sensation of tightly leashed speed, the feeling of power that surged under her command. In her element, Emily watched the dark landscape flash past the window, her self-confidence returning as she drove, glad to be in control again.

Ross woke when the car stopped. He looked around. There was a full moon lighting a small building a few yards from the car. Checking the luminous hands of his watch, he saw it was two-thirty in the morning. "Where are we?"

"At the house." She was calm, a smile of contentment on her face.

He sat bolt upright, smacking his head against the side of the car, shocked into alertness. "Already? How fast did you drive? What the hell kind of a driver are you?"

"Yes, ninety, and good."

Ross was quick on his feet but it took him a moment to apply the answers to his questions. When he did, he felt like strangling her. "Ninety isn't good."

"It is if you're a competent driver."

"How do I know you are?"

"We've arrived in one piece, haven't we? Besides I took a race driver's course."

"What? In your big wheel when you were two years old?"

"No. Eighteen." His scorn bounced off her. "Fully old enough to graduate at the top of the class."

"I suppose they designate top of the class for speed freaks."

"Jealous?"

He shot her a look calculated to reduce her to rubble. "I'll bet they were glad to see you go."

"Let's just say the instructor muttered something about creating a monster."

Her tone was unmistakably smug and he felt a small jolt at the victorious smile on her face.

Ross could feel a laugh begin somewhere deep inside and choked it back. The last thing the woman beside him needed was encouragement.

FOUR

Ross got out of the car and stood, motionless. The night was bright with moonlight. He could see the cabin clearly some yards away. It was a low structure, with a small, front-facing porch. He turned as he heard Emily moving behind him.

"Stay put," he ordered. "I'm going to look around."

"No one could possibly know we're here," she protested.

"Remember the so-called deserted farmhouse in Pennsylvania?" he asked, then began to move without waiting for her reply.

Emily watched as he approached the building and stopped, his body in a listening pose. He was in motion again, his shape blending with a darkness edging the cabin. Then he was gone. She shivered in the cool air as she waited. After a few moments, a rustle came from her left. It was Ross and she relaxed.

"Everything okay?" she whispered.

"All clear." He spoke in a normal tone.

She retrieved her purse and jacket from the back seat. Hefting their suitcases from the trunk, Ross asked, "Is this place left open?"

"No. I need a key. I know where the hunters keep it." She bent by a faucet in front of the porch, and scraped in the dirt at its base. She located a thin wire and dislodged it from the tamped down soil. A small object dangled at the end. "See?"

"Why go to so much trouble?" His voice was dry. "I thought this was the last place on earth."

"To most everyone it is, but people still cross the country on foot looking for work." She mounted the porch steps. "My father regards this as a subtle tribute to civilization. Maybe if people see the door is locked, they'll leave the lodge alone.''

''Have they?''

''Nope.'' Emily peered in the darkness toward the door knob. ''It's entered at least a couple of times a year. But Dad believes in holding the line against the forces of chaos. He's a perfectionist.'' She inserted the key and turned until it clicked.

''And you take after him,'' Ross said, pushing the door open.

''Probably,'' she returned, unruffled.

Ross entered behind her, putting the suitcases down. He could hear her hand patting the wall to her left. ''Looking for this?''

Light flooded them and she held up a hand shading her eyes. ''I despise people who can instantly find light switches.''

''Comes in handy sometimes,'' he replied, stepping past her.

''I'll just bet it does. You probably find yourself in some pretty strange places.''

Along with some pretty strange people, he could almost hear her add.

Emily made a sweeping gesture at the interior of the cabin. ''Well, this is it.''

They were standing in a large, bare room which served as the kitchen, dining, and living area of the house. Ross had to admit it wasn't exactly what he'd envisioned.

A white, enamel stove was in a corner next to a long, badly chipped Formica counter. A low humming noise came from an ancient refrigerator on the stove's other side. In the middle of the room stood a deeply scarred wooden table and two benches. Light shone down from a bare bulb hanging at the end of an electrical cord directly over the table. Unpainted wood walls were covered by black, peeling tarpaper, and the foundation listed noticeably. Fading strips of linoleum lurched across the floor, its rose and trellis pattern assaulting the eye. At the far end, a rock fireplace took up most of the wall. The only other furniture was provided by two armchairs squarely placed before the hearth, their cushions sagging from years of use.

"Doesn't look that bad, does it?" Emily said, eyeing Ross's skeptical expression.

"You pick the linoleum?"

"Very amusing. The hunters did, probably out of a catalog."

"Hope it was in black and white."

She grinned at the jibe. "I don't imagine they cared as long as the floor got covered. People who come this far to hunt believe they're rugged individualists but conveniently forget they have heat and electricity. I might as well go ahead and get unpacked. Save time in the morning." Emily's voice was brisk.

God, she seemed wide awake and ready to take on the world, Ross thought, his mood souring. He was feeling old and beat up while she looked as though she'd slept a full eight hours instead of flying through the night on four tires. He stifled resentment at her youthful ability to thrive under adversity.

Once upon a time, he'd thrived under similar circumstances, fueled by idealism. Nowadays, however, his personal generator was running low on that particular commodity.

After pausing to drop her purse and jacket on a chair, Emily walked into the other room. "Take your pick of beds in here," she called back. "Dibs on the one in the corner."

Ross followed, his glance taking in the second room's plan. It was large and rectangular with another crude rock fireplace at one end. Six beds were lined up against one wall, and bare shelves hung over the beds. There was a doorway near the fireplace.

It opened to the bathroom, Ross discovered, as he glanced through it. A small window over the tub looked out on a barren patch of ground. "Where exactly are we?" he asked, stepping back into the bedroom, watching as she began to unpack.

"Eight and a quarter miles from the nearest town, at an elevation of four thousand three hundred fifty feet. There's a mountain range immediately to the west of us approximately seven thousand feet high and a valley to the east, which runs north and south, intersected at irregular intervals by low ridges. The approach is winding but visible from the house.''

"You must have been a cartographer in an earlier life.''

"You asked me where we were 'exactly.' I figured you'd want to know everything about the place so you could make plans.''

"Thanks.''

Emily tilted her head. "Was that sarcastic?''

"Nope.'' Ross selected a bed on the other side of the room and heaved his suitcase onto the mattress. His practiced eye calculated the likelihood of comfort to be garnered from the bed. "Merely observing you saved me time. I should have realized you'd know.''

"I don't think I like the way you said that.''

"Sorry.''

He wasn't, she thought, keeping the hurt off her face. He made her sound like an egghead. "So you would have asked for the information if I hadn't told you?''

"It's my job to protect you. Details can make the difference between leaving a place feet first or walking.'' Ross leaned over the bed, putting his palm on the mattress. He pressed down. Nothing happened. An eyebrow rose. He tried again. The bed gave slightly. He put his suitcase on the floor with a small sigh.

"I imagine you'd feel safe anywhere in the world,'' Emily said, "whether you had anyone else's help or not.''

"I wish that were true,'' he said.

Emily paused, holding a stack of clothing. "That's not very confidence-inspiring. You're supposed to make me feel secure.''

"I'll do better,'' he said evenly.

She frowned. He looked exhausted, his face lined with fatigue. She didn't know what assignment he'd been on before she met him but he obviously hadn't had a break in a long time.

After a small hesitation, Emily smiled, offering a diversion. "Actually you do make me feel secure. Like at the airport. You saw something you didn't like and took countermeasures.''

"How's that?"

"You kissed me." She could still feel the countermeasure on her mouth. "Wasn't that the whole point of the exercise?"

"Right."

Ross's face was bland but Emily felt a ripple of emotion from him. His ambiguity made her uneasy. Right about what? That the kiss was a legitimate safety device or only that he'd said it was?

"Do you know if there's any food here?" he asked.

"There isn't. We'll have to get some in the morning."

"Fine." Ross yawned prodigiously. He picked up a blanket from the foot of the bed, and draped it over himself as he lay down, fully clothed. Emily saw him slide a gun under the pillow.

"One more thing. I locked the door from the kitchen to the porch. See you in the morning." He shut his eyes and settled deeper in the mattress. Then, unbelievably, he was asleep.

Emily shook her head in wonder at his ability to seal himself off from his environment. She studied him a moment longer then went to the kitchen and turned out the light before going back to bed. She lay down, her gaze moving to the window over her head.

Moonlight streamed in, laying a cold, white blanket across her. The wind was still, the only sound in the room Ross's quiet, steady breathing. Her ears tingled in the unaccustomed silence.

At any hour of the day or night in Manhattan, someone was sure to be walking along a street, slamming a door or yelling from his car, or tripping over a garbage can that seemed to roll forever. When she'd first moved to New York, she'd had to get used to the endless barrrage of sounds. It struck her as ironic that now she couldn't sleep because of the quiet. And the loneliness.

It had been years since she'd slept in the same room with someone. Memories surfaced of whispered jokes, murmured stories, quiet giggles shared with her brother.

She remembered her nervous laughter, afraid their parents would overhear. Emily had enjoyed that closeness. She'd been unable to duplicate it since.

From the looks of things, she wasn't going to be able to now either. She and Ross were physically together but emotionally apart. He'd given a reason for his aloofness, but his excuse of professionalism didn't ring true. Emily turned over, punching the pillow a couple of times to even out the lumps.

She shifted under the covers, pulling them more snugly around her shoulders. Once the good guys found out who the bad guys were, she could go back to her life in New York. That was what she wanted, right? Emily shut her eyes.

When she woke the next morning the cabin was silent. Rising, she went onto the porch. The car was where they'd left it the night before. She went back inside, heading for the shower.

Fifteen minutes later she emerged, her hair hanging in damp curls around her scrubbed face. She dressed in the cramped bathroom, donning a pair of old, faded jeans and an open-collared shirt. Padding to the kitchen, she saw Ross seated at the table.

Her hands toweled her hair. "Did you sleep well?"

"Fine." He gave her a comprehensive glance, then focused intently on the gun he was cleaning. He pulled a cloth from the leather case on the table beside him and wiped the weapon carefully until a sheen of oil lay on the barrel.

"You all right?" She walked in front of him and peered down at his bent head. Ross was wearing jeans and a dark flannel shirt.

"Yep," he said.

"If you're worried that I took all the hot water, don't. I turned on the water heater last night, so there's plenty left."

Ross grunted noncommittally. Shrugging, Emily sat down. His movements were economical. His hands, long-fingered and powerful, were precise and deft. His touch on the burnished metal was gentle as he stroked it with the cloth. Emily had a sudden vision of those same hands on her bare skin, caressing her with a lover's touch.

She almost jumped. What on earth was the matter with her? This was the second time her imagination had produced erotic images. And the kiss he'd given her only added color and texture. She felt a funny tingle in her belly. She dropped the towel and propped her chin on her hand, staring at him unblinkingly.

Ross finished and put the gun away, along with the kit. "I'm going to town in a few minutes. If there's something in particular you want from the store, make a list. We should be here a day or two, but I won't know for sure until I reach someone in Washington."

Emily straightened and surveyed him with disfavor. "What do you mean you're going? You're not moving an inch without me."

Ross returned her look. She looked soft except around the eyes. He leaned negligently against the table. "Why not?"

"Because it wouldn't be safe for me to stay here alone."

"Not safe? This is the hideout you picked, if you'll remember."

Ross wondered if he'd missed a clue somewhere. She didn't look worried yet her words implied otherwise.

"That doesn't mean I want to be abandoned."

Emily wasn't about to tell him she'd dreamed during what was left of the night—dark, confused dreams where someone chased her down a long corridor. Footsteps pounded after her, closer and closer. She'd awakened trembling.

"Besides," she added, "you're the one who told me earlier we were going to stay together. Don't you think you'd have a hard time protecting me while you're gone?"

"True, except presumably the risk to you here is less than the risk in town where you could be recognized."

"No one will ever connect me with the old Emily Brown." She gave a light laugh. "The last time I was here, I was fifteen years old with pigtails, braces, and knobby knees."

"I suspect there are other differences as well."

Heat bloomed in her cheeks as his look drifted over her. Ross's fingers thumped on the table. "All right, but you have to do exactly what I tell you."

"Of course." She arched an eyebrow in mute question.

"Get ready and we'll go."

It was still early, and the morning breeze was fresh as they walked outside. She stopped just past the door, her head cocked. A quail chirruped then fluttered its wings and flew up the slope to join the rest of the covey. Emily smiled.

This was the time of day when she'd missed the ranch most. The desert became harsh and unforgiving at midday but in early morning and near sundown, a gentler radiance softened the contours of the mountains, blurred the spiky edges of the plants, and filled the high desert with peace. The air felt soft for a time, making promises the rest of the day rarely delivered.

"God, I've missed this," Emily said huskily as she lifted her chin and inhaled deeply with closed eyes.

Ross, watching her, thought her upturned face held the warmth and color of a beautiful woman's awaiting a lover's kiss. He gave himself a mental shake and deliberately cooled his voice.

"Why not move back?" He went around to the driver's side of the car, and got in as Emily opened her own door.

"I might, but not to the ranch. My brother is best suited to run it. Besides, my skills aren't very useful out here."

There it was again, Ross noted. The implication she didn't fit in, even in the place she called home. He started the motor and drove slowly down the curving, rough road, wincing as he felt the bottom scrape over the high center.

"How do your parents feel about you living in New York?"

"They miss me but they understand. They've never tried to hold me back. They knew it was best for me to go somewhere else." She looked at him. "Do you see your own family much?"

"No."

"Why not?"

"Just because," he said, his tone unmistakably closing the subject.

Emily hitched sideways in the seat, her eyes angry. "What's with you anyway? It's fine for you to ask me any personal question you like, but when I do the exact same thing, you slam the door in my face. Are you going to tell me your past is classified?" She watched as a muscle bunched in his jaw.

"Anything I want to know is directly related to the job I have to do. I need to know about your background, your habits, likes and dislikes, because it could be very relevant. On the other hand, nothing about my past has any bearing on our situation."

Her lip curled derisively. "At least it makes a good excuse." She pointedly turned away from him and stared out the window.

Ross's hands tightened on the steering wheel. How could someone like Emily, coming from a loving family, comprehend his own?

They'd abandoned him when he was twelve. Arnie and Betty Harding blew with the wind from one side of the country to the other. They'd picked oranges in Florida, cotton in Georgia, and lettuce in California. Then, pockets jingling with change, they'd moved on. Ross had been dragged along behind them, accustomed to grabbing sleep in the back of cars, on benches, or sitting upright in hard chairs while his parents negotiated for the sale of whatever item they had to barter, as they scrounged for the next day's cash. Finally, they'd left him with Anna Bazinsky whom they'd met when she was cooking at a soup kitchen. Anna had died shortly before he graduated from the Ivy League university he'd attended on full scholarship. That second abandonment, even though involuntary, had been more painful than the first. She at least had cared about him.

"Which way?" Ross asked as they reached the pavement.

"Take a left."

He braked and pulled onto the highway.

"By the way," he turned toward her, smiling faintly,

"thank you for letting me sleep during the drive. I might have hurt my eyes otherwise." He saw he'd gotten her attention.

"How could you have done that?"

"From constantly watching my life flashing past."

She rewarded him with a similar smile and Ross felt his tension ease. Why it mattered, he didn't know. But it did. The town came into sight a few minutes later and he slowed at the outskirts. "It's only seven-thirty. Why don't I make my call, then we'll find some coffee. What time does the store open?" he asked.

"Probably around eight. There should be a phone at the gas station at the other end of town."

Ross drove where she indicated. About to dial straight through to Washington, he stopped and hung up, his expression thoughtful. Walker's phone was too vulnerable. The day before when he'd called, he'd known they would be out of the area before being traced. Now, he couldn't afford to leave an unnecessary trail. He picked up the receiver again and dialed the work number in New York of Mike Reynolds, an old friend from his army days. They'd kept in touch ever since. It looked as though Mike's job with a long distance service company would come in handy.

"Mike, this is Ross," he said, hearing the familiar voice.

"Great to hear from you. I thought you were overseas. When did you get back?"

"A couple of days ago. I need a favor."

"If I can. Shoot."

"Can you patch me through to a Washington number without leaving a trace?"

"No problem. Give it to me and the number where you are and I'll call you back in two minutes."

"Thanks. I'll owe you one."

"No, you don't. You saved my hide from that little necktie party. We're not close to even yet."

Ross grinned. The necktie party had consisted of a band of guerrillas who'd captured Mike when he was on a reconnaissance mission. The noose was already secure when Ross stepped in with three smoke bombs and a grenade. He remembered Mike's white-lipped nonchalance as Ross untied the rope from around his neck.

While he waited, Ross turned his head to watch Emily's profile through the car window. She'd had an air of vulnerability when she'd asked to accompany him to town. He didn't know what was behind the unlikely fragility. He'd have to find out. The conversation with Mike came back to him and his expression darkened. He'd hate to see Emily's slender neck with a noose around it.

The phone rang and Ross stayed on the open line while the call went through. As soon as a voice answered, Ross tensed because it wasn't Walker. He gripped the receiver tightly.

"Who is this?" the man at the other end demanded. "Speak up."

"Ross," he said. "That you, Galloway?"

"Yes," Frank Galloway responded. "Where are you?"

"Nowhere in particular. Where's Walker?"

"Out for a while. If you need to talk to him, why don't you leave a number? I'll have him get back to you."

Ross heard a tightness in Galloway's voice. "I'm going to be moving around a lot. I'll call later."

"When?" Galloway prodded.

"I don't know." Ross severed the connection. He'd heard a click on the line and Galloway had sounded frightened.

That was bad. Very bad. Galloway was normally unflappable. But he shouldn't have answered the phone since Walker had promised to man the line himself. What the hell was going on?

Emily took one look at Ross's face and asked, "What's wrong?"

"I tried to reach my boss and he wasn't there."

"That's serious?"

"Yeah. He'd told me he'd be manning the phones personally. Instead, someone else answered."

"Could your call have been traced?"

"No. I routed it through another line."

"Do you want to go back to Washington?"

"Not yet. If I don't get in touch with Walker by the day after tomorrow, we'll leave." He started the car. "Where can we get coffee?" he asked.

"There's a cafe down the street."

Reba's Round-Up was two blocks down, and there were a couple of dusty pickups pulled up in front of the door.

Before they went in, Ross took her by the arm and pulled her to a halt. "If you meet anybody you think you know, tell them you're on your way to your folks' ranch."

"Fine, and how do I introduce you?"

"Your devoted husband, of course."

"Name?"

Ross could see someone from inside the restaurant turn to look at them. "I'm Ross. But not Harding. Try Jones."

"Really has the ring of truth," she said dryly.

He released her and opened the door.

Two tables were occupied and Emily headed for a third one at the back of the restaurant, safely out of earshot. She stole a quick glance at the patrons, didn't recognize anyone, and slid into a seat across from Ross. Not that she'd expected to see someone she knew, but coincidence was a strange and pervasive phenomenon.

Looking around her, she felt immediately at home. Booths, upholstered in bright red plastic and deeply indented with buttons, were ranged against the walls. The radio blared a cowboy lament in keeping with the western scenes hung above the tables. The odor of fried food drifted from the partially enclosed kitchen and she heard snatches of the song from someone, probably the cook. Emily smiled, welcoming the unselfconsciousness of the place. She'd gotten tired of trendy spots where the ferns and cutely folded napkins looked crisper than the patrons. Here the napkins were honest paper, and the condiments were still in their original bottles.

The waitress, a tired looking woman in her late thirties, popping gum noisily in one ruddy cheek, ambled over to them. She propped an elbow on a jean-clad hip and held out menus. "You folks know what you'd like?" She shifted her gum to the other cheek.

Ross surveyed the selection. "Two eggs over easy, link sausage, orange juice, and coffee."

Emily was still reading. She heard Ross move impatiently in the seat but didn't lift her eyes from the plastic covered sheet.

"I think I'll have the waffles," she began, then stopped and looked up. "How are the blueberry pancakes?"

"Fine, honey." The waitress popped her gum. "Want a plate?"

"Uh . . . no, on second thought I think I'll have the scrambled eggs, bacon, and toast. And coffee."

"No pancakes." The waitress made a note on her pad and left.

Emily raised her eyes to find Ross staring at her. "Well?" she demanded.

"Performing cosmic calculations with the menu?"

Her eyes narrowed. "I like breakfast to be just right."

He knew her well enough already to realize she thrived on order. But you didn't always get what you wanted. He frowned. Although twenty-eight, Emily looked almost like a kid, fresh and untainted by life's dark underbelly. So far.

Their food arrived after a few minutes and they ate. Emily was on her second cup of coffee before she spoke. "I should call my parents. We usually talk once a week. If anyone called about my apartment, they're going to be out of their minds with worry."

"I can probably arrange it," he said easily.

Why should she have been surprised he'd agreed so readily, she wondered. He really wasn't cold or unfeeling, no matter how impenetrable the toughness seemed on occasion.

She drank her juice, then leaned back against the seat and gazed at her keeper. He sat almost indolently, his broad shoulders relaxed, his forearms on the table. But his pose was deceptive. Ross never truly let down his guard.

In Pennsylvania, she'd seen every muscle and nerve pitched to a high degree of tension, yet he'd moved smoothly, silently, and with impressive control. Now, his gray eyes were sleepy, and a small smile curved his mouth upward, but she knew if anything out of the ordinary occurred, the other Ross would be triggered.

As they left the restaurant, he said, "Want to call your parents now?"

She nodded. "Yes. If it's not too much trouble."

"We can use the phone over there." He pointed across the street to a telephone booth and they walked to it. He stepped in to make the connection, going through the same procedure with Mike, and gestured to Emily to get in with him.

She stood in the small enclosed area and Ross tilted his head, covering the mouthpiece of the receiver with his hand. "Just a sec." He listened, then removed his hand. "Go ahead." There wasn't a spare inch of space between them, she realized. She tried to back away.

Helen Brown came on the line.

"Mother?"

"Emily, where on earth are you? I've been getting mysterious telephone calls from different people. They said your apartment was destroyed by fire. Are you all right?"

"I'm fine. There was an accident but no one was hurt. Don't worry about a thing."

Ross pressed his back against the hard wall of the booth while Emily's breast brushed his chest each time she breathed. Morning sun streamed through the dusty glass, beat down on his shoulders, and heated up the space between them. Her faint perfume, warmed by their closeness, seemed to rise in a steamy mist, locking them together. He inhaled sharply and looked down to the open-throated shirt, to the arching curve of Emily's neck. He saw the tender skin of the swell of her breast. His mouth dried.

The booth was suddenly stifling. He shut his eyes briefly. He should have been worrying about Emily, and the very real danger they were in. Instead he couldn't keep his mind above his waist.

Ross put his hand back over the mouthpiece. "Your mother's been contacted?"

Emily tried to pry his fingers loose. "Yes. Let go, damnit."

"The phone could be tapped," he hissed. "Don't say anything else. Tell her you'll be in touch later."

She glared sideways at him. He released his grip. "Sorry, Mom. I was having trouble with one of the machines here," she said deliberately. She felt his body shake. "I've got to run. I'll talk to you in a few days."

She hung up and pushed against Ross. He didn't budge.

"What did she say?"

"Will you move?"

"What did she say?"

Emily rolled her eyes. "I'm surprised you couldn't hear every syllable yourself. You couldn't get much closer," she said, then he shifted against her. Emily bit her lip.

Oh, yes, he could.

All the while she'd been talking, she'd been acutely conscious of his body against hers and she'd barely dared breathe. Her hips had been jammed into him and she'd felt his unmistakable response.

She went on hurriedly, "Mom said that she'd been getting calls from people asking where I was. She already knew about the apartment." She pressed her upper body away from him, resulting in her waist and hips tilting forward. His body hardened.

She blushed. "Will you let me out!" Emily felt something akin to panic race through her veins at his knowing expression. Her knees felt funny and she locked them. She felt like a little kid caught playing with fire—attracted but wary, fascinated yet scared. She'd definitely burned. And he'd known.

Ross shifted and stepped through the door. "I'm sure her phone is tapped although we weren't on the phone long enough for a trace. But the pressure's on." And it came from more than one direction, he thought. "Come on," he said crisply.

She followed him back to the car, the turmoil inside subsiding. As she moved around to her side, she said, "Sounds like I'd better get to work right away on the message I received."

"Yes. Maybe then we'll have something to bargain with. Where's the grocery list?"

"Right here." She patted her shirt pocket and saw Ross' eyes follow her movement. Emily dropped her hand.

"Give me the list. I'll get what we need. No use in running the risk of anyone spotting you."

Emily agreed, still shaken by the intense sexual arousal she'd experienced when he'd stared at her, a flash of something hot that disappeared at once from the eyes she'd originally thought so cool.

By the time he returned, carrying two grocery bags, Emily had convinced herself that he hadn't behaved out of character in the phone booth. She'd simply misread things.

"Did you get everything I needed?" As he leaned in, putting the sacks in the back seat, she said threateningly, "Blood will be spilled if you didn't. And it won't be mine."

"Keep your shirt on."

"I always do," she said sweetly, then froze at his arrested expression.

——————— FIVE ———————

"I don't think I'll pursue that," Ross said, his mouth quirking upward, as he got in and slammed the car door.

Emily's composure slipped. She'd never been the type to engage in sexual innuendos. But honesty compelled her to the conclusion that, subconsciously at least, her choice of words had been deliberate. After a last, thorough look at her, Ross drove out of town. The trip back was silent, Emily vowing to keep her mouth shut before she got herself in more trouble.

You'd love the trouble, a mocking inner voice gibed.

As they turned into the dirt road leading to the cabin, Ross slowed, and rolled down his window, putting his head through the opening.

"What are you doing?" she asked, relieved she no longer felt flushed.

"Checking for tracks." His eyes scanned the road in front of them. "No one has been through here since we left."

"You surely don't believe anyone knows where we are?"

"No. But it pays to be careful." He pulled into the spot the car had occupied the night before. "I'm going to look around. Be right back." He reappeared a moment later. "All clear."

She got out. "How do you know?"

"I left twigs in a couple of places, smoothed the dirt clear in others, rigged a home made alarm system by two of the windows, a few things like that. The building is far enough from the surrounding brush that anyone approaching would have to leave cover and walk across open ground," he said, pulling out the groceries.

Emily followed him up to the porch and into the house.

66

She put away the food. As he stashed the empty sacks in a space by the refrigerator, Ross said, "Before you got up this morning, I looked over some of the area but I'll feel safer once I've made a complete circuit of the hillside."

"Okay. I have things to do here."

Emily watched through a window, reflecting on the man who was leaving.

He oozed sexual magnetism. But she didn't know why. On the surface, he wouldn't have seemed to possess charm. True, there was humor in his face, but a counter-balancing grimness had left its mark as well. And his behavior was equally ambivalent. Yet the total added up to a compelling attraction that baffled while it intrigued.

Sometimes she was positive she detected warmth, even a subtle tenderness, only to have that certainty dispelled by an unexpected retreat. As he'd just done. She gave a wistful sigh before turning away from the window.

Forcing herself into action, she retrieved the clothes she'd worn the day before. She'd remembered to pack detergent and a short time later had her underwear and shirt hanging over the tub.

Outside, Ross forced his thoughts away from the woman inside. He inhaled deeply of the fresh, pine scented air as he walked around the cabin, cataloguing the approaches. The place was defensible, if you had an adequate notice system. While he walked, he took care not to dislodge any rocks and avoided stepping on open areas of soil. He preferred to leave few traces of his passage, although he knew an expert tracker could have followed his path. An hour later, satisfied he had evaluated the most likely risks, he walked uphill.

A half mile above and beyond the cabin he sat down, and leaned against a rock that had been warmed by the sun, surveying the structure below. The building snugged against the steep slope, its tin roof glinting in the sunlight. Rocks and loose shale around it made hiking slow and noisy but were an advantage for defense. Mesquite, a scattering of pinon, the outstretched spidery arms of ocotillo, and other desert plants dotted the hillside. Nearby, a lizard stared at him unblinkingly, half his body in shadow, and when Ross remained motionless, edged further into the sun.

He didn't understand how Emily could leave this for New York City. Ross managed to stand Washington for short stretches, but only because time in the field made it bearable.

Although that was less true lately. At thirty-six he supposed it was time for him to look into another line of work. Reflexes, eyesight, and hearing—they'd all changed over time. His instincts, nurtured by experience, were essential.

A second's delay, an unheeded warning, and you were history. And Ross didn't know if he had what it took any more. The disaster in Berlin five years earlier had eroded his self-confidence, forcing him to question his ability to judge people. Although he'd been fine in Afghanistan. Hell, he'd been damned near superb.

And the rebels had been magnificent, fiercely determined to keep their homeland, and eager to acquire the training he could provide. He'd been placed with competent men and women who were used to living on the edge of existence, their lives narrowly held from extinction by happenstance. Will the helicopter gunship come this side of the gorge or the other? Will it come when the late afternoon sun highlights my rock or someone else's? The mountain people believed in fate. If it was meant to happen it would and the smiles behind huge mustaches accepted either.

But after Berlin, life had lost its savor. Yes, he'd performed well in Afghanistan, but without fire, without enthusiasm, and even worse, without commitment. Professionalism had been what had saved him. Would it be enough now?

His thoughts shifted to the woman in the cabin below. Emily had a naivete about the real world allied to a sense of invincibility. Like Marta. He knew only too well how the combination produced disaster under the right circumstances.

He rose to his feet, telling himself he was unnecessarily

worried. Walker was temporarily misplaced, the mole would be found, and Emily could go back to her safe existence. As far as his own life was concerned, he would have to make some decisions, and soon.

Quickening his step, he turned towards the cabin. Opening the door quietly, he hesitated as he saw Emily in the living area. Her head bent, she was writing on a pad of paper. He passed through to the bedroom and unbuttoned the top button of his shirt, planning on a shower. Just inside the bathroom door, he stopped cold.

A bra in the color of palest champagne, the cups edged with scallops of lace, was draped over the shower rod. It was alongside a filmy pair of panties, in the same intoxicating color. Both were damp. The blouse she'd been wearing the day before dripped gently onto the mat on the floor beneath.

Ross reached out his hand, and ran a finger slowly over the ribbon strap of the bra, sliding down to where the lace swelled before jerking his hand away as though burned. He was having enough trouble keeping his mind clear without having mental images of her slim body covered with only bra and panties. He backed out, telling himself he felt anger at the invasion of lingerie. Not desire. Not a growing need.

Emily stretched her arms over her head and looked up in surprise to find Ross watching her.

His mind swam with the image of bare, damp skin.

"I didn't realize you were standing there," she said with a lazy smile that caused his throat to tighten.

"Sure." Like hell she hadn't known, he thought, keeping his eyes away from the way her shirt had risen when she'd stretched, exposing inches of soft skin. The woman knew how to drive him mad.

"I often don't hear what people are saying if I'm concentrating. I was busy trying to remember all of the words in the message," she said, waving the yellow pad at him.

"Oh." He rubbed his tight neck.

"It's not all that hard."

Oh, yes it is. He shifted.

"Fortunately," she said, "I have close to a photographic memory. The problem is that I have to reconstruct several pages of technical data.''

"I won't bother you then," he said and turned on his heel.

"What in Sam Hill is the matter with you?" Emily stared in amazement at Ross's back.

"Not a damned thing." In a second, he was out the door.

"Don't you walk out on me," she yelled. Emily stalked across the kitchen after him, slamming the door behind her for emphasis, enjoying the slight twitch of Ross's shoulders as she came onto the porch. She sat next to him on the top step, and thumped him on the arm. "Look at me. What's wrong?"

"Cabin fever," he said shortly.

"Cabin fever? You've been here five minutes," she said.

More like Emily fever. "I guess I'm just feeling antsy."

Emily shot him a glance, but couldn't read anything from his face. She controlled her exasperation. He was being ridiculously volatile. She leaned back, stretching her legs in front of her then caught her breath. Ross's gaze was traveling up her body slowly.

"Am I bothering you or something?" she demanded finally as the silence lengthened.

"Yeah." He didn't take his eyes off her.

Emily wet her lips, her throat tightening. "How?" God, he was making her breasts hard, she realized in stupefaction. With just a look.

Dark blue eyes were focused directly on his, and Ross saw her pupils enlarging, expanding, as she stared at him in fascination.

Damning his inability to resist, he muttered, "This way. Making me ache." He told himself she was driving him to it. He pulled her against him as urgency hammered through his blood.

His mouth came down on her bare, soft lips, and his heart thumped at her gasp. Ross gripped the nape of her neck, holding her head steady as he kissed her. She whimpered as he probed at her closed mouth with his tongue, pressing until her lips parted.

She was magic. The softness of her mouth, the feel of her erect nipples against his chest, they were driving him wild. His body hardened and he thrust his fingers through the silk of her hair, wanting to crush her against him. Her moan penetrated the fog and he stiffened. He raised his head.

He was out of his mind. He'd been on the verge of losing control, he realized in shock, as he tasted her on his mouth.

For the second time. He gripped her harder for a timeless moment then released her.

"Wha-at?"

Ross rose and moved to the other end of the porch, hands jammed deep into his pockets. "That was a demonstration to show you what happens when we're in close contact. It's too dangerous."

"It is?" She fought disorientation.

"Right."

"You mean you find me appealing and contact between us is dangerous?" Her eyes were bright.

"Yeah." Ross bit back a curse. Her hair was mussed where he'd run his fingers through it and her mouth was curved in a smile.

"Wonderful."

"No, it's not."

The light dimmed from her face. "Let me recapitulate what just happened so I understand. You find me attractive, you kissed me, and we can't do it again. Is that correct?"

"Essentially."

"Why not?"

It was always the simple questions that did you in. "Because we're who we are."

Emily bent her knee, lacing her fingers around it. "So?"

"Being attracted to you means my objectivity is compromised. I won't be able to deal with an emergency as quickly if I'm worrying about your reactions. Things could go wrong.''

"This is great. You're now going to predict my future.''

"Hell, lady, if I don't read your future, there might not be one.''

"Or at least not one with you?''

Ross sighed. "I shouldn't have kissed you. I'm sorry.''

"Or you should only kiss me to make a point, like to persuade an impartial observer that we're involved, when we're not? The way you did at the airport.''

"Exactly.'' His ears felt hot.

"You're not finding this at all confusing? I sure am.''

"Let's stick to serious issues like saving your neck. That way no one gets their wires crossed. It's cleaner and easier.''

"For you, perhaps.''

Ross looked away from the hurt and naked vulnerability he saw in her eyes.

Emily was motionless, then she gave herself a brisk shake. She wasn't about to put herself through an emotional wringer. If he wanted distance, fine. She would be professional. "I've been thinking about our predicament.'' Her smile was humorless. "I mean our real predicament, not the one you've dreamed up.''

"And?'' He didn't let himself react to the flash of pain on her face.

"Yesterday, you told me I'd received a message by mistake that carried a hidden code in it to disrupt Canadian government.'' He nodded. "Okay. As I told you, I've been trying to remember all of it. It was rather long.''

Ross turned sideways to face her, and settled against the porch post. "Right, but there's one thing I don't understand. Why would a New York arm of N.S.A. be dealing with this anyway? Wouldn't the Fort Meade headquarters have taken care of it?''

"Normally.''

"So why did you get this one?''

"Because it came straight to New York. Canada doesn't generally send messages into this country deeply encrypted. We're a major trading partner, and we observe an unwritten gentlemen's agreement not to probe into their transmissions. Although," she added, "with the situation heating up because of separatism, we've begun paying more attention."

He frowned. "So they send coded messages?"

Emily nodded. "The Canadians know we've got decoders as well as data from our own satellites, so for the lower-level signals, they don't go to extreme security lengths."

"And this is still going on?"

"Yes. Any nation wants to be able to communicate securely with their foreign offices."

He nodded in agreement, his own experience confirming her words. "Could two copies of the message have been sent?"

"Sure. Canada is scheduled to have discussion at the U.N. over their trans-border status, and presumably their Washington office as well as New York staff would be alerted. So most likely I wasn't the only one at the agency dealing with the material." She was quiet for a moment, then added, "Unless Washington never received the duplicate because the sender realized he had mistakenly encoded critical material. He might then have cancelled the second transmission to Washington."

Ross considered the possibility. "If you're right, that would confirm you're the only one who saw the message. No one at headquarters took a crack at it." He paced the length of the porch before turning back to Emily. "All right, what about the message itself? Was it strange in any way?"

"It contained the reference to 'Rocket.' "

"What's unusual about that?"

"Because I think it indicated an individual rather than a thing, and besides, I've never seen a Canadian message to the U.S. about missile launches."

Ross pursed his lips in silence. "Who would have known that was an aberration?"

She shrugged. "I didn't consult with anyone else."

"If it had gotten to Fort Meade, would anyone there have spotted it as an anomaly?"

She looked at him sharply. "If it had been received,

yes . . . but I just explained that I don't think the message was duplicated. You'd be worried about someone else besides me.''

"I'm not willing to rule anything out at this point," Ross said. "What time of day did it come in?''

"As I remember, and this was almost ten days ago, it was about nine-thirty in the morning.''

He stood at the other end of the porch, head bowed in thought. "In your opinion, should this transmission have been handled differently?''

"Absolutely," she replied unhesitatingly. "Based on what you've told me, this message was critical, and shouldn't have come in with normal traffic over telephone lines, even encoded. Whoever sent it should have buried this so deep I wouldn't have stumbled across it. The fact they didn't is significant.''

He rubbed his chin with a long-fingered hand. "What else could have been done to conceal it?''

"They could have sent it across a spread spectrum," she explained, "transmitting on several frequency bands. Part of the message would be at 150 megaHerz for example, another at 50 kiloHerz, and a third at still another level. Anyone listening wouldn't be sure they had put together all the pieces of the text. You might have two separate parts, without a middle to link them. It's not hard for the sender to do but a nightmare for anyone decoding.'' She laughed. "I have to admit they're fascinating.''

He was fascinated both by the information and the glimpse of the inner workings of Emily's mind. "How was this one transmitted?''

"As a digital transmission in a bit stream, sent in a microburst of sound. We run this type at varying speeds on the computers and sooner or later a pattern emerges. It really isn't such a big deal although the equipment for it is expensive.''

Ross remembered what Walker had said about a possible funding source being Libya. "You said it was significant that it came in so easily, even though it was in code. Why?''

"Because somebody slipped up and sent it without adequate protection . . . or that someone tried to warn us by using a simpler method. It's routine to scan all international calls. I mean, everyone does it, us, the French, Russians, you name it.''

"We've considered the possibility of a warning." Ross tugged at his lower lip thoughtfully. "Do you think you can get the message down verbatim?"

"I've been trying, but I'll need time."

"Don't quit," Ross said soberly. "You said earlier your memory was nearly photographic. Walker was clear we don't have any other option but to work this out on our own. There's no point in rushing to New York until we've narrowed our list of possible suspects." He got up. "I'll leave you to work."

Emily returned to reconstructing the material, shutting off all thought of Ross and the kiss. At first it was difficult until she reminded herself that he wanted, even demanded, professionalism. She was absorbed in her work when Ross called her to come to lunch.

"I had no idea it was this late," she said, as she saw him putting their plates on the table.

She picked up her sandwich and had started to eat when Ross asked idly, "By the way, do you know how to fire a gun?"

"Yes," she said.

"How well?"

"Very. Why?"

"It might be useful," he said. "Let's see after we eat."

"Fine." Sooner or later Ross would learn she didn't lie.

After lunch she followed him outside to a place he'd marked in the dirt, near a stand of stubby trees.

He pulled a black automatic out of his shoulder holster. She noticed it was a 9 mm., the same one he'd had in the car.

"I've put five shells in it," he said, as she hefted the gun.

"All right. That should be enough." She ejected the magazine, counted the bullets, then rammed the magazine home.

"You didn't believe me?"

"It's safer not to take chances."

Ross pointed to a small juice can he'd propped against a rock over a hundred feet away. "See that can? Use that as a target."

She nodded and shifted until her balance was steady then took aim. The first shot was wide of the mark. She drew in a breath, and adjusted her sights. The second shot made the can jump. Shots three and four put it in a spin and the fifth shot sent it spiraling out of sight. She turned, carefully handing Ross the weapon.

"What other nifty skills do you have I don't know about?" he asked expressionlessly.

"Depends on what you'd call nifty." She grinned.

"I can hardly wait."

She knew that was a lie. Her grin widened, as she enjoyed the sight of Ross off balance.

He tucked the gun back in the holster. "Are you at a reasonable stopping place with your work?"

"Probably. Why?"

"I'd like you to take a walk with me."

"Why?"

"You've been sitting for the last day and a half, and if you're going to do any productive thinking, we need to keep your blood flowing."

Emily forbore to tell him that he got her blood flowing without exercise. "I happen to be in pretty good shape," she said.

Ross couldn't agree more. "That doesn't mean you'd have the stamina to make a run out of here if we get in trouble. Let's go."

He set off at a brisk pace, his legs covering the ground in long strides. Emily hurried after him and caught up just past the car. Ross surged up the steep incline as easily as if he were on an escalator. She was only slightly over five feet eight inches whereas Ross was almost six feet two. She envied the extra inches.

She did a lot of walking in New York to and from the subway, and around her neighborhood, but she hadn't done this kind of hiking for years and she could feel the pull on her muscles.

Ross, however, was in top condition with long, heavily muscled legs, powerful shoulders, and a superb backside. With a sense of amazement, Emily realized she hadn't paid so much attention to a man's body in her life and bit her lip. It was disconcerting to find her mind focused on physical rather than mental attributes.

Earlier that morning Ross had seen a small stream he wanted to reach before stopping. Stealing a glance over his shoulder, he saw Emily hurrying to keep up, her hair sliding over her eyes. He slowed immediately. She needed to be exercised, not exhausted.

As he continued to climb, he contemplated the enigma of Emily Brown. On first glance, she appeared prim, then out of left field a wicked sense of humor would surface. And she had dogged determination to succeed. In everything, he suspected. She was a formidable woman, intelligent, logical, and tenacious.

Most definitely a woman, he acknowledged, remembering the feel of her in his arms. Cresting the ridge, he heard Emily's feet slip behind him on the slope. He turned and reached for her, pulling her up the last part. He released her as soon as she regained her balance. The stream was under a clump of trees and he walked over and sat down on a flat rock, shaded by an overhanging cliff.

"What was the point of this? To kill me? Get it over with quickly?" She tried to regulate her breathing.

He leaned back in a relaxed pose. "You never know when you have to depend on your own two legs to get you out of trouble."

Her smile was a little strange. "I know exactly what you mean about walking." She sat down. "This looks great. I'm going to take my shoes off." She gave a blissful sigh a moment later as she immersed her feet in the cool water.

The cry of a lone bird, perched in a low, dense bush to the left of the stream, broke into the still air.

Ross stirred. "Do you know who lives over there?" He

pointed to a distant house across the valley, its tin roof barely visible.

"A rancher, Arnold Bartlett. At least he used to," she added.

"You told me you were never here. How did you know?"

"Mr. Bartlett was nice to me once when Dad brought me and my brother here. I don't forget when someone does me a kindness."

He was fairly sure she was sending him a message. He ignored it.

"Besides," she added, "in this country, everyone remembers more or less where people live."

"Unlike New York. No one knows who their neighbor is."

She nodded, her expression thoughtful. "It's an impersonal society. Strangers are viewed as a threat. Ever notice how people on the streets in Manhattan take great care to avoid direct eye contact? It used to bother me when I first arrived."

"And now?"

"I've gotten used to it."

"That's not necessarily good."

"No. It's not," she agreed.

A comfortable silence fell as they absorbed their surroundings.

"It's quieter, too," he offered.

"That's how I like it." She lowered her voice. "See the deer, moving along the ravine? And the quail next to the ocotillo."

He followed the direction of her hand. "I imagine the very lack of people means you have more wildlife."

"I'd like to keep it that way. Any time I hear about a huge influx of people out here, I get the willies. I'd just as soon this part of the world stayed forgotten."

"But it won't. At least not forever."

"Probably not. One benefit of isolation now is how much you can see. About dusk, it's wonderful to sit in the shade of an overhanging rock and watch the deer come down the slope to water. They're completely graceful and unselfconscious.'' She jumped.

"What's the matter?''

She laughed, pointing to a small school of minnows that were swimming rapidly away from her bare feet. "We scared each other.''

"By the way, what happened to your leg?'' He pointed to a thin white scar that ran halfway up the side of her left calf.

"Some of the wildlife you're talking about. A rattlesnake bit me when I was a kid and it took a long time to get to the doctor.''

"Where were you when it happened? Were your parents around?''

"No. I was checking a water trough and almost stepped on the snake. He didn't take kindly to my near miss.''

"How old were you?''

"I'd just started driving, so I'd have been about thirteen.''

His eyebrows ascended another notch. "Your parents sent you off on your own at that age?''

"Sure. Why not? What was going to happen to me?''

"Something did.''

"Well, it could have happened anywhere.''

"What did you do?''

Emily lifted her chin to the breeze and felt the sun's warmth on her cheeks. "I couldn't do much except get back to the ranch as fast as possible. I was about four miles away and it took me almost an hour walking since I didn't want to run.''

"Walking?'' Ross was stunned. "I thought you were driving.''

"The truck wouldn't start. I couldn't wait around.''

"My God.''

"You said it. I was terrified but I got over it. I mean, what good was being scared going to do me?'' she added. "In fact, I decided that the more frightened I got, the greater the chance of speeding up my heart rate and pumping the venom even faster. I couldn't panic so I didn't.''

The unwelcome image surfaced of Emily as a terrified

young girl, drawing on her own reserves of willpower
and sheer guts. "I imagine you spent some time in the
hospital."

"Yes, but we took so long to get there that the poison
had taken hold." She shrugged. "But it came out all right."

A muscle jumped in his cheek. He'd seen small children
brutalized by war but he never got accustomed to it. Emily
hadn't been in a battle, but she'd demonstrated her own
brand of courage.

"What about you?" she asked. "Ever get bitten by a
snake?"

"No. But I've seen men die from their bite and it isn't
pleasant."

"Where?" He shot her a look. "I get it. This was in
your persona as super spy. What kind are you anyway?"
she asked, and sent him a teasing grin. He didn't answer
and her grin widened. "James Bond type? I can see it now.
Women in every port. Secret infiltrations in the dark.
Right?"

Secret infiltrations in the dark had a nice ring, he
thought. If Emily were being infiltrated. "Maybe I'm just
a babysitter."

She shook her head. "Nope. I can't buy that. Don't try
to kid me. So which type are you?"

He laughed shortly. "Not 007 for sure. The places I've
been, the women were concerned with other issues."
Except for Marta.

"Where have you been?"

"All over."

"You're not going to tell me," Emily said chal-
lengingly.

"You don't need to . . ."

"Know," she finished. "How could I have forgotten?
You'll parcel out information on a need-to-know basis.
Your background and any small insights into what makes
you tick are off limits."

Without answering, Ross straightened. "We've rested
long enough. Time to go back."

Emily stuck her tongue out at him. She didn't enjoy
being alternately slapped and stroked, and the fluctuation

was wearing. Sooner or later she'd find out what made him react the way he did. It wasn't simply professionalism as he'd claimed.

The breeze had picked up, shifting around to the north. Clouds were piling up in bulky clumps on the horizon. Blue sky had given way to gray and Emily shivered. Ross's hand reached for her several times on the way down the rocky slope, then released her the instant she had regained her footing. By the time they were within sight of the cabin, her teeth were chattering.

"I should have brought a jacket," she mumbled. "I'd forgotten how rapidly the temperature can drop."

"Looks like we might have a storm."

"Every rancher," she said, "is probably hoping so. They need a spring weed crop. Although storms can be threatening as well."

She walked into the cabin, grateful to be out of the wind.

"I'll get a fire started. Why don't you sit there." Ross indicated one of the chairs.

Emily wrapped herself in an aging quilt she pulled off a shelf and watched while Ross piled up kindling, paper, and logs. Within a short time, flames were roaring and she stretched her hands out to the warmth gratefully. Cave men must have been ecstatic when they discovered fire, she thought, her eyes half-closed as the heat dispelled the chill.

Ross's voice interrupted her thoughts. "You look bushed. You drove last night while I slept. How about a nap?"

"Sounds wonderful. Maybe my brain will be sharper when I wake up." She rose from the chair. "In fact, since this room is warmer than the other, I think I'll just rest here."

"You're not going to be very comfortable on the floor."

"The way I feel, I won't even notice." She smiled wearily. "Don't let me sleep more than an hour. I've got to work."

Hesitantly she slid down onto the small rug in front of the fireplace and let her eyelids droop closed, feeling him drape a blanket over her. Emily relaxed. The security of his presence was soothing and moments later she was asleep.

Ross watched her as she lay before him, almost frightened at his rush of feeling. She appealed to him in some deeply emotional way that he didn't dare analyze, afraid if he did, his resolution to maintain a careful distance would go soaring out the window.

Unwelcome memories rose in his mind and he frowned. The line between civilian and professional was narrow but clear, not to be crossed. The only time he had, Marta had died.

Ross could still remember when he'd met her and the others who were working to help people escape from East Berlin. What an irony it was, he thought with bitterness. Just a year after she died, Gorbachev came into power and tensions eased markedly. The number of people trying to escape from behind the Iron Curtain had dropped as legal exits became possible. Eventually the Berlin Wall itself had fallen. His mouth tightened at the renewed realization of the incredible waste her death had been.

But when he'd met her, the status between East and West had still been very tense. And Marta had been ready to take up the battle. She'd announced that she was the granddaughter of a veteran resistance warrior. Her head had been raised proudly as she said she was taking her grandfather's place.

Slim, blonde, and delicate, Marta seemed incongruous in the group. Quelling his misgivings about her civilian status, Ross had ignored his better judgment. He'd known that civilians had no place on missions. Marta had pointed out that she was perfectly capable of taking care of herself, reminding him that she knew the streets of Berlin better than he. Like a fool, he'd agreed, and convinced himself nothing would go wrong. And of course, everything had.

He'd watched her fall backward, pinned by the guard's bullet near the Berlin Wall, her life over because he'd disobeyed the most basic rules of the trade. Forget emotion. Forget impulse. And don't get involved with civilians. Now Emily threatened his resolve, with lethal consequences for a mistake of judgment.

SIX

Emily woke and felt stiff. Turning her head, she saw that the sun had moved below the horizon and it was dusk outside. She rose and stretched. According to her stomach as well as her watch, it was time to start dinner. She went into the kitchen and began assembling ingredients and soon had a Mexican feast bubbling away.

Ross sniffed as he entered the cabin. Emily was stirring something at the stove, her face flushed. She looked relaxed. He was glad she at least could forget the outside world. Unfortunately, their circumstances were never far from his mind.

"Smells good," he said.

She grinned. "Doesn't it? My mother made terrific Mexican food. All sorts of interesting odors—cilantro, cumin, chiles, other spices—filled the house until your mouth watered."

"Did your mother teach you how to cook?"

"She tried," Emily answered. "She cooked by the dab and pinch method, while I preferred a more scientific approach. So many ounces of this, so many of that. Dabs aren't very precise."

"I imagine not. I suspect the two of you had a number of interesting conversations about your respective styles."

Emily laughed. "Sometimes our tempers were hotter than the ingredients. My mother refused to provide written recipes. I had to learn her way or not at all. Made for intense negotiations."

Ross grinned at the image of a young, earnest Emily trying to absorb her mother's more cavalier approach. He watched as she upended a spice jar, tapping on the bottom. And again. His eyebrow rose when she tapped a third time then stirred the mixture.

83

"Want a taste?" Emily twisted her body toward him.

"Definitely." Her mouth was inches away.

Emily felt heat rise inside her. at the look in his eyes and swung the spoon, narrowly missing his chin. He clasped her wrist.

"Let me." He tugged, pulling her whole body to him. For a moment neither moved, bound together by a spiraling tension.

Emily stared up at him, feeling his hardness against her belly. He shifted and she inhaled sharply at the surge of desire that rippled through her. He was too close. Yet not close enough.

When his thumb gently rubbed the skin on the inside of her wrist, her fingers shook and her mouth dried. Her stomach felt weak and she knew in another minute her knees would give way.

Then he closed his mouth over the spoon and she saw him swallow. His eyes widened in surprise. He released her and stepped back. His face suffused with color. "That's really . . . great."

She frowned at the huskiness in his voice. "Like it?"

"It's very . . . tasty." He pulled a soda from the fridge.

Her brow puckered as he drank deeply. "If it's too hot, I can try to dilute it."

Ross lowered the can. "Don't do anything on my account."

She took a taste from the pan and said, "Seems okay to me."

"Fine," Ross said bravely. "Emily," he said confidingly, "you've got a new future. The world needs weaponry. You're it. The army's secret lab in California will make a spot for you." Her eyes widened then narrowed as she stared at him. "You could be sent to foreign missions, come in, smile innocently, and take out whole field staffs with a taco or two."

"Damnit, Ross, now just a minute . . ." Her temper was perilously close to snapping, and her expression was furious.

"Don't you think that's a good idea? I'm very appreciative of your efforts to keep me on my toes. You win, lady. I've imagined being killed by a gun, maybe a bomb or a knife. But a pepper? Never. Just goes to show you can't be too careful."

Emily spotted it. Perfect. Every instinct that had urged lifelong caution was suddenly mute. Her knuckles whitened as she picked up her salad plate and sailed it through the air. It missed him. Ross stared in stunned surprise. The second plate was closer.

"I was just kidding," he said, dodging the saucer that whizzed past his ear. Her loss of control floored him. She took further aim. A platter burst into pieces against the wall. Ross flinched.

She was still furious but couldn't help laughing at the look on his face. A glorious sense of freedom swept over her as she threw another cup. It felt wonderful to just let go. She did, and the missile landed with a satisfactory crash. "You wanted weapons? You got 'em," she said with a full-throated laugh.

Ross lunged, and saved the saucer resting in the palm of her hand, tilted at a threatening angle. "I apologize," he said, his arm wrapping around her waist. Neither moved, although the room seemed to spin momentarily. "I'm sorry, Emily. I was just teasing. I didn't think how you might take it. We've both been under a lot of stress lately." When he spoke, his mouth was near her ear. "You don't have to be a superstar at everything." He hugged her gently, trying to ignore how good she felt. "I like you the way you are. Come on, let's eat." He released her and filled his plate.

After dinner she went into the kitchen.

Following her, Ross said, "I'll do the dishes." He grinned. "Those that are left." He motioned her to the side and began to pour soap into the sink. "Go sit on the porch. I'll be right out."

Emily obeyed, biting her lip. She'd overreacted but Ross had handled her gently. She was staring upwards, her back against one of the posts when she heard Ross walk onto the porch.

"Here," he said, draping his jacket around her shoulders. "You're going to be shivering in a minute."

She was, but it wasn't from the cold. His scent and the warmth of his body permeated the fabric she pulled around her. She gathered her wits. "I apologize," she said, "for losing my temper. It won't happen again."

"Don't worry about it. You just needed to let off steam."

"You could say that." She laughed. "I'll bet you were surprised when I threw the first plate."

He grinned. "Yep." Emily had glowed with anger as well as passion. He'd been dangerously close to kissing her. That would have been a bad idea but an appealing one. He shifted his gaze.

"It's peaceful out here," he said quietly.

"Yes. It's a great place for thinking." She pointed up. "See the sky? When I was a kid, I would imagine how it stretched past the edge of the world, sweeping into space. The changes in color from lighter blue to a dark, intense almost black at the outer limits, seemed to draw me with it." She smiled. "When you're in a city your horizons are limited. Not here." Emily's voice softened. "Infinity as a concept is virtually impossible for a child to grasp. Yet the vast reaches of heaven and land in this part of the world stretch your view of the possible. I remember having grandiose ideas as a kid about what I was going to do when I grew up." She looked at him. "I'm not sure now I fulfilled any of those dreams."

"What adult does?" he said soberly. "Everyone at some time in his childhood creates a future. The trick is in living up to it. I suspect you've done as well as anyone." He reached over and rubbed her arm. "You're cold. Come on in. I'll rebuild the fire."

She sat down on the least battered of the two chairs, watching while he squatted in front of the fireplace. He bent forward, and the muscles in his thighs bunched. Her gaze moved upward. His back was broad, and it tapered into a narrow waist. She wondered what he looked like nude. Undoubtedly beautiful. And all man.

There was something comforting about watching a man build a fire, she thought. He was providing warmth, security, and a sense of well-being. Ross sat back, then moved to the side as the flames roared. He stared away from her, his expression abstracted.

Her voice was soft. "For a while today, I forgot why we're here. It was nice but unrealistic." She sighed. "When do we leave?"

"Soon. There are still some things to do before we can."

"Like what?"

"Decipher the message."

"I'm working on it."

"Good. And we also have to find the mole before he finds us. We're not going to be able to get any real help from my agency. So it's up to us. Let's get started with the mole. I want you to tell me about the setup of your office in New York."

"We're a relatively small staff. Only three of us decode."

"Who are the other two?"

"Hugh Johnson and Ernie Lukas. George Rand, the head of the office, used to but he's now tied up in administration."

"Is it unusual to quit decoding?"

"Not really," she said. "Cryptanalysis requires énormous powers of concentration and sometimes people burn out."

"Who else is in the building?"

"A technician in the radio room and a runner. Plus George has a secretary, Teresa. There's also a receptionist on the ground floor. She's supposed to screen visitors." Emily laughed. "We've got one of those misleading signs outside."

"Sub-Saharan Research Arm of the U.S. Department of Agriculture?" he joked.

"Worse. 'Joint Effort for Research in Kinesis.' "

He gave a small grin. "Great acronym."

"Yeah. J.E.R.K. Some birdbrain in Washington dreamed that up without putting the initials together."

He laughed. "Typical." His face sobered. "Getting back to the office, how do you get your assignments?"

"Directly from the computer."

"What about Ernie and Hugh?"

"Same way."

"Who decides which of you gets a specific message to analyze?"

"No one. There's a computer program that sorts incoming messages in a random sequence."

"This particular message could have been received by anyone?"

"Right."

"Could Hugh and Ernie have decoded it easier than you?"

"Probably not. I have a particular facility for decoding. They could both have solved it, but it would have taken longer."

"So the person most likely to work the message out was assigned the job. How long did it take to decipher?"

"About a day and a half."

"Has it ever happened that you couldn't decode something?"

Her face sobered. "Just once. One came in through a spread spectrum, the kind I told you about earlier. It happened during the height of a nasty stand-off in the Arabian Gulf. I was pretty sure I hadn't gotten it all. A few weeks later, I was able to fill in the missing spaces based on analysis of actual events."

"Why not let it go?"

"I couldn't," she admitted. "I'd never failed before, and I needed to figure out why."

She sat curled up in the chair, chin propped on her hand, her face relaxed. Her tenacity was invisible but real. "What helped you break the code?"

She shook her head in remembered chagrin. "They'd alternated Russian phrases with a dialect from one of the Japanese islands. I hadn't studied Japanese," she said matter-of-factly.

"But you know Russian?"

"Yes, and French, with a smattering of German."

"How about Ernie and Hugh? Do they speak French?"

"Both do, plus Russian, and Ernie even speaks Arabic."

Ross filed that away for future reference, making a note to pursue it later. "And Rand?"

She shook her head. "No French or Russian. In fact I wondered why he was ever assigned to New York, since his specialty is German and there's not much work in that language."

"We'll have to check into that." Ross leaned forward, his attention on the flickering fire behind him. He picked up a stick and poked at the coals, sending flames upward. Emily settled lower in the chair, the heat from the fire soothing.

It occurred to her that Ross's interrogation technique was effective. He spoke in a low, even voice and never indicated any haste or urgency. She knew if she tried it on him, he'd clam up.

Turning back to face her, Ross said, "Let's talk about George for a minute. Is there anything unusual about him?"

"No." She shrugged. "He's always been nice to me."

"Ever seen his house or apartment? Do you know if he lives beyond his means?"

"No. I don't even know where he lives. However, I've heard he's a car nut. He's had a BMW, Audi 5000, and now he owns a Mercedes, but I imagine he earns enough to afford them."

"What about Hugh and Ernie?"

"I don't know. We all work hard, and after hours I don't socialize with them. Oh, once in a while, we'll all go out for a drink. But that's about it. They don't seem to want to have a lot to do with me . . . nor I with them. They don't notice me much."

She missed the narrow-eyed look Ross gave her. Were the men in her office blind or stupid or both? Her beguiling, innocent sensuality raised his own blood pressure about twenty points.

Her hair shone in the firelight, and her mouth was pursed slightly in concentration. Dark blue eyes surrounded with long, silky lashes were narrowed in thought. Ross shifted in his chair, cursing his overactive libido. He couldn't stop wanting her.

Jerking his thoughts back with an effort, he asked, "You don't work with them closely enough even to chat?"

"Not usually. Ernie and Hugh confer sometimes and come to me once in a while for help, but I don't consult with them."

A log shifted in the fireplace and fell, sending up a shower of sparks, lighting the room in a soft glow. Ross damned the firelight. It produced all sorts of insane thoughts. About rugs, bare skin, and warm hands. And Emily lying there, hair spread out, pale skin gleaming under his touch. He stood and began to pace.

"Do you deal with anyone at headquarters on a routine basis?"

"All of us know people there since we were trained at Fort Meade, but we don't have day to day contact. Once or twice a year there are meetings on advances in the field."

"Do you still have friends there?"

"As a matter of fact, I do. Dana Phelps and I went through the ten week training period together. And a woman, Virginia Harrison, took us both under her wing, helping us get settled."

"Did you know Dana before?"

"No. We became friends after the training course."

"What about Virginia Harrison? Is she also an analyst?"

Emily laughed. "No. She thinks I'm crazy. She's in administration. I think she started as a secretary and worked her way up. Now she's Assistant to the Deputy Administrator."

"Do you see any of the headquarters staff more often than the once or twice a year conferences you mentioned?"

"No. I'm not close to anyone else. Occasionally Dana and I call each other, or Virginia might come to New York, and we'll have lunch. It really isn't very often," she said, almost in apology.

"Let's go back to the New York office. Who else is there?"

"Jody Donaldson, our messenger boy—about twenty, just a kid. He delivers documents to the U.N. sometimes or to other offices."

"What else does he do?"

"I'm not sure. Teresa has him run errands, but I don't see him much. Every so often he pops into my office to say hello. I think he's pretty lonely."

"Anyone else?"

"The traffic coordinator, Paul Wilson. He keeps to himself up on the third floor, monitoring the radio equipment."

"Who are his friends in the office?"

"I don't know. Since my work is fed to me straight through the computer, I'm fairly isolated."

Emily realized with an inward start that the life she was describing to Ross was sterile. She might as well be attached to her computer for all the human contact she experienced. The reflection was sobering.

"So you have little contact in person. What about through the computer? Can anyone find out what you're working on?"

She shook her head emphatically. "Absolutely not. We each have a complicated layering of passwords to go through. In addition, there are safeguards to let us know if anyone has been trailing us through a program."

"Do you change passwords?"

"Every few months, randomly. The system cuts us off from each other, unless we actively look for help. Then we have to record that we're conferring. That way, we've got documentation of how many people know what we're doing."

"What about this particular message? Who else knows about it? Someone had to for it to get back to Ottawa that you'd stumbled across something you shouldn't have seen."

"That's just the problem. No one knows . . . or at least, no one I can think of had access to this message."

Ross turned to face her. "That can't be true."

"I'll telling you, I didn't discuss it with anyone. It came into my computer the normal way. If anyone read it, I can't tell you who. Or," she added after a moment, "if I read it, anyone could have since I can't figure out what happened."

"You're saying it could have been George, Ernie, Hugh, Jody, or even Teresa."

"Yes. If I don't know how the system was penetrated, then I'm not going to be able to figure out who could have done it."

He rubbed his hands over his face. "I know you can't be sure who got into your system, but you're going to have to rack your brains." He crossed his arms. "We're leaving something out."

She threw up her hands. "So far I can't come up with a single person. The mole thing is like the mist. I can't get my hands around it or touch it. Just feel the intrusion as a presence."

"There may be more than one person involved. Remember the problems in Pennsylvania."

"I know. That reminds me. You implied that the two men you saw there were amateurish."

"Yes."

"Is that reasonable? Why not send someone better?"

"Could be for any number of reasons. The person in New York who knows you read the text may be so deeply buried he can't make contact with any professionals. Plus, he had to move swiftly." Ross paced. "And ended up with two jerks. Or he may want us to believe the entire operation is being bumbled."

"I still can't understand why there would even be a French-Canadian agent already under cover at N.S.A."

"The U.S.-Canadian relationship is of the most vital importance to both countries: politically, economically, and strategically. Whatever upsets that balance is disturbing to Ottawa as well as Washington. Imagine a scenario where a separatist group several years ago placed somebody in our intelligence community to determine how we reacted if unrest developed in Canada."

"They wouldn't have had to do that if they could buy help."

"Right, or they could do both."

"You mean insert an agent who was eager for cash and without scruples." He nodded. "That could mean almost anyone," she said finally.

"Yeah, that's the hell of it."

Both were silent.

Ross surveyed her thoughtfully after a moment. He remembered the impression of fragility he'd had earlier in the day. "This morning when you insisted on going to town, something was bothering you. Want to tell me about it?"

She smiled faintly. "I had a dream. I was being chased. It unnerved me. In the morning I was still reacting."

"It's perfectly normal for the stress to get to you."

"I don't think it's the danger itself that bothers me so much as the uncertainty," she replied. "I want to know who's after me. That would be much easier to deal with."

Ross was momentarily surprised. He'd had an initial impression of tremendous control. Yet now, she willingly revealed her fear, the anxiety that obviously had burrowed deep inside. Her willingness to confide in him was as unexpected as it was disarming.

"You'll have a better handle on that once we find out who's running the operation, so keep working on who could have learned about the message. Have you made any progress with it?"

"Some. Obviously the part about 'Rocket' is the key but it's in a sub-code. The problem with a sub-code is that, for example, you and I could agree to call Walker . . ." she hesitated then smiled, " 'Skunk.' Unless we put in the appropriate sub-text to indicate 'Skunk' knew you, or you worked for him, how could anyone else tell who we were talking about? I need a larger context."

Ross nodded understandingly. "Let's put that off until the morning. We'll sleep on it." He paused. "We're going to have to get a lot more background information on everybody before we can begin to sort them out. I'll have to think about how to obtain it since we can't go through either my office or yours."

"What can we do?"

"I can call on a couple of friends for some temporary

assistance. I'll think about it." Ross stood. "More coffee?"

"Yes. Mine's gotten cold." She started to rise.

"No, you sit there. Be back in a minute."

Emily turned in the chair and watched him move around the kitchen. His muscles bunched and rippled under his shirt as he readied the coffee and she remembered again how those same muscles had felt, pressed against her in the confined space of the phone booth that morning. She doubted whether he even knew how much of a distraction he was.

She nibbled on her lip. Her concentration at work was legend. Now she could barely remember to keep two thoughts in sequence because whenever Ross moved, she was instantly aware of him.

Ross returned in a few minutes, holding two cups. "Here."

Gazing at him over the rim of the mug, Emily decided the flow of information had been one way for too long. "We've been talking about me and my life forever. It's my turn." He opened his mouth to object but she cut him off. "I don't need another supposedly logical argument why you won't talk to me. Everything's changed. Look, Walker isn't going to help us. My office is full of suspects. Your office is equally riddled. So it's you and me. I need to learn about you because I'm going to be relying on you."

Ross looked at her. "Fair enough," he said finally.

"Pretend I just met you. Where did you go to college?"

"Yale."

She raised her eyebrows. "Did you like it?" she asked. He didn't strike her as the Ivy League type. His polish was of a subtler kind. Ross exhibited an unselfconscious easiness about himself that was very effective—and a bit daunting because it was allied to a powerful personality that he kept in check. Most of the time. She'd bounced off his force field a time or two.

"Yale was all right," he said.

"And," she prodded.

"Nothing."

"Come on. Talk," she said. "What did you major in?"

"History and philosophy."

"Why?" Emily struggled to keep surprise off her face. She would have pegged him as someone comfortable only with issues sharply defined in black and white. History and philosophy painted events from a richer palette, raising questions and feeding on curiosity. She gazed at him speculatively.

"I thought we could learn from our past about our future. I hoped I could do something that would make an impact." He shrugged. "I can't."

Idealism gone astray, she thought. "What did you do after graduation?"

"Joined the army. Served in Vietnam, was discharged, and went to work for the agency."

"What about your family? Were they proud of you?"

There was a definite hesitation before he answered and Emily watched as his right hand closed in a fist on his thigh.

"They had better things to do than raise me." His expression was closed. "They worked crops all over the country. I guess they got tired of me as I grew older and bigger, requiring more food and clothes. They dumped me on a woman when I was a kid." His voice softened in recollection. "Anna took care of me the best she could, and it wasn't always easy." A shadow crossed his face. "She died my senior year in college, right before graduation."

His mouth tightened and Emily wondered whether that loss had not in fact been greater than his parents' absence.

"Have you ever heard from your parents since that time?"

"No. They wouldn't know where to find me. They're probably dead now anyway."

"No other relatives?" she persisted.

"None."

"How old were you when they left you?"

Ross shifted, and leaned back against the wall by the fireplace, his face in semi-darkness. "Twelve."

"Did this woman have a family of her own?"

"No. Not until me." His smile was bittersweet.

"Why do you suppose she took you in?"

"I suspect because we were alike," he replied quietly. "I was used to being alone, she'd lived alone for years." He shrugged. "Perhaps she saw a certain kinship between us. My parents were thinking of leaving me with a trucker when Anna stepped in. After that, we took care of each other."

She could imagine what he'd looked like then. Signs of his height already apparent, probably thin, with dark hair carelessly ruffled, and eyes that were distant in a wary face. Sympathy for him smote her. "I imagine you were appealing as a kid," she said with a small smile.

"Hell, no. I was scruffy. No one would want me."

Emily didn't miss the quickly masked pain. "Anna did. Perhaps you provided something in her life she'd missed. Companionship at the very least. Besides, if you smiled at her the way you've smiled at me a couple of times, there's no doubt in my mind why she wanted you. You have a very nice smile. Occasionally," she said judiciously.

Ross looked at her incredulously. "Nice smile?"

"Yes. Ever heard that?" Mockery gleamed in her eyes.

"No. Anna used to say that if I ever smiled my face would crack. She was probably right."

"Too bad. You should have. Perhaps you're not aware of the effect you have on other people." Like me, she added mentally.

"I assure you I'm well aware of my effect on other people."

"Perhaps. Perhaps not," she said obscurely. "Anna didn't have you as a baby, but during much of the critical part of your life, at least you were with someone who loved you."

A strange expression crossed Ross's face. "I don't know about that."

"Fine, but that's what I think." She shifted in her chair. "Looking back now, would you do things differently if you could?"

"Yeah." He smiled thinly. "Probably major in business

and work for a big company. Maybe end up in mergers and acquisitions.''

''Get into leveraged buyouts?''

''Why not?'' he replied carelessly. ''Might be exciting.''

She didn't believe it for a minute. The man sounded like a closet idealist retreating from disillusionment, and now he was talking like a Wall Street shark. What was he hiding? She studied him unblinkingly. ''Why business?''

''Money and power,'' Ross said. ''Get a pile of loot.''

His expression was casual but she noted his hand was still in a fist. ''If you felt that way, why go into the army at all?''

''Because it was there.''

His look of discomfort increased as she stared at him. ''And the agency? You could have gone into business then.''

''Because.''

''They didn't teach you to speak in complete sentences at Yale?'' she demanded.

''Yes.''

She shot him an exasperated look, missing the flicker of a smile on his mouth. ''What did you do in the army?'' she inquired.

''I was in military intelligence in the field.''

Now that seemed like the Ross Harding she was beginning to know. She already knew his brain was skilled at analyzing potentially lethal situations and then getting out safely. And physically he would have been prepared for almost any contingency.

''What exactly does military intelligence cover? Sneaking around in overcoat and fedora? Tapping phones?''

''What you're thinking about is a spy.''

''What's intelligence if not spying?''

''I did other things as well.''

''Give me a break. What? Look, maybe I'll need to know about your specialized talents. How will I know when I can count on you?''

That was the question, wasn't it? He rubbed his cheek. ''Let's just say I was a facilitator. If people needed assistance in training or gathering intelligence, I provided technical input."

"Explain. Facilitator sounds like one of those people at conferences who introduces each speaker."

"Just proves how different your world is from mine." He brushed his hand across his forehead. "My job was to fire any weapon I was handed, glide on my belly through the underbrush, often with my face ground into the dirt. Sometimes I was lucky and could stand up. But I was usually dressed as a native. The tricky part was dealing with the police who asked for identity papers. I could never betray fear." But he'd felt it, every time. "Not exactly a desk job like yours."

"No," she admitted. "But I'd like to understand. Did you work all over the world?"

"Primarily in Eastern Europe at first. I'd learned Czech and Polish from Anna. Later I went to other places."

"Do you plan to stay in this line of work?"

"Ask me in two weeks. Things will look brighter then."

"Do you really believe that?"

The intensity of her gaze momentarily unnerved him. "Probably not," he answered slowly, honesty compelling his words. "You're still fresh and shiny. I'm not. It's no wonder if I feel a little old, a little used sometimes. Tainted even." His voice deepened on the last phrase and Emily's heart twisted.

"I still have hope," she said.

"That's not necessarily realistic."

She was wrong. What was real were the dark places inhabited by people like him. Civilians, if they got close to the dark zone, were sucked into it and vanished. Just as Marta had.

For a moment, there was only the sound of the fire as the last of the log snapped and sent up another shower of sparks, briefly lighting the room again.

"Time to go to bed. I think you've gotten enough background about me." Ross broke the silence. "You're probably tired even with the nap this afternoon. I am. See you in the morning."

With a fluid movement, Ross rose to his feet and went through the doorway into the other room. Emily could hear him moving about. Her expression was thoughtful. The man she was beginning to know possessed surprising facets to his personality. By turns warm, yet aloof, with flashes of long suppressed idealism that colored his views; he was fascinating. Now that she knew about his past, she didn't find his unapproachability so baffling. No wonder he kept her at arm's length, for with the exception of Anna, his experience with intimacy had been fraught with emotional disaster.

That was why he'd deliberately described his past in such vivid terms. To frighten her—demonstrate the gulf between them.

But Ross was going to be surprised if he thought he could get away with shutting her out again. Before he'd left, he'd stared at her with a look she was beginning to recognize. Desire mixed with resistance. Want blended with withdrawal. And for a moment, he'd reached out to her, even if he only shared the surface of his life. She suspected he'd wanted more.

Emily's mouth curved in a little smile.

She was going to give it to him.

SEVEN

Emily was deeply asleep when she heard the noise. She jerked awake at once, her heart pounding furiously. There it was again. A deep guttural sound. The hair lifted on the back of her neck.

The cabin was faintly illuminated by moonlight and she stared across the room. The noise came from Ross's bed. He moved, and it was repeated. Emily rose and walked silently over to stand next to him, peering down through the dimness as her eyes adjusted.

His face was contorted and he was sweating. His T-shirt was soaked, drawn up above his waist. The covers were bunched around his hips, baring tanned skin covered with fine silky hair.

Some powerful emotion had tightened his throat and he was mumbling hoarsely, his head thrown back against the pillow. Emily bit her lip then reached out tentatively to touch his shoulder.

With shocking suddenness, Ross came fully awake, his hand in an iron band around her wrist, jerking her to him. Emily managed to brace herself on one palm before falling forward. Heat from his body poured onto her skin, scorching her through her pajamas.

"What's wrong?" His fingers tightened.

Emily tugged. "You were having a bad dream and I tried to wake you." She could see the shine of his eyes and felt the clasp change, loosening, but not releasing her.

"Never wake me unexpectedly. I could have hurt you."

Ross sat up, the covers sliding further down. Emily's gaze skittered over his chest and lower then stopped. Her pulse thudded and she knew Ross could feel it.

"I wasn't worried," she muttered, dragging her gaze upward.

"You should have been." His fingers opened, freeing her, and he pulled the sheets higher.

Emily knew he was talking about something besides waking him. She remained bent over him. Urged by a compulsion she couldn't resist, she raised her hand. Her fingertips gently drifted from his cheek to his chin, then to the corner of his mouth.

"What the hell are you doing?" His voice wouldn't come out right. Emily sat, her weight depressing the mattress. He could feel himself sliding and grabbed the side away from her. It didn't help. It was as though she were a magnet, pulling him to her.

She stroked his skin, fascinated by the texture of the whiskers on his face. He felt totally masculine, irresistible. Her thumb gently touched his mouth, absorbing the softness of his lips. Her fingers tingled as heat raced up her arm.

"Emily," he warned, his voice rough. "You don't know what you're doing."

"I'm only touching you."

The utter simplicity of her words made him swallow hard.

The darkness made things possible she would never have contemplated in the daytime. She felt free, liberated from the person she'd been for years, shedding caution and past habits like so much excess clothing. She sucked in air and her pajamas tightened over her breasts.

"You're playing with fire." His voice was dark and deep.

"God, I hope so," was all she had time for.

With a swift movement, he pulled her down beside him, his mouth covering hers. The night air flowed over her body, following the path of his hands as he deliberately smoothed her top upward. His tongue gently probed at her closed lips and entered slowly, sensuality mingled with a disquieting tenderness.

She'd expected power. She received gentleness.

She'd asked for a response, and he overwhelmed her.

His palm covered her breast eliciting a gasp. Sensation

surged in the wake of his hand, as fingertips plucked at her waiting nipple bringing a reeling dizziness.

She felt his chest rising unsteadily and heard his rapid intake of breath. His lips sucked gently at the curve of her neck, his tongue brushed against the lobe of her ear then plunged inside. Her body bucked in reaction at the desire surging through her.

Ross gave a quick tug and her pajama bottoms slid away with a quiet rustle. Suddenly she was bare. He thrust his leg between hers, and a deep heaviness throbbed in her belly. He was hard, pressing against her, and she moaned.

She needed him to fill the aching void at her center.

With devastating slowness, his hand cupped her completely before he slowly slid a finger into her warmth. She was burning up. Heat sliced through her. Emily gave herself up to the sweet torment of his hand as her hips rocked against his touch. Clutching his shoulders, her mouth blindly sought his. Desperate for release, she tightened her grip. "Ross," she managed, feeling as though she were spinning out of control.

Ross's body stilled. He made a harsh sound almost of pain then he withdrew his hand. He rolled away and lay beside her, his breathing still rough, one arm over his eyes.

"I'm sorry about that." Ross's voice was very quiet.

She turned and saw the gleam of his eyes as he stared at the ceiling. He shut his eyes briefly before he swiveled his head and gazed at her. With a sigh, he pulled her shirt down over her bare breasts. Silently he handed her the pajama bottoms he'd removed.

"This won't work." He spoke over her bent head.

Emily fought to control the humiliation that colored her cheeks. She'd fallen all over him in bed, literally. She'd practically seduced him, driven to behave uncharacteristically by her own urges. She'd wanted him, hot and hard inside her and he'd known it. Undoubtedly pity was a powerful aphrodisiac.

Emily moved to the edge of the bed, swung her legs to the floor, and sat up. "Certainly not," she muttered, her eyes stinging. "No problem. I understand completely."

She was babbling but couldn't seem to stop. Tears threatened and she bit her lip.

"You don't understand one damned thing, Emily." He pulled her chin around, forcing her to meet his gaze. He gave a short laugh. "Hell, I can't even keep my hands off you. You make me lose control faster than any woman I've ever met. Another second and I'd have been inside you." The image made him pulse briefly. He'd barely been able to stop, and he cursed the attraction he couldn't resist.

Or satisfy.

"The more intimately involved you and I become, the greater difficulty I'll have in protecting you. I can hardly see straight much less think logically when I'm around you anyway." The way he was feeling now had a hell of a lot to do with the libido and not much else. He rose and walked to a chair, pulling on jeans. Turning, he added, "I'm not supposed to get embroiled in a hot love affair."

She managed to get out, "You don't love me. So what's the problem?" Love?

"Figure of speech." He ran his fingers hastily through his hair, frustration in the gesture. "Don't pick apart everything I say. Just take my word for it. This won't work. It can't."

"You're sure of that, aren't you?" She gave him a thin smile. "Seems to me we simply behaved like adults who wanted each other. Tell me what's really bothering you, because it can't be that you got the hots for me." She forced nonchalance. At least he'd said he wanted her.

"All right." He hesitated as he stood before her, the moonlight casting his body in silver. "A few years ago, I allowed personal feelings to get in the way of professional judgment. I learned a bitter lesson when the woman died."

"How?"

"About five years ago I had to get some people out of East Berlin. Years before the Berlin Wall came down. Anyway, things were still tight. Something went wrong. Marta showed up to help," he explained. "I took one look at her and knew she didn't have the necessary experience to handle it. But she said her family had been involved for years. I should never have agreed.''

''Why blame yourself? She persuaded you.''

''Yes, but my judgment was at fault. I was attracted to her when I shouldn't have been.'' His eyes narrowed in remembrance. ''I was given the responsibility for the safety of the mission.'' Ross's mouth tightened. ''I watched while she was shot by a guard as she tried to help the refugees cross.''

Goosebumps rippled up Emily's arms at the starkness of the words.

He continued. ''The hell of it is that just a year or so later, it probably wouldn't have happened.''

''You mean because of the changes in Russia?''

''Yes.''

She drew in a shaky breath. ''Did you sleep with her?''

''Yes.''

''Did you love her?'' That word again, she thought, feeling a pang.

''No. But I could have.''

Neither moved for a long moment.

''Don't you think she knew and accepted the risks?''

''You don't know reality until you're actually confronted with it. Imagination is a notoriously poor substitute for experience. I had the experience to know the situation was tight. She couldn't handle a sudden emergency.''

''Perhaps, but you're denying her free choice after the fact. She chose to do it. Going to bed with you was something she decided to do . . . just as she decided to do the other. You're acting as though you're safe only if you're sealed off from the rest of the world, but that won't work. You and I are interdependent, whether we make love or not. If I mess up, you're at risk. This is mutual. A relationship between us can't make any further difference.''

''I'm sorry, but I don't agree. The fact I slept with her clouded my judgment.''

''That's your view. Marta went into it with her eyes open.''

''In some sense that's unimportant. She wasn't experienced enough to know what she was getting into. I was.''

He looked drained. "She's dead and can't speak for herself. What I know is that I didn't exercise proper care because I wasn't thinking straight." He moved away. "You'd better get some sleep."

She rose silently and walked across the room, unaware of the desolation in his eyes. As she lay in her own bed, the sheets cool after being thrown back to the night chill, she couldn't stop trembling. What she was feeling, she realized eventually, was sexual frustration. She'd never thought she would.

And it was Ross's fault. He had caused the ache between her thighs. Her emptiness was his responsibility. And her bittersweet pleasure. A faint smile curved her mouth. Should she thank him or tell him to go to hell?

He confused intimacy with danger. He was wrong. She would prove to him that the only safety he would ever have lay with her.

Turning on her side, she hitched the covers higher on her shoulder. Sleep finally came but it was troubled.

When Emily woke, daylight was pouring in through the window and the cabin was empty. Ross had left without waking her. She rose and dressed, deep in thought. Perhaps Ross was not the only one who had to face reality. Of a different sort.

As Ross walked back inside, he saw Emily standing by the stove. He walked past her, every nerve alert. She was different in some subtle, undefined way, and his nerves jumped in reaction.

Gesturing at the pot, she said, "Have some. At least I've been able to drink a cup." She had concluded friendliness was the opening wedge in her campaign to get through to him. She smiled, noticing his wariness increase. "Did you sleep well?"

"Yes."

"The rain didn't keep you awake?"

"No." She had.

As he'd lain in bed during the night, listening to her restless movements, he'd convinced himself that he'd done the right thing continuing to keep her at arms' length.

That hadn't prevented his imagination from placing her

naked in his bed, wearing only a smile. Sleep hadn't come easily.

Emily shifted her weight to one leg, and involuntarily his gaze was drawn to the gentle swell of her hip. She stared at him over her shoulder as she lifted the coffeepot. Moistening her mouth with her tongue, she asked, "Ross? Coffee?"

He was worried. Emily had ridden the pendulum from drab to dynamite and hadn't even gotten dizzy. He had.

"You're doing this deliberately, aren't you?" he finally said.

"Doing what?"

Her attempt at innocence failed.

"You know."

She smiled. "You're not worried about me, are you? You're tough, resourceful, used to facing difficult situations. What's the problem dealing with one woman?"

Damn her, she even looked amused. His eyes narrowed. Emily was wearing jeans and a velour shirt in a deep emerald green. The shirt, by accident or design, had slid off one shoulder. A champagne colored band of lace lay across her pale skin.

The woman within kissing distance bore only the faintest resemblance to the woman he'd first seen days before.

This Emily Brown had gleaming hair, gorgeous dark blue eyes, skin that smelled good enough to suck on, like an all day lollipop, and a smile that heated his blood faster than an acetylene torch.

"You're asking for trouble," he said.

"At the very least."

Her expression sent his pulse wild.

Emily walked toward him, her eyes unwaveringly on his. She came closer and stopped.

A mere kiss away.

"I've already eaten," he said gruffly, feeling his body react. His damned jeans were going to kill him if she didn't let up. He walked around her, telling himself he wasn't a coward. "You finish your coffee. As soon as you're ready, we can take another hike. Then we'll go into town and check on Walker."

Ross hadn't planned to go anywhere but being cooped up with Emily was impossible. He walked out the door, feeling pursued.

When she appeared on the front porch a few minutes later, Ross said, "You'll need a coat." He looked down at her feet. "And I'd suggest you change into different footgear. The ground is pretty muddy."

Her smile mocked him gently. "Of course. I'm glad you're thinking about my welfare."

He ground his teeth. For the next hour he showed her the possible routes someone could use to approach the cabin, and how those same routes would take her away.

The cabin sat near the middle of a range of mountains. The town was directly north. "If something happens, go over the top and get help." He paused, looking straight at her. "Whatever you do, don't wait for me. Just get out."

"Where will you be?" The good humor of the morning had dissipated like early fog and she shivered. Ross's hand tightened on her shoulder before he answered.

"If you're in trouble, it'll be because I'm not here to help. You'll be on your own." He turned her to face him. "Can you handle that?"

"Yes. But you don't believe me."

"Probably because I don't think you have the faintest idea of what kind of world these people inhabit. You sit in an office, working on arcane codes, oblivious to the outside environment. The people I'm talking about don't understand either logic or mercy."

She knew Ross had seen and experienced things she could only imagine, but she hadn't been deluding herself when she said she wasn't afraid.

Perhaps facing death at the age of thirteen when she'd been bitten by the rattlesnake was the reason for her feeling of security, but more frightening, she realized, was the prospect of a barren existence without . . . Ross. "If I have to face it, I will."

He gave a noncommittal grunt. "I hope it doesn't come to that. Let's go on back."

At the base of the mountain, he preceded her, motioning

her to remain behind. He walked into the cabin, but not before Emily noticed that he scanned the area for signs of intruders as he'd done the day before. When he motioned, she followed him.

Ross opened the cupboard and got a glass. Filling it with water, he drank thirstily. She saw the movement of his throat muscles as he swallowed. Her own mouth dried in reaction. It occurred to her that seducing Ross could prove as wearing on her own control as it was on his.

His look caught her and the glass stayed at his mouth. His eyes darkened, and she froze. Emily took a deep breath and moved, breaking the invisible bond.

"I'd like to discuss the message with you, if you don't mind." She saw relief on his face at the neutral topic. With wry amusement, she considered that a positive sign of progress.

"Do you think you've remembered the code?"

"Most. At least the important part." She went to the kitchen table, and sat down, pulling over the pad she had been working on. "I'm convinced that the remainder of the message is just what it looks like—material about the upcoming presentation of the U.N. The critical part seems to be the inserted text."

"What makes you say that?" He sat across from her, stretching his long legs under the table. By accident their feet touched. He turned sideways at once.

"Because a slightly different code was used. I'm going to read it out to you. By the way," she said with a slight smile, "you're going to wonder why I took so long. But I had to be sure I'd reconstructed the entire message within the message. Here goes." She lifted the pad. "Ten-forty star two plus light crescent Rocket."

"That's all?"

"Except for something else which I took to refer to the Ottawa government. 'Chimera dead.' That was surrounded by spaces."

"Why would 'Chimera' refer to the central government?"

"I'm guessing because the separatists have felt for years that they were engulfed, swallowed up, by the majority in the country. That their distinct identity was slowly vanishing," she said. "At least that's the reason I've seen this reference before."

"So you think something is going to happen in Ontario?"

"Yes. Got a better idea?"

"No, although I seem to recall a different meaning for it. I'll try to remember. At any rate, we may not have much time to deal with this," he said thoughtfully. "You mentioned 'Rocket.' Any idea yet who it refers to?"

"No one would have gone to the trouble to encode this name for a minor player. Something is going to happen to Rocket, whoever he is. For all we know, it could mean the Prime Minister."

He stared at her silently, then nodded. "It could. The impact would be devastating."

"I know, but we can't be sure yet."

"All right. Let's put together what we've got so far. First we have a man, code-named Rocket." She nodded. "What about the rest of the text?"

"I think the ten-forty refers to a time."

"That makes sense. It wouldn't be a date because if it were the tenth month, October, there isn't a fortieth day. And reversing it, there isn't a fortieth month."

"Exactly," she said. "Besides, the French write the month last if they're using only numerals."

"The star you mention could refer to a general. Virtually every military force puts stars on epaulettes to denote high rank."

"Or it could refer to a place or thing," she commented, "assuming Rocket is a person. The message might not have two personal references."

He rubbed his hand wearily over his eyes. "This isn't exactly easy, is it?"

"No. Now you can see why cryptanalysts retire early. They get tired of working on words they're never sure they got right."

"Let's not throw in the towel just yet. What about 'crescent?' "

"That could refer to a Middle Eastern connection, but

again, without a context, I can't tell," Emily said. "The crescent and scimitar are often used in flags or insignia of Middle Eastern nations."

"Right. I think there may be a link to Libya—they may be bankrolling this operation." Ross told Emily what Walker had said about that likelihood. "On the other hand, I don't know that it fits right here. From what I know about this, the text is strictly French-Canadian."

"Maybe. But I've learned never to rule anything out."

"How about 'light?' Have you given that any thought?"

Her tone was somber. "Sounds like a bomb. Perhaps even a nuclear detonation that creates a lot of light."

The horror of what she'd said filled the room.

"I see," he said as he looked at her.

"I wish I could be more positive, and say I had the words with their precise meanings. But I don't. Anyway, we don't even have the date yet when whatever is going to happen takes place."

"That thought occurred to me, too." Ross's face was tight. "I'd bet the people who are after you think you know more. I'd like to get more information on the people in your office. It's possible that might help with the actual message. Maybe we can dig up something to help us identify who knew what you'd found. I want to make a call from town and see if I can enlist some assistance."

"I'll be ready to go in a second."

"Fine. When I get Mike on the line, I can start a search for background on all of the names you've already given me. But I'm going to call Walker's office once more to see if I can get a reading on that situation."

When they reached the small community, Ross pulled up to the now familiar telephone, saying, "Do you want to call your mother?"

"No." She smiled. "But thanks for asking."

He nodded and left the car.

When Mike answered, he said without any preliminary, "By the way, I've been hearing rumors about some funny things happening in your home town."

Ross stiffened. Mike kept an ear to the ground through a network of old army friends. "What kind of funny?"

"That maybe someone you know at work is having a problem."

Curses erupted under his breath. "That's bad. Means all the agencies have got wind of something."

"Yep."

"Any specifics?"

"No, but you know how the bloodletting can be between competing fiefdoms. Half the time the warfare is just for territory. They'd be snooping for kicks if they thought your group was in real trouble."

"Thanks for the warning," Ross said. "I may have to call you back."

"Anytime." Mike put the call through to Walker then disconnected.

When the telephone rang, it was picked up on the third ring. Walker's voice came on, very calmly. "Hello?"

"Ross here."

There was a pause then Walker said smoothly, "Nice of you to check in, my boy. Hope things are fine in your area."

The "my boy" stank to high heavens along with everything else. "Yeah. I'm having a nice vacation. How are things at your end?"

"Oh, just wonderful," Walker said with uncharacteristic airiness.

Ross could almost see him, eyes alight with glee at the prospect of outwitting an opponent. There was a loud suck on the phone. The infernal pipe was being given a workout.

"By the way, have you seen anyone from the Chase Corporation lately?" Walker asked.

"No," Ross said slowly. Obviously the hunt was intensifying. "Should I have?"

"Seems to me you might be getting a wire soon from our friends, so you need to be on the lookout."

"How soon?"

"Massive efforts are being made to get the material together to send you as soon as you check in. Probably late tomorrow. You might bear that in mind," Walker warned obliquely.

"Got it." Ross hung up. After a momentary hesitation, he picked up the receiver again. "I have some friends I'd like to have checked out," he said quickly when Mike answered.

"Non-standard channels?"

"Absolutely."

"Go ahead."

Ross read the names of the personnel in Emily's office.

"You'll be calling in?" Mike asked when Ross finished.

"Sometime tomorrow."

"It may take me a little time. I imagine you don't want any waves with this."

"None."

"Fine. Watch your back, buddy."

"Yeah."

Ross hung up and returned to the car.

Emily looked at him as he approached. His face was lined and there was a new hardness about him. "You'd better tell me what happened," she said quietly.

Ross got behind the steering wheel. Leaning his head back, he rubbed his neck. "Walker answered the telephone this time. He tells me the hunt is in high gear. It's broader in scope than anticipated and he thinks they're getting close."

"But he doesn't know where we are, does he?"

"Not yet."

"And there's no doubt that they're really coming after me?"

"None. The agent has to take every reasonable precaution to save his hide and position. The stakes are too high. If he can find you, or his men can, he's home free."

"What do you want to do now?"

"Make plans to move on. I put out a request for background material on the people in your office. We'll get something later tomorrow."

"I'd rather that weren't necessary."

"There's no way around it, Emily. This is a matter of survival."

"Can we really investigate without using either your agency or mine?"

"We'll manage. We have to." He started the car. "Let's plan on getting out first thing in the morning."

"Can we wait that long?"

"I think so. Walker said he thought we had that much time." He gave her an assessing look. "We're going to be glad of a rest now. Things could get bad," he added.

Nodding, Emily looked out at the passing landscape unseeingly.

As they turned onto the dirt road, Ross pressed the accelerator gently. The nose of the car tilted upward as they headed up the last slope, and he stepped slightly harder on the pedal to gain traction through the mud that coated the road from the previous night's rain. He heard a grinding noise as the wheel lurched in his hand. Ross cursed under his breath and the car slowed to a crawl.

"What's wrong?"

He grunted and kept driving, his expression forbidding. "I won't know until I can stop." He pulled the car in front of the cabin. "Why don't you go inside and see if you can work on the text some more while I check the car." He turned to her. "Unless you're an auto mechanic as well?"

"Not yet."

He snorted.

Peering out the window a few minutes later, Emily saw Ross's feet under the car.

Checking her wristwatch, she noted it was almost noon and decided to throw a couple of sandwiches together in case Ross was hungry. The door opened behind her as she finished the last one and put the plates on the table. She turned and saw that Ross was covered with mud. His expression was bleak. He unbuttoned his shirt and pulled it off, draping the garment on the doorknob. Moving to the sink, he quickly washed his hands and chest, removing the worst of the dirt. Droplets of water splashed and glistened on his skin as Emily watched.

"Well?" she inquired, trying to keep her eyes off his bare chest. She remembered the feel of his skin under her cheek, the strong masculine scent of his body, as he'd held her on the bed. Then she'd wanted to take the taste of him into her mouth. Her mouth dried. She imagined his flavor. Like heaven. His next words took a moment to sink in.

"We've got a problem with the transmission. The linkage is bent."

"Can we drive without repairing it?"

"No. So I have to go back into town. There's a garage there that should have the necessary tools. I could go later today."

"Isn't that risky? Seems to me you'd attract more attention being seen two times the same day."

"The only other choice is to wait until morning, and we don't know how long the repairs might take. We need to be out of here first thing tomorrow."

"I understand, but we were in town yesterday for breakfast. We went back today and used the phone. If you go in again this afternoon, someone is bound to remember you. You'll have to talk to the mechanic at the garage. He'll ask questions. If you wait until morning, we'll be leaving so quickly we couldn't be traced anyway."

Ross grunted and lifted the towel off the counter but he couldn't prevent a niggling sense of unease. Walker had better be right. He put the towel away and sat down and picked up his sandwich.

Ross got up immediately after he finished lunch. "I'll be back later," was all he said, before moving toward the door.

Emily had stared at his bare chest throughout lunch and he'd felt an unaccustomed warmth in his cheeks at the open desire in her look. Buttoning the shirt, Ross muttered under his breath as he stomped off the porch. Maybe a walk would cool him off.

The vast emptiness that stretched out away from the mountain range where the cabin nestled was vaguely soothing. The wind blew gently, and grasses that had faded to a pale gray bent before it, their heads waving above the earth.

He suspected the ranchers in this part of Texas watched

the clouds scudding across the sky, hoping for rain, but prepared to survive without it. The men he'd seen in town had been battered but not broken, and were self-reliant because survival wasn't possible otherwise. Only those with the ability to endure would last.

His thoughts turned abruptly to Emily. She knew something about self-reliance, he thought, as he walked slowly back towards the cabin. Snakes, guns, and fast cars, they were all part of her upbringing. Telling himself he wasn't hurrying back for her, he quickened his pace.

Emily was in one of the two armchairs, writing on the ubiquitous yellow pad. She hadn't heard him and he stopped quietly at a position behind and to the side of her chair. He could see the gleam of her hair on her bowed head and the clean line of scalp. He inhaled, drawing in the sweet scent of Emily, soap and perfume. His gaze moved. Faint freckles marched across her straight nose and bluish veins made a delicate tracery under pale skin.

Her head turned suddenly and she saw him. He saw pleasure, a flare of desire, and then her expression became shuttered.

She shifted, pushing her hair behind one ear. "Been here long?"

Not long enough. "Not very."

"Where were you?"

"Around, checking on a few things. I'm going to pack my things tonight. You should, too."

"Where are we heading tomorrow?"

"New York. There's no point in going to Washington until we have the mole identified."

Emily told herself he was right, but all the same she couldn't suppress a strange feeling in the pit of her stomach. Maybe due to nerves, maybe not: Whatever the reason, the sensation was unaccustomed and unwelcome.

Ross sat in the other chair, stretching his long jeans-clad legs in front of him. "I think we ought to review the people whose names you gave me one more time. You never know what will pop into your mind. It's possible a word association will trigger something to give you a clue with the code."

"Fine." She shrugged. "Let me put on coffee. I was feeling so drowsy after lunch I was afraid I'd fall asleep." She stood and stretched unselfconsciously.

He swallowed hard as the velour strained across her breasts, outlining their shape.

"You want any?"

Did he ever. He jammed his hands in his pockets.

When he didn't respond, she said, "Ross, do you want coffee?"

"Please." He watched in silence as she got cups, coffee, and put on the water to boil.

"Any person in particular you want to start with?" she asked from the kitchen, turning to him.

"Let's go over your first days at N.S.A. and see if we get anything."

She raised the heat under the water and said, "Okay." She walked over toward him and sat down again. "I was only nineteen when I was hired. It doesn't seem possible that I've been with the agency almost nine years. Seven of them in New York."

The kettle in the kitchen whistled and she got up to make the coffee. Coming back a few minutes later, she resumed. "Anyway, I was hired for the Fort Meade headquarters. The ten week training program was a preliminary overview of the agency's functions. They shifted us around, from computers, to cryptography, to languages, and so forth. I seemed to have a special aptitude for both computers and languages, which was useful in cryptography, so when the time came to pick my area, that's what I selected."

"Have you ever regretted it?"

"No. I like puzzles, and a piece of code is just that. The satisfaction I have from solving one is enormous. Or at least it was until recently." She gave a half-smile.

"I can imagine," he said dryly. "Go on. You mentioned yesterday a woman named Dana. Were you both assigned to cryptography?"

"No. She decided to go straight into languages. She studied Chinese with the hope of working on publications and other documents out of China that would give us a hint of the country's political leanings."

"Is that the section she's still in?"

"Yes. And before you ask, I know she's happy there."

"Do you keep up with anybody else from the class?"

She shook her head. "No. If it weren't so dangerous, I'd be laughing at the idea that a single person I know from N.S.A. is trying to harm me. It's scary knowing someone is lurking out there and I can't do one thing about it."

"You're wrong. We are going to do something." His voice hardened. "Go on."

"I stayed in Fort Meade for two years after finishing training. When an opening came for the New York office I grabbed at the chance."

"Is Manhattan considered a plum?"

"Sort of. The opportunity of working with a small staff away from headquarters is a plus, although the cost of living is astronomical. The positions are hard to get but I got lucky."

"I doubt it."

"What does that mean?"

"Just that I suspect you were considered more deserving than your competitors."

Color rushed into her cheeks. "Is that a compliment?"

"Yes." Emily reacted with such visible pleasure to his words that he felt even more of a heel when he had to push her away.

He continued. "How were you treated when you first arrived?"

"Fine. I came on as a junior colleague and wasn't a threat. I've been there ever since, doing more work, rising a little higher."

"And you're satisfied?" There was a curious gleam in his eyes.

"Yes and no. I don't really know what else I'm qualified for. All my training has been scientific. The only problem is that I'm getting bored. And the backbiting is awful."

Ross grinned for the first time that afternoon. "Bureaucrats."

"Exactly. And since I'm not the type to like office intrigue, I've been on the outskirts of everything."

"Have you dated anyone from the agency?"

"No. That's frowned on since it can lead to internal problems. Just like they refuse to have family members working there. I guess they figure you'll be more loyal to the relative than to the agency." She stared at him. "Why did you ask?"

"You'd be an ideal target for a seduction attempt by the other side."

She choked then recovered. "I see." She wondered if she'd call his phrase a breakthrough.

Ross had to get up. He shouldn't have used the word seduction. Damn. He moved across to the fireplace, and stood with his back to the stone. "Look at this objectively." Sure, buddy, he thought, just like you do. "You're bright, well placed to do your country a disservice, single, and alone. Why not make a run at you to see if you could be turned?"

"You mean become a traitor?"

"That kind of thing has happened before," he replied.

"Not to me," she said, stoutly.

"Obviously not, but it might have. That's why I asked about your fellow workers. Being objective, it would make sense to try to get closer to you."

A sense of letdown hit her. She was beginning to hate the whole concept of objectivity.

"Can you think of anything at all about the people in Maryland or New York that stands out? Anything at all?" he asked.

"No-o-o, I don't think so. I realize this isn't very helpful."

"If you can't come up with anything, you can't. But don't give up. Sometimes you'll have a nugget of information you don't even know you have. Knowledge often lies buried for weeks, even months."

"I don't think we have that kind of time. Speaking of which, would you like me to fix dinner?"

"No. I will. It's my turn anyway."

EIGHT

Ross pulled out two steaks and set them on the counter, his thoughts uneasy. The attraction he'd felt for her had grown steadily, careless of his efforts to stamp it out. Hopes and dreams were a steady diet to the woman standing within easy reach. She didn't need a tired Cold War soldier to keep her warm.

"Do you want anything else in the salad?" she said, gesturing toward the refrigerator. "I could add more celery."

Ross deliberately shook off his dark mood and walked over to peer in the bowl. "That's fine. I'll put the steaks on. How do you like yours?"

"Rare."

She smiled and he felt his heart begin a triphammer beat at the look in her eyes. "Back in a minute."

He went outside and worked on the grill. Damn her. She knew what it could be like between them. Her expression had been ample proof. Electric. Hot. Dangerous.

He cursed as the match burned down to his fingers. A small dark smear was on his thumb and Ross's mouth twisted in wry acknowledgment. He'd burn more than his fingers if he didn't leave her alone.

Adults are smart enough to exercise prudent judgment, he told himself. So stay away from her. Prudent judgment is boring, an inner voice riposted. But safe. Ross grunted in silent acknowledgment of that bit of wisdom. He stomped up the steps to the cabin.

Dinner was quiet and relaxed. They took their plates close to the fireplace and sat on the floor, letting the heat flow around them. Flames flickered and a sweet sense of peace crept over Ross.

Memories of other fires drifted behind his eyes. A

campfire in the desert, hawknosed men staring at him with barely controlled ferocity, long rifles across their laps. The sound of the wind as it caught the edges of tents, snapping the heavy material. A sky pierced with stars above the rolling sands.

The men weren't friends, not foes either. Just customers for the kind of religion Walker espoused. Peace at the point of a sword was an old tradition, except today it was a gun or a missile.

His memories flowed seamlessly to the last time he'd seen Marta before her death. A marble fireplace in a small hotel in East Germany as she sat in a velvet covered armchair across from him, sipping a dry Rhine wine. The comfort of the fire had been false.

Emily's words broke the silence. "Why haven't you ever married?" She hesitated. "Or perhaps you have?"

"Never felt the need."

Emily waited and Ross finally looked up. She was sitting forward, one elbow on her knee. "Is that how you view relationships? They're based on need?"

"Sexual attraction plays a large part, if not the most important part, in any relationship between men and women. It's a biological urge sanctified by society through marriage."

"All right. I'll grant that may be part of it. But what about mutual giving?"

He shrugged. "I'm sure that's often included but it doesn't seem to be an essential element. Most people link up with someone because the other person fills an emptiness, rounds out a rough spot in the other's personality. They actually need that other person."

"You're saying you haven't ever felt that kind of drive? That's why you haven't married?"

"Right."

Her expression was disbelieving. "That sounds more detached than I think you are. You just won't admit you've ever felt that way. I bet you think it fits your image." She grinned suddenly. "But I still remember when you picked up that junk heap in Pennsylvania."

He smiled. "The one you liked so much?"

"The dice were a big attraction," she agreed wryly. "I was more interested, however, in the fact you passed up a nice family sedan. I think you gave in to a charitable impulse." She swore she could see a hint of color on his high cheekbones that wasn't caused by the fire.

"You'd be wrong. The car wasn't suitable."

Emily grinned. "And a noisy, attention getting jalopy was?" She laughed. "Stop trying to kid me, Ross. Or more importantly," she said, sobering, "stop trying to kid yourself. Everything about you yells that you're tough. But you make a point out of it."

"My life hasn't permitted anything else."

"Your particular job or because you keep on the move?"

"Both." He ran his fingers through his hair, frustration in the gesture. "Don't make me something I'm not. We started this talking about need. And people. I don't need people in the sense you mean." The lie rolled off his tongue effortlessly. "I've got a better question. Why haven't you married?"

"No one's asked me."

He saw acute discomfort flash across her face. "Why not?"

"How should I know?" she asked flippantly. "Maybe I'm not attractive enough. Maybe I'm too smart. Who knows?"

Maybe she'd never let anyone see past the brain to the woman. Was her intellect a defense mechanism or a barrier she couldn't overcome, or both? Because she sure as hell was a woman underneath.

"Would you like to be married?"

"I guess, but I've never envisioned it as part of my future." She shrugged. "I've got my work, and while it's not an all consuming passion, it satisfies me."

"That's enough?"

"You said it would be for you."

"We're not talking about me." He felt like shaking her. "You're entirely different. You should get married, settle down. What about having a family?"

"You must have spent a lot of time watching Ozzie and

Harriet reruns,'' she said dryly, ''if you think home life is that easy for everyone. I had a great one as a child, and I'm not going to settle for less. I'd have to find someone who wanted me, not the great brain, the mind that doesn't stop. I haven't so far.''

His heart twisted. ''For God's sake, Emily, give yourself a break. You say that as though no one will ever want you.''

''You don't,'' she said simply. ''You may desire me, but there's no place for me in your life.''

He was stung. ''Anything having to do with me and you is irrelevant to you and another man. I can't have a relationship with you. You're confusing the issue.''

''You've given me that song and dance number more than once already. I'm not buying it. You use it as an excuse instead of telling me you don't find me desirable. I'd rather you were honest.''

''It isn't an excuse,'' he replied quietly. ''Men in my profession don't make very good husbands or long term lovers. We're gone too much, our minds aren't with our wives even when our bodies are. And our work poses a threat to families.''

''You don't have to stay with it forever. Make a leap of faith. Aren't you saying almost the same thing to me?''

''This is pointless, Emily.''

She turned away, her eyes stinging at the rebuff. ''Fine.'' The rest of dinner was silent. When the meal was over, she offered to wash the dishes and completed the task in record time, turning over the conversation in her mind.

He'd slipped. That much she knew. He wasn't immune. She hadn't been mistaken that he wanted her. A gleam of pure desire had been visible in the depths of his eyes at one point but he was working overtime to deny it.

Nerves that had been quiet started to jump and she walked over to stand in front of the fire, restless, her thoughts churning. Ross leaned against the wall above the fireplace, his foot propped on the edge of the hearth. Emily shot him a sideways glance.

She'd always achieved whatever goal she'd set for herself. Now she wanted a man. Not just any man, but Ross.

The very qualities that set Ross apart, making her want him, also made him terrifying. Self-sufficiency was stamped on his features, along with an uncompromising maleness. The glimpses of gentleness, verging on tenderness had been few and far between.

She had to believe they were a real part of his character. More than her ego was at risk. Her awareness of herself as a desirable woman was on the line. If Ross turned away, could she handle it? Her hands felt clammy and she wiped them down the sides of her jeans. She hoped to hell he really needed her. Because she needed him.

"Ross," she said quietly.

He looked down at her. "Yes?"

"Kiss me."

He closed his eyes briefly. "That's not a good idea, Emily."

"Yes, it is."

"No. It's not."

She sucked in air. "We're leaving tomorrow. I don't know what's going to happen in New York. Neither do you. I'm not asking for a commitment. Just one night to be close to you."

Ross's mouth dried. Emily's face was open for him to read. Desire, fear, pride. All there. And a heartwrenching vulnerability. An irresistible combination.

"Oh, Emily," he began.

"You can say no," she whispered. She tried for a smile. "After all, I can hardly overpower you."

"You already have." He gently stroked the hair from her forehead, feeling his detachment splinter. "You're so unbelievably trusting. Why can't you be tough? So I can say no."

"Let me make it easy for you. If you don't want me, just tell me. That's all I ask. I don't think I could bear for you to lie to me about that." Her face was uncharacteristically solemn.

Ross shook his head, helpless in the face of her extraordinary honesty. "I've wanted you for what seems like forever, Emily," he finally muttered in a voice made harsh by need.

She reached out with a trembling hand and touched the material of his shirt tentatively. With a brazenness she didn't know she possessed, she gripped his collar and tugged his head down.

Ross discarded discipline for desire as he took her mouth in his. How much more could he be expected to take? God, she tasted sweet! He gently brushed his tongue across her mouth, and felt her respond with a sudden, greedy passion that took his breath away.

Her hands clutched him, fingers digging into his shoulders. He moved deeper into the cradle of her hips. Ross stared down. Emily's head was thrown back, her neck arched, and a flush lay across her cheekbones. Her eyes were hazy as she looked up.

He felt the pressure in his groin increase at the open hunger he saw. Deliberately, he undid the first button of her shirt. Emily's mouth slid along his neck. His hand trembled. Ross ran his fingers along the fine skin under her collar bone and undid the second button. Then the third. The fourth laid her bare to the waist.

She was wearing a silk teddy in a pale beige that hugged her firm breasts and covered her body, disappearing into her jeans. It was about to drive him out of his mind. Her nipples hardened to peaks and jutted against the silky fabric. His thumb brushed a crest.

Emily moaned, her mouth blindly searching. He did it again. His left hand tightened around her waist as he felt fine tremors rippling through her. His hand continued to move across her breasts, and then Emily felt his tongue wetly on a nipple.

Ross's arms were hard around her as he swept her off her feet in one smooth, powerful movement. Emily gripped his neck, tucking her face into his chest, aware that she'd have fallen if he weren't holding her.

"Are you sure?"

Ross's voice was husky, and Emily realized he was asking her a question. He'd stopped moving, and was holding her above the bed in the other room, his eyes almost black as he stared at her.

"Sure about what?"

"That you want this."

She lifted her mouth, begging mutely for a kiss. "I'll never forgive you if you leave me now."

A groan ripped out of him as he cast every reservation to the wind and laid her down on the bed. His fingers fumbled briefly on her zipper. With hands that stroked and caressed, he slid the jeans down her thighs and over her feet.

The perfume from her skin rose in a mist around him, and teased his senses. Emily raised her hands to him from the bed and her eyes glowed with need. "Come here."

Ross could feel the last vestige of control slipping away as he put his knee on the bed and bent over her.

She tried to unbutton his shirt and gave up. She tore the shirt open. Buttons popped. "You shouldn't have made me wait," she said, a slow smile curving her lips. "I've wanted to do that for a long time."

"What?" He took in a deep breath.

"Tear the clothes off you," she said.

She saw Ross's throat convulse as she stretched slowly under his intent gaze, her nipples erect, the line of her body sleek.

He moved away, and swiftly removed his pants. With an almost desperate lunge, he was on the bed beside her, his hands holding her fiercely. "I want this to be perfect for you," he muttered, his mouth pressed against her skin. "Tell me if I do anything wrong."

"There's nothing you could do wrong, Emily," he managed, as her hands found a sensitive spot.

He kissed the tender junction of shoulder and neck, then the hollow under her collarbone. His tongue rasped as it lapped across her breasts, followed by strokes across her belly. Then lower. Emily panted harshly as his tongue probed and teased.

"Please, you're . . . I can't stand it. What are you doing?" Emily's eyes were wild, as she stared down at his dark head.

"Loving you."

She screamed as he found her.

"I can't hold back any longer," he groaned and then was inside her, the heat and slickness of her welcoming body almost pushing him over the edge. Ross stiffened on his elbows and bent his head, searching for control.

Emily surged up to meet him, sealing him tighter within her, and he began to move, his arms holding her tightly, his breath coming in great gasps.

"I . . . can't . . . I don't know how," she said.

"Yes, you do," he said, his hands gripping her to him. "Now," he commanded, and Emily could feel it happening, harder, faster, and then she was gone with him, over the top.

Ross's breathing slowed finally. He couldn't move. Emily's thighs held him securely and he gently stroked the damp hair from her forehead. "Are you all right?" Emily opened her eyes slowly and smiled up at him, the blue of her eyes blinding him.

"It's not exactly described this way in the biology texts."

For a long moment there was no sound in the room, then Ross's voice broke the silence. "Bio . . . biology texts?" he sputtered, his body shaking with silent laughter.

"Don't laugh, I want you to stay inside me." Emily sounded aggrieved, and her legs tightened around his calves, her hands digging in at his hips.

Ross gasped and restrained himself, her request making him pulse briefly. "I'm sorry," he said.

Emily said quietly, her fingers gently stroking the skin of his back under her hand, "How long before we can do it again?"

"Not long." A surge of pleasure at her question arrowed down his middle. He felt himself harden again, still buried within her and his pulse rate picked up, its rhythm matched by the beat he could feel deep within her body. "Not long at all."

"Are you sure? This fast?" Her voice was thin.

Ross pressed his hips deeper and watched the passion fill her eyes. "Yes."

When he finally moved from her, he drew up the covers of the bed, covering them both. She lay on her side facing him, one arm thrown over her head, totally vulnerable to him in her openness. Ross closed his eyes for a moment at the sight. He placed his hand on her throat and gently began to stroke downwards, over her beautiful breasts, across her flat belly and down to the curls between her legs. He let his hand rest against the warmth he felt there and quieted a shudder of want that flickered to life again.

"You're quite a surprise, Miss Brown," he said lazily.

"How's that?" She yawned.

"You've got a gorgeous body that you hide most of the time under very deceptive clothes. The first time I saw you, you were wearing a horror of a dress. Brown something."

"That's one I wear to work. It's appropriate."

His dark eyebrow quirked as he glanced down at where his hand rested. "How so?"

"I'm the egghead of the office. I dress like one. Simple."

He was astounded. "You mean you deliberately look like . . ." he searched for a word that wouldn't offend her.

"Drab? Plain?"

"No, just not eye catching."

"How diplomatic," she teased. She yawned again.

"Why do you do it?"

She shifted into the curve of his arm, and sighed. "It's elementary, my dear Watson. Starting from high school, or even earlier, I decided to lower my profile as it were. Can you imagine how awful it would have been if I'd been gorgeous and smart?" She shuddered dramatically. "I would have been hated. This way, no one found me a threat, at least not a real one. The girls at M.I.T. who were older than I was, and not as smart, could console themselves with the thought that poor Emily really wasn't very attractive. I just dressed to fit the misconceptions."

"Or opted out?" he said shrewdly.

"What does that mean?"

"You're damned smart. You're also sexy as hell.

You're a very desirable woman,'' he stressed, his hand pressing on her still heated skin. "But you don't act like you know it. You should.''

Emily bit her lip. "You drive me crazy when you do that.''

"You do the same to me.''

"Really?''

He gathered her close, hugging her to him. "God, yes, Emily.'' His laugh turned into a groan. "I thought I made that clear. I've shown about as much self-control as a teenager.'' He put her back gently. "Honestly. You make my knees weak. That's very rare and very wonderful.''

Her eyes filled with tears. "You don't know how that makes me feel.''

His heart turned over. Her vulnerability reached deep. He inhaled shakily. If anything happened to her . . . it didn't bear thinking about.

Emily stretched, her eyes focusing on the suddenly grim face of the man at her side.

"What's wrong?''

"Nothing.'' Ross forced a smile and watched the worry leave her face. He had to touch her. His forefinger smoothed the lingering trace of anxiety from her forehead, then trailed down her throat to the pulse throbbing beneath the skin. He rolled onto his side and propped his head on an elbow as he gazed down at her.

"What is it?'' she asked with a little laugh. "Something on my face?''

"Yes, the glow of a woman who's just made love.'' His smile was very satisfied and Emily grinned. "Can't imagine why.''

"Huh.'' He stroked her belly, enjoying the slight hitch in her breathing at his touch. "There's something I've been wanting to ask you. You obviously love it out here. Why have you stayed in New York?''

"Because I feel alive there. The work has been chal-lenging, and I've enjoyed having to stretch to the limit.'' She bit her lip as his hand trailed lower. "I'd love to have both lives, the ranch and the city, but can't think of any reasonable way right now." His hand paused in its movement then lifted.

"You weren't challenged at home?"

"My mother did her best. She made me and my brother hit the books all morning, then do ranch chores in the afternoon. I think she worried I'd end up a bookworm. I have almost, but at least I've developed a lasting appreciation for life here, and the values shared by people on the land."

"Such as?" He had a suspicion what she'd say but wanted to hear her anyway.

"Knowing your limits, establishing independence. You're on your own out here in a way few people are. You can't run next door for a cup of sugar."

"Or for a doctor to take care of a bite."

"Nope. Distance breeds strength. My parents wanted me to have that feeling."

She had it in spades. Sometimes. Ross felt his throat tighten with an unfamiliar sensation and his eyes stung. Damn her. Why did she have to come into his life now? Too many years, too many lives too late.

Emily's hand caressed his lean cheek. "Come here. You've gone away."

Ross felt his pulse kick.

"I just want to kiss you, not start something," she teased and he leaned over, a smile deep in his eyes. Emily's lips pressed a soft kiss on his mouth then she looked up at him, her expression one of complete satisfaction. "I'm ready to sleep."

She sighed deeply as he drew her close, one hand possessively on her hip. After a moment, she slept, her breathing light and even. The flush that had invaded her cheeks during passion had faded to a warm tinge. His arm tightened as he closed his eyes, a hard knot in him easing at the regular sound of her breath.

The sun was laying pale pink ribbons along the horizon when Emily woke up, disoriented, something hard holding her down. Then she remembered. Ross had made love to her the night before, his mouth and hands saying things to her she knew he wouldn't say aloud.

Perhaps couldn't, she admitted. But the aching tenderness, the gentleness she'd known was there, he'd made her feel both.

She turned her head and looked at him. Dark hair flopped over his forehead as he lay on his side facing her. His expression was calm and relaxed, and one lean hand still curved over her breast. Emily looked at it and felt, astonishingly, a surge of sexual heat in her middle and her eyes opened wider.

For so long, she'd been sure there was little to the biological process between men and women. Was she ever wrong, she thought smugly, a satisfied smile tilting her mouth. After the night she'd had, she wouldn't have believed herself capable of a bottomless well of desire.

She was, though.

The nipple under Ross's fingers stiffened and she watched in fascination as, still without opening his eyes, his fingers stroked the sensitive skin as it puckered under his touch. Her gasp jerked his eyes open, to see her watching him with unwavering intensity, her lip caught between her teeth.

"Does this go on forever?" she asked.

His fingers continued their torment. "With you, anything is possible."

The reaction of his body drove everything from his mind but Emily and slaking the thirst that welled up endlessly.

He moved closer and she shivered in anticipation as one hard muscled leg slid between hers causing her stomach muscles to tighten, and heat to pool between her legs. She was ready for him, opening at once to his slow, powerful thrust.

"What you do to me," he got out between his teeth, "should be either outlawed or bottled."

They burned together, then slept.

The sun beat gently on her closed eyelids and Emily smiled. She put her hand out on the sheet. Nothing. Her eyes snapped open.

Ross stiffened from his position by the side of the bed.

Without saying anything, he turned, presenting a smoothly muscled backside to her as he walked to the other side of the room where he'd left his clothes. She propped her head on her hand and watched him. She thought she saw a muscle leap in the side of his jaw, and a pink color painted on his ears.

Ross left the bedroom and walked into the kitchen. He leaned tiredly against the counter, self-disgust pouring through him. The night before had been a mistake. Like a complete fool, he'd thought he could make love to her and then back away. Worse, his selfishness had been at her expense. No matter what she'd said, she'd deserved better than he'd given her.

He could no more view her dispassionately than he could walk on water. His smile was mirthless. He just hoped a similar miracle wasn't called for.

When Emily had offered herself to him he couldn't have turned her down even if he'd wanted to. And God knows he hadn't wanted to.

He was stirring eggs in a frying pan when she walked in a few moments later. Toast was on the counter ready for butter and Emily smelled coffee.

"Why don't you set the table," he said without looking at her.

Emily hesitated then got out the forks, napkins, and juice glasses. A few minutes later breakfast was on the table. She was beginning to get angry at his continued silence. "Did you enjoy my body last night?"

Ross's hand slipped on his fork and it clattered to his plate. "Did I what?"

"Did you enjoy my body last night?" she repeated calmly, carefully keeping anger out of her voice.

"You know I did."

"No, I don't." Emily's throat hurt. "If you did, you wouldn't be shutting me out. Making it seem as though nothing happened." She lowered her head.

What had happened was cataclysmic and a mistake. How could he tell her that? He rose and came to stand beside her. When she didn't speak, he squatted next to her, his eyes peering under the fringe of hair that had fallen over her forehead.

"Last night was wonderful."

"Then why are you being like this?"

He heaved a sigh and placed his hand on hers, enfolding it tightly. "We're adults. I've made everything clear. I didn't think I needed to say anything else." He realized he sounded like a complete bastard. Color tinted his cheeks.

"Made everything clear?" she repeated, matching flags in her own cheeks. "Like mud."

He felt defensive. "I mean . . ."

"You've been having second thoughts, probably even third and fourth. Now you're trying to dream up suitable words to tell me. I told you before that you and your boss liked to wrap up things in phrases. Just be blunt. I prefer it." Her eyes glistened with tears. "What you mean is that last night you did me a favor. Made love to me because you felt sorry for me. After all, I'd just been whining about my lack of desirability and you decided to give me an instant cure. Right?"

The pain in her face was enormous.

"No, damnit. I made love to you because I wanted to."

"Or because you decided you'd better?" His fractional pause gave her the answer. Emily's face paled and tightened. "I shouldn't have forced the issue, Ross. You have my sympathies."

She rose from the table and moved to the sink, her shoulders rigid. Ross felt sick to his stomach. He'd hurt her.

"Emily . . ."

"I think we've said all there is to say." She didn't turn. "You'll just make it worse."

She was probably right, he thought bitterly. He seemed to have a true gift for destruction but at least he'd stopped before she was hurt any more.

"I'd better get into town to have the transmission repaired," he said finally when she didn't turn around. "Get your suitcase ready and we'll leave."

"I'll wait here."

"I'd like us to stay together. That was the plan yesterday."

"And I'd rather not. Things change."

What she didn't say was that just then she couldn't have

stood being in the car with him. But he read it from her expression and his jaw tightened and deep lines bracketed his mouth. He turned on his heel and walked out of the room. Emily wondered dully if her legs would continue to support her by the sink.

She had dried the last of the dishes by the time he was ready. He left his suitcase standing in the middle of the floor.

"Be careful, won't you?" She spoke quickly, almost as if she regretted saying the words aloud.

"I will. You, too." Almost involuntarily, he walked toward her and pulled her to him, his breath hissing in as her body sagged against his. He gave her a swift, hard kiss, his fingers gripping her shoulders before putting her away from him.

She followed him to the door and held it open as he strode to the porch.

"Ross."

He stiffened, his back to her.

"You do need me, no matter what you think."

"I won't."

He was out the door and in the car before Emily could draw breath to protest. She watched the car ease slowly away from the cabin, feeling an acute, disturbing sense of abandonment.

He'd said, "wont," not "don't." Why was he so blind? Her fingers trembled as she touched her mouth, remembering the touch of his lips on hers. Pain speared her and she almost doubled over from its force.

She felt like dying. Her eyes misted and it took a moment for her to regain control.

Ross was running scared and she was going to have to be strong for both of them.

Emily walked into the next room, aimlessly touching things, running her hand over the pillow where Ross's head had lain. She lifted it, and smelled the clean, masculine aroma, then laid it carefully down. She packed her clothes, placing them in the suitcase, her thoughts far away.

By the time Emily cleaned up the cabin, she saw it

was almost ten o'clock, and she frowned, beginning to be concerned. Ross had left shortly after eight and she expected him back by now. She checked her watch and listened to the faint ticking she could still hear, then walked outside to wait on the porch.

The crisp air of the morning had warmed up under the sun's heat. The heavy dew that had lain on the ground and dotted the plants with bright droplets of water had been absorbed by the thirsty leaves of the plants. A doe stepped across the clearing in front of the cabin and Emily held her breath, motionless.

She had a fawn at her side and the pair weren't aware of Emily's presence. Emily's eyes shifted behind the deer but couldn't see a buck.

The doe's ears flicked forward, and her head came up quickly, her dark eyes focused on something behind the cabin. With a seemingly instantaneous spurt of energy she jumped away, the fawn following, tail held high.

Emily sat up quickly, her nerves jangling. Something had spooked the deer. She looked around, all senses alert, but couldn't see anything out of the ordinary. Then she heard a deep voice behind her.

"Don't move."

NINE

Emily's head whipped around. She met the detached gaze of a tall man dressed in a plaid wool shirt and blue jeans. He was dark haired with a pleasant smile. She froze when she saw what was in his hand. He was holding an automatic, its muzzle pointed straight at her.

Her mouth dried. "You're on private land. I won't press charges if you leave right now." She could tell by his expression her bluff hadn't worked.

"Please be quiet, Miss Brown," he said, his smile narrowing slightly. "Harry, come here."

The fact that he'd used her name more than anything told her that her time had run out. There was a faint scraping sound and another man appeared around the edge of the cabin. This man was shorter, younger, probably in his early twenties, good looking, with blond hair. He had a look of almost boyish excitement . . . except for his eyes which were empty. They made her blood run cold.

"Be sure she's not carrying anything, Harry," the first man said.

"No sweat." Harry reached out. Involuntarily Emily stepped back. His expression tightened. "Stay put," he ordered.

This time she stood still, controlling a nervous flinch as his hand patted under her arms, around her waist, and then edged upward toward her breast. She inhaled sharply.

"Easy, Harry," cautioned the other man.

"She's clean," he said, giving her a narrow-eyed glance.

The first man turned to Emily. "Miss Brown, Harry is new at his job and sometimes a little impulsive." His gaze flickered away to Harry then returned to Emily. "I'd suggest you comply with his requests. It will make things easier . . . for all of us if you stay in one piece until we're finished.''

There was an almost inaudible grunt from the younger man and Emily felt sweat running down her side in a cold trickle.

''Come on. Let's get out of here,'' the older man continued.

''We need to take any of her clothes?'' Harry asked.

''What for? We're just going to ask questions. That shouldn't take long.''

Bill's tone was devoid of emphasis but Emily shivered.

Harry looked at her and smiled. ''I'm sure she'll cooperate sooner or later.''

She fought for control. With enormous effort she forced herself to think calmly. They meant to torture her then kill her. What else could Bill have meant? There's always a chance, she repeated to herself. Always. Emily drew in a deep breath and deliberately kept her expression blank. She wasn't giving them the satisfaction of knowing she was scared.

Bill turned and walked away. Harry took her upper arm in an unbreakable grip and shepherded her after him.

''Where are we going?'' Emily asked, her gait unaccountably clumsy. The pressure of his arm increased.

''You'll see.''

Bill headed up the slope at the back of the cabin and Harry pushed her in that direction, staying close behind. When she stumbled his grip on her arm tightened painfully.

Prodded by Harry, Emily managed to keep up the pace set by Bill, although she had to scramble to maintain her balance on the uneven ground.

As they crested the ridge, she looked down and saw a Jeep canted at an angle. She cast a brief glance toward the paved road in the distance, praying she'd see Ross's rental car returning.

Nothing. She clamped her lips shut, willing herself to stay calm. Where on earth was he?

Harry pushed her from behind, and she skidded. Showers of white rocks cascaded under her feet. He pushed again, and swore when she tried to jerk away. His voice grated in her ear.

"I may be new at my job but I'm good at it. Don't push me away."

Emily clenched her teeth. Calm. She had to stay calm and remember these men were just a different kind of snake than she was used to. She was sweating and wiped the moisture from her forehead.

"Get in." Bill stood waiting by the vehicle. "You sit in the back, Harry. Keep your gun on her. I'll drive." He motioned Emily to take the front passenger seat.

The trip down the hill was slow. Several times the Jeep's tires slipped before grabbing for traction. Emily held on tightly to the door handle aware of Harry behind her.

Bill spoke without inflection over his shoulder. "Don't try to jump. I'd just have to shoot you. Probably in the knee so you couldn't run. I'm sure you'd prefer to stay healthy."

For how long? "Where are we going?" She'd noticed Harry hadn't answered earlier.

"Mexico," Bill replied.

"Why?"

"Because I need to ask you some questions and you may not want to answer." He glanced at her briefly, his face blank. "We'll need privacy," he said.

"Questions about what?"

"Your job."

"You have the wrong person."

"Miss Brown, don't make it harder than it has to be." He looked at her then glanced away.

She almost thought there was a note of sympathy in his voice then dismissed the idea as ridiculous. Emily forced herself to ask, "Do you have to do this? Can't you just let me go?"

Bill barked a laugh. "If you don't talk, I not only don't get paid, but I take a risk of someone coming after me. Someone who's going to be mighty unhappy if I don't produce."

"Will you let me go afterwards?" She deliberately injected a note of panic into her voice.

Bill shrugged. "Depends."

His tone was unconvincing and Emily wiped her damp hands on her jeans. At least she wouldn't make it easy for them. "By the way, how did you find me?" she asked after a short silence.

"It doesn't matter. We did," Bill said curtly. "That's enough talking for now."

Ross paced along the concrete apron of the garage. The mechanic had promised him the car would be ready a half hour earlier and the guy was still tinkering with it.

Muttering a curse under his breath, he glared at the reclining man under the vehicle. After a moment the dirty figure slid out and stood up. The mechanic wiped greasy hands on his overalls and smiled.

"Ready?" Ross raised his eyebrow.

"Sure is. Had to do some last minute adjusting but I think it'll do you fine."

"How much?" Ross pulled out his wallet.

"That'll be sixty-seven fifty."

Ross paid.

"Much obliged."

Ross got into the car, and drove out of town. For the last few minutes he'd been feeling increasingly anxious about Emily. Logically, he knew she should be all right. If Walker was correct about the searchers and the time frame.

But if Walker was wrong, Emily could already be in trouble. By the time he reached the cutoff, every instinct tingled.

As the cabin came into view he slowed, his eyes rapidly surveyed the area. No tracks in the road. Everything was quiet.

Too quiet. Where the hell was she?

Ross got out of the car in one swift movement, his gun in his hand. His breath left in a whoosh as he saw the marks of a man's soled foot in the soft dirt.

He leaped up the steps to the porch. He was inside the cabin and out in seconds. She was gone.

His face darkened with anger. He slammed his hand against the upright of the porch, pain stabbing through his palm. He didn't know how big their head start was, but he had to find her fast.

He went back into the cabin, came out again with the suitcases, and threw them into the car before slamming the door. Ross circled the cabin, looking for signs of the direction they'd taken. He'd already spotted two pairs of tracks, coming from above the cabin, both deep enough and large enough to have come from men. Cresting the mountain, he put binoculars to his eyes.

There, in the soft dirt at the base of the mountain, were faint tracks. He sharpened the focus on the eyepieces and squinted. Tires that looked like those for a Jeep. Ross turned and swiftly returned to his car. A few minutes later, he'd left the dirt road and was on the highway.

A muscle jumped in his jaw as he concentrated; his eyes flicked every so often to the gauges as he kept the car steady on the dark, gray surface unfurling in front of him like an endless ribbon. When he came to the crossroads he slammed on his brakes and contemplated his choices.

The kidnappers could first turn either east or west then drive south to get her to Mexico. Or they could head north towards Midland and an airport. He decided Mexico was the more likely option. While West Texas was sparsely populated, it still presented more risks to the kidnappers than comparable areas on the other side of the border. They undoubtedly planned on questioning her, then killing her and dumping her body. And deniability was the name of the game.

It was one hell of a lot easier to stonewall questions about events in Mexico than on home turf. He'd learned that a long time ago, and undoubtedly the men who had Emily had, too.

A quick check of the map told him that the nearest Mexican towns were Ojinaga to the west, and Boquillas to the east, which was hardly more than a crossing. The only other possibility was Ciudad Acuna, even further to the east, across from Del Rio.

It was more likely they'd take her there than risk entering a small border village where their presence would be more easily noted. Logic dictated they'd want to know how much Emily knew before disposing of her, and Ross was pinning his hopes on that frail reed.

He looked at the signs one more time and decided.

This operation had all the earmarks of a rush job. If Walker had been even partially right, the trail had suddenly heated up and the opposition had risked rushing in, rather than missing their quarry. Worse, the men who had taken her could be feeling pressured. Haste made for mistakes. Final ones.

The attempt in the subway station and then the fire in her apartment had been clumsy, but real. Someone had meant to kill her then. But not now.

Instead, she'd been snatched. Something significant must have happened in the last few days to make whoever was running the operation change his mind. Otherwise she would have been left in the cabin. Dead.

And that indicated Emily was in for a bad time, unless he got there first. His mouth dried as the image of Emily's anguished face rose in his mind. She'd try to hold out. But no one could. These men would be under pressure to get results in a hurry and it wouldn't matter how.

His knuckles gleamed white as he gripped the steering wheel.

Two more towns, more like wide places in the highway, flew by as he pushed the car to its limits, but he didn't notice.

Pictures flooded his mind. The demons he'd fought in the long nights mocked him, and sweat poured off him. Phantoms from the past laughed gleefully. What he'd dreaded was happening. Torture, pain, terror. He knew them all. Now Emily would.

He drove as though he were fleeing from nightmarish visions, tearing across the landscape, hoping to escape. He couldn't.

Ross drove on, finally nearing the outskirts of Del Rio.

Mesquite and sagebrush dotted the brown earth and a few low lying brown hills could be seen in the distance. The entire area appeared desolate, almost barren, and his eyes darkened.

He slowed. Traffic intensified. Thirty minutes later he had passed through the city itself and was at the international bridge, ready to cross into Mexico. He flexed his stiff fingers, reminding himself of the job ahead.

He'd have to be cold. Cold as ice. Or it would all blow up in his face.

He stopped at the border station and pulled out his identification. The guard's expression changed when he saw the official seal.

"How may I help you?"

"Have you seen a Jeep come through here with two men and a woman in the last hour? She has brown hair, blue eyes, and is wearing slacks and a yellow shirt. She's in the front," he added, figuring the men who'd taken her would have a gun pointed at her from the back seat.

"No, señor, but I just came on duty."

"Anyone from the other shift still here?" Ross asked.

"I think so. I will find out."

The guard walked to the small building and stuck his head inside. A moment later he came out, followed by a second man.

Ross repeated his question and the new guard nodded. "The Jeep you describe just came by about twenty minutes ago. The men were arguing and the woman was quiet."

Ross's pulse accelerated at the realization he'd guessed right and was closing in. Until this moment, he'd been unwilling to contemplate the possibility she was dead. "Did she look okay?" he asked, holding his breath.

"Yes." The guard smiled, gold fillings shining behind his dark mustache. "She was in the front seat and I could tell she was mad about something because her eyes looked so fierce."

"Do you know which direction they took?"

The man nodded vigorously. "They asked me for a hotel and I told them about one near the downtown. It is brand new." He shrugged. "It is a good place and is run by relatives of mine."

"And just where might this be?"

"Past the second street. There is no longer a sign. A drunk took it out three days ago. No one has had time to fix it." The guard lifted his shoulders in another shrug. "The hotel's name is La Huerta, the orchard, and is written on the front. My cousin likes trees," he added as an afterthought.

Ross nodded and left after thanking both men. He drove slowly over the bridge and into the town, dodging potholes and children, as he cruised down streets that were dusty and littered with refuse.

It was not yet one o'clock and if he were lucky, the men holding Emily would want something to eat before beginning their interrogation. A full stomach would make them less prone to mistakes.

He saw the street.

The hotel was halfway down the block, its name on a large sign nailed to the front of the building. Ross parked in front of a big truck which hid his car from view. He left the car unlocked, figuring he might need to make a hasty exit.

The hotel sat well back from the curb. A high wall surrounded the grounds and a white painted door marked the entrance. Ross walked past without turning his head, rounded the corner and struck paydirt.

The Jeep was parked about eighty feet from the corner. Ross peered inside then stiffened. Emily had pulled out some of her hair leaving it as a marker, a few shining strands tied in a knot lying on the front seat.

He lifted the hood, and within seconds had disabled the engine, then quietly lowered the hood and walked back to the hotel. As he was about to enter the building, he spotted a kid wearing baggy khaki shorts and a dirty, ripped shirt stopping passersby, trying to polish their shoes. The boy was probably no more than ten with a sharp intelligence lurking in his black eyes.

"Want a shine, mister?" He carried a small box with

a rag hanging over the edge. His English was heavily accented.

"No, but how would you like to make some money?"

He looked warily at Ross. "Doing what?"

"Just find out what room some friends of mine are in," he said, pointing to the hotel entrance. "It's kind of a joke."

"That's all?" The boy's expression was disbelieving.

"That's it. They checked in a few minutes ago. It's worth five dollars." He held a bill between thumb and forefinger.

"What do they look like?"

"They're Americans. Three of them. One woman, tall, brown hair and blue eyes. She's wearing jeans and a shirt. Two men."

"You don't know what they look like?" Black eyes eyed him consideringly from under the mop of hair.

"You're going to earn the five dollars by being sure you find the woman." Ross waited, his face hard, his hand outstretched.

"All right," the boy said slowly, his expression shrewdly calculating. A grimy hand come out and took the money, cramming it into a pocket. "You want me to meet you here?"

Ross said, "I'll be around the corner, that way." He indicated the intersection. The kid nodded, then turned and walked across the street and disappeared inside the hotel.

Checking to be sure no one had spotted him, Ross went down the side street, surprised at how little traffic there was. The very lack of people was both good and bad, because it meant no one was interested in him, but it also made it harder to hide in a crowd.

He heard the sound of running footsteps and turned quickly to see the boy coming towards him.

"They're in room sixteen, señor. That's on the inside courtyard, second floor."

"Did anyone inside ask why you wanted to know?"

"There was a girl at the desk. I told her I was delivering something."

"Thanks." Ross gave the boy another dollar.

The boy looked over his shoulder as he walked away. "You need anything else, just ask for Tomas. I'm always on the street."

Ross nodded, his attention on the problem of getting into the hotel. His mind made up, he moved towards the building.

After Bill had checked them in, he'd left the room to use the telephone, telling Harry to stay put. Emily sat on a straight-backed chair pulled up beside a small, round table in front of the room's only window, her hands clasped together in her lap.

The drive to Mexico had been fast and silent. Emily had felt Harry's eyes on her the entire time. Now he was watching her from his reclining position on the bed. Emily kept her head turned towards the window, avoiding his unceasing stare.

It was more than menace, she decided, that frightened her. He seemed dangerously on edge, as though whatever controls he had were wearing thin. She'd felt safe with Bill although she knew he intended to dispose of her. At least he'd be quick about it.

The door opened and Bill came in. "We'd better get to work."

Emily's mouth dried and she managed to inject pleading into her voice. "Couldn't you just ask me your questions and let me go?" Everything depended on their willingness to believe she'd cooperate.

"Sure."

Bill's smile left ice in her stomach.

"What say we get down to talking now?"

His tone was totally pleasant and her fists clenched.

Harry sat up. "I can help."

Her jaw tightened from the strain of holding back a shudder. "Before we start, could I have some lunch? I'm starving." She let a smile tremble on her lips.

Bill waited, his gaze assessing her. He nodded. "All right. No reason we can't wait a few minutes."

Harry grinned at her. "Let's not wait too long."

Bill's face changed, and his lips barely moved as he spoke. "That's enough, Harry. I told you before we came on this little jaunt that you were getting on my nerves. Remember Wilson?"

Harry's eyes widened. "I didn't mean anything, Bill."

"I hope that's right," Bill replied quietly, his look never leaving the other man. "All right. What do you want to eat?" he said to Emily, after a long moment.

"Anything is fine," she answered. "I like Mexican food."

"Okay. Harry, while I'm gone, don't do anything you'd be sorry for. Get me?" Bill's eyes were deadly as he focused again on the other man. Harry nodded. "I'll be back in a few minutes." Bill's eyes shifted back to Emily. "And you. Don't do anything to rouse Harry."

"I won't," she said, hearing her voice shake.

After Bill left, she remained unmoving in the chair, while Harry continued to watch her with the unblinking intensity of a guard dog.

God, if Bill would only come back.

The irony of it struck her and she fought nervous giggles at the realization she wanted one murderer to come and rescue her from another. Bill's politeness only added to the bizarre quality of the situation. Were murderers taught manners? If so, Harry needed a refresher course.

The room wasn't hot but it was airless, and Emily felt sweat bead on her temples. Bill had ordered the windows shut and it was stifling. Neither man had thought to tie her hands but she knew she didn't have a chance against them physically, unless she could outwit them. She cleared her throat, her heart pumping rapidly.

"You travel with Bill much?" She turned to look at him and plastered a smile on her face. Maybe she could get around Harry.

"Yeah. You in the mood to talk?"

"I just wondered how often you did . . . jobs . . . with him." What on earth did you call kidnapping and murder?

"We've been together some." His tone was suspicious. "Why do you want to know?"

"I thought it might make the time pass more quickly if

we knew something about each other. Seeing as how we're in the same room.''

"Sure." Harry turned expansive. "Me and Bill have done a lot of jobs." He grinned. "Know what I mean?" Emily nodded. "You and me, now, we could have a real good time. Before things get rough.''

"Sure." She kept her voice even and listened for the sound of footsteps.

He looked briefly surprised and she caught a glimpse of excitement. He rose from the bed and began to walk toward her.

Emily smiled and rose from the chair. He reached for her and she backed away until she felt the dresser against her thighs. He frowned. Her smile widened. "Can't you read an invitation when you see one?" she asked teasingly.

His expression cleared. "Yeah, sure."

He took her in his arms and Emily felt her stomach lurch. Moistening her lips, she looked upwards. Harry's eyes held a bright gleam and she shut her eyes briefly. He pulled her close and she lifted her arms to his shoulders.

As his face lowered, she let one hand drift from his shoulder, behind his back, to the top of the dresser. Her fingers closed around the brightly colored, triangular ashtray and with a sudden movement, she slammed it against his head. He shuddered and sagged against her. Swallowing hard, she hit him again.

Harry slipped to the floor unconscious. Emily was breathing quickly as she stepped away from his still form and went to the door. She listened for a moment, then with a swift turn, she had the door open and was out in the hall.

Emily started to run down the dark hallway towards the lighted area near the stairs when she careened into a large, dark figure. It was a man. She staggered and his hands grabbed her in an unbreakable grip. She opened her mouth to scream when a hand clamped tightly over her mouth and she was lifted off the ground.

She flailed at the arms holding her, panic giving her

strength. She heard the breath hiss out of the man behind her as her elbow slammed into his midsection.

"Damnit, stop that," he said with an angry rasp.

"Ross?" She melted into him.

"Who the hell else?" He hauled her limp body around the corner, and planted a hard kiss on her mouth. "Where's the other guy? You all right?" he asked softly. His eyes scanned her anxiously for any sign she'd been hurt. His fingers stroked her face and neck.

Emily turned into his hand, overwhelming relief flooding her. She felt his grip tighten before he put her away. "I'm fine and one of them is inside on the floor. I knocked him out."

"Why doesn't that surprise me? Where's the other one?"

"Downstairs, getting me some lunch." She thought she heard him laugh.

"Stay here," he ordered then released her.

Emily felt rather than heard Ross leave, go around the corner, and move noiselessly towards the room she'd just left. There was a low thud. She didn't move and in a moment heard footsteps approaching. Her pulse beat more rapidly. She relaxed only when she saw Ross's tall silhouette against the faint light behind him.

"I tied him up. I want you to wait on the balcony while I round up his buddy." He took her hand and pulled her after him.

The double windows at the end of the hall were open. Pulling a curtain aside, he motioned for her to go out to the shaded balcony immediately outside. "I'll be right back."

Emily stepped quickly through then turned. She peered through the parted curtains and stiffened. Bill was standing outside the door, carrying a tray in one hand. He'd raised a hand to knock, and Emily saw a dark figure launch itself at him. There was a clatter of dishes and falling cutlery as Bill swung a punch at Ross.

She heard a grunt and quickly stepped through the opening, and pressed against the wall, holding her breath.

Emily saw Ross's fist come up. There was a terrible

sound as it met solid flesh. Bill doubled over. Ross brought his hands up again and Bill dropped to the floor.

She ran towards Ross, her heart still thudding painfully in her breast.

Ross said, his voice hard, "I thought I told you to stay outside." He stepped over the body on the floor before he went into the room without a backward glance. "Get in here."

Emily went. Harry was laid out cold on the bed. His hands were tied with a belt. Ross looked around the room, focused on the curtain at the window. With one jerk, he pulled it down, tore a long strip off, tested it, then left the room.

A minute later, he was hauling Bill in by his feet, then tying him expertly with the length of fabric while she watched.

"I want you to go downstairs," he said, surveying her over his shoulder.

"Why?"

"I need to do something in here."

"Oh. All right. I'll be back in a few minutes."

"Make it about fifteen."

Emily walked out and shut the door behind her. She stood listening for a moment but the room was silent. She went to the lobby to wait, returning upstairs after checking her watch.

Bill was lying on the floor under the window, his eyes shut, and his face pale. His mouth was drawn tight with pain. Ross rose from beside him, shooting her an unreadable look then sat down on the other bed. He picked up the phone and started to dial.

"Who are you calling?" Emily asked.

"Washington." After a short delay he was through. "I've got the package safe and sound." He listened. "Right. Can you arrange transport for two others? The accommodations don't have to be great. Anything else?" A pause. "Fine." He hung up.

"Well," Emily demanded, "what's going on?"

"Walker has things under control at his end. He's arranging with the Mexican government to get these yoyos back to the United States.'' Ross had been tempted to send them back in body bags but he'd cooled off after he realized Emily was unharmed.

"Did he say anything else?"

"No. He wouldn't risk it without a scrambler."

"Won't it matter that he knows where we are? After all, you had to tell him so you could get help removing Harry and Bill," she said logically.

He shrugged. "We won't be here. We're going to fly back to New York."

"And use me as bait when we get there."

"No." Ross walked over to the window, where he stood, looking out the window. Emily followed.

"I don't see any other option," she argued. "I'm tired of being on the run. I never know if I can stick my face out of a door for fear someone is going to come along and grab me. This kidnapping taught me one valuable lesson. All I've done the last couple of days is react. Now it's time to turn it around."

"You're just upset because of what happened."

"Shouldn't I be?" She waited until his eyes met hers. "I'm not running any more. Ever. The only choice left is for me to show up, alive and well. That should flush someone out. You and I can gather information until hell freezes over, but I'll bet that once we've narrowed the list down, we're still not going to be absolutely positive whom we're after." He didn't reply and she fought exasperation. "I'm right, Ross, and you know it. Until someone comes out in the open, we're not going to be sure. I want to get back to my life and not worry if my oven is going to blow up."

"We'll handle it another way."

"No, we won't." She was as determined as he was. "My stake in this is bigger than yours."

Ross stepped away from the window and looked at her, gray eyes boring into blue. "If you don't think they've made this very much my business, you're mistaken. I've chased you and these two thugs all over Texas and I'm going to finish it. Without involving you."

What a lie. She'd invaded his mind and couldn't be dislodged.

"You can't do it without me," she said. "And I won't cooperate unless you agree."

She was right. The two men who'd kidnapped Emily had told Ross nothing useful although he'd presented a powerful incentive.

"We'll see." His tone was noncommittal.

"Did you bring my clothes?"

"They're in the car."

Surprisingly quickly, two soldiers from Laughlin Air Force Base as well as two Mexican Federal Police showed up to take custody of the prisoners and Emily and Ross were free to go.

Walking out of the hotel into the bright sunlight, Emily managed to avoid shooting obvious glances around the area. She couldn't help but still be uneasy after the way she'd been taken hostage at the cabin. Ross swung open the door of the car and waited until she was seated on her side.

"I've got a suggestion about getting back," she said when the silence lengthened. "Let's go separately," she said. "By now the mole knows I'm with someone. If I'm a lone woman, that may be safer."

It went against the grain of everything Ross knew. "I'm in a better position to look after you if we're together."

"Unless your very presence is the key that makes me noticeable," she argued with faultless logic.

Ross started the car, feeling the familiar tension building. He was damned if he did, and damned if he didn't. Leaving Emily on her own would mean she'd be defenseless. On the other hand, being with her might alert the opposition to her presence.

"We'll compromise," he said, as he turned the car around, before heading back across the border. "We won't travel together, but I'm going to be dogging you every step of the way. Once we get to New York, we'll join up. At that point, we'll have to go to ground until we can be sure we've narrowed the list of candidates."

Emily examined the idea for flaws and slowly nodded

her head. "All right. But if it becomes clear we have to change the plan, then we'll do it. I've got another idea."

She quickly laid it out—obtain telephone bills on everyone in the New York office, then cross-reference them to see if there were patterns.

Ross agreed, his brain considering the options. It was just possible that the mole had left a trail through the telephone.

He drove to San Antonio, and let Emily out at the airport. "Get reservations on the first flight to New Orleans. We'll work our way up the East Coast. Once we get to New York, we'll go through several hotels until we've found one I think is safe. I'm not running the chance of being picked up by a tail the minute we land."

Emily got out, and leaned back in the opened door on the passenger side, her eyes concealed behind dark glasses. "It's going to be all right. Don't worry."

Before she could straighten, he moved. His hand captured her nape and pulled her close. Then he kissed her. His mouth was hard and firm, and she felt an instantaneous flare of heat in her stomach. She felt her lips soften, parting under the pressure.

Ross released her. He surveyed her before putting out a finger to stroke her mouth. Emily shut her eyes briefly at the powerful surge of desire.

"Take care of yourself," he muttered, his voice rough. "I'll be watching."

She straightened and shut the door behind her, before walking quickly into the terminal. Ross had the uncanny ability to put her off balance. One minute, he made her knees wobble. The next, he was totally professional.

She bought her ticket then found the lounge area to wait for the flight. When Ross appeared a while later, she didn't turn her head, nor did he acknowledge her presence.

The flight was uneventful and she managed to doze. After landing in New Orleans, Ross walked by her on the way off the airplane, muttering, "Delta, Atlanta," without breaking stride. Emily followed more slowly and saw him get into line ahead of her at the Delta counter.

They followed the same procedure through Atlanta,

Washington, and then to Newark. It was almost dark by
the time they landed in New Jersey, and Emily was standing on the curb waiting for a taxi when she heard a familiar voice behind her.

TEN

"Mind if I share your cab?"

It was Ross.

Emily replied coolly, "No." They'd agreed to behave as strangers for the benefit of anyone watching.

"You looking for a hotel in town? I can recommend one." He named one she'd never heard of.

"Thanks."

Ross gave the address to the taxi driver and didn't speak again. Feeling slightly irritated at his ability to maintain the act, she looked out her window. Emily had a feeling things were about to happen. And she wasn't prepared. She had to unravel the mystery of the text quickly. Perhaps then her understanding of the code would provide some measure of control to a situation that threatened to get out of control.

Something about her first interpretation of the message didn't ring true. Had she missed a vital clue? She must have, she decided. Because nothing else explained events.

Initially, the intent of the mole had been to dispose of her. The safe house and the explosion in her apartment testified to that.

But Bill and Harry provided a twist. They'd made it clear she was to be interrogated then killed. What had she missed that was so important? She frowned, deep in thought.

The taxi halted at a small hotel. Ross directed her into the lobby and without a pause out the side door. Emily raised an eyebrow but said nothing. The tactic was repeated. Three hotels and twelve long blocks later, her feet were hurting and she was having trouble keeping up with his longer stride.

"How many more?" she gasped, her hand tightening on her suitcase.

"The next one. Only a couple of blocks."

She groaned and Ross slowed down to look at her. "Didn't I tell you that you had to be in shape?"

"Yes," she puffed, "but that was to walk out of the ranch. Not all over Manhattan."

"Same difference," he replied, fighting the urge to hug her to him. She'd been on the run continuously for hours. For days, he reminded himself. She had no home, since her apartment had burned. No friends she could turn to with safety. She couldn't even contact her family for fear of involving them. The only person she could depend on was standing next to her. And he was wearing her down.

Abruptly, Ross turned and hailed another taxi. One veered across traffic, braking with a screech beside him. Ross gestured at her. "Come on, get in."

"We're just a couple of blocks away."

"You're dead on your feet."

By the time she was standing in the middle of the room, she didn't care how or why they'd arrived, just so long as they had.

"Do you promise this is the last one?"

"Probably."

She turned, putting her hands on her hips. "What kind of answer is that?"

"A realistic one. If something happens that I think warrants a move, you can be sure we're leaving."

"Great," she said, fighting a temptation to stick her tongue out at him. Nothing better happen, she told herself, as she stepped out of her shoes. Emily shut the bathroom door behind her and turned on the shower, her mind on the man outside.

Aside from the kiss before they got on the plane, Ross hadn't by so much as a word or gesture indicated what he was thinking. But the kiss had held a hint of desperation, as though Ross were in the grip of a powerful struggle. Perhaps she was imagining things.

Emily stopped as she caught sight of her body in the mirror. A flush rose in her cheekbones. She wasn't Miss

Universe but he'd seemed to find her attractive . . . to a point. Her eyes stung and she drew in a ragged breath. Nothing was going to get accomplished by standing around. The shower was quick, hot, and removed some of her tiredness. After toweling off, she came out of the bathroom in her nightgown feeling unaccountably shy.

Ross was in the big double bed, his bare chest visible. The sheet was pulled up slightly above his waist. The silence stretched as she stared at him. She couldn't read his expression but she thought she saw a flash of pain in his gray eyes before he pulled back the covers.

"You're tired. Come here." He patted the bed. "Come on."

She went. "This is bliss," she said as she crawled in beside him. For a moment she considered not touching him then threw caution to the winds. She reached over and put her hand on his arm, feeling him stiffen. Emily froze. She was not going to cry, she told herself fiercely, as she jerked her hand back. She could feel his gaze on her averted face.

"Damnit, Emily," he said, "stop making me feel like a bastard." She remained silent. "All right," he sighed, "I am." He gave a laugh that sounded suspiciously like a groan. "But I can't help it." Liar, he told himself.

Ross's arm curved around her shoulder as he hauled her close, aware that for the first time since that morning, he finally felt his tension ease. "Go to sleep. We've got a lot of things to do tomorrow."

His voice rumbled under her ear and Emily rolled towards him, her blood heating deliciously, making her feel almost light-headed. He felt wonderful. She smiled secretly against his shoulder.

"I'm feeling more awake by the minute," she said.

"So am I," he muttered, as she deliberately thrust her leg between his. Muscles that had been dormant stiffened.

"I was scared to death today when I came back to the cabin and you were gone," he admitted hoarsely, as she wound her arms around his neck.

"But you don't have to be any longer." She pressed

her mouth against the hollow of his throat. "I'm here now."

"I know." His grip tightened. Was this to be the last time? As her hand stroked across his belly, he warned, "You're liable to get what you're asking for." He damned his lack of resistance as her fingers quested lower.

"I sure hope so," she exhaled.

"This isn't smart."

"Stop thinking so much," she counseled. "Just feel. Things are on the verge of slipping out of control and I want you to want me. That at least is real, isn't it?"

"God, yes." Every piece of advice he'd told himself, every admonition to pull away, vanished in that instant. He stared down at her, his gaze roving over her face. Desire rose in a flood. He gripped her shoulders fiercely. They had so little time left.

With a breathless passion, he pulled her to him, driven by a greedy need. His mouth and hands were almost desperate as he made love to her. Gone was tenderness, to be replaced by a blinding heat. Gentleness was a thing of the past.

Caught up in his desire, Emily met his with her own. Their pants and moans filled the silent room, as they surged together with an explosiveness that left them trembling in its aftermath.

Emily slept in his arms, limp from their lovemaking. Ross closed his eyes, admitting at last what he'd hidden from so long.

He loved her. As he'd never loved Marta.

The devastation he'd experienced at Marta's death would be a pale reflection of what he'd suffer were Emily to be hurt. His eyes shut. She had to be out of it. As soon as possible. There was no other choice.

The following morning Emily awoke to the sound of Ross's voice. She opened her eyes to find him talking on the telephone.

"I appreciate it. Yeah. I know." His look shifted to her. "I'll call you later and see what you've got."

She sat higher in bed, pulling the covers over her. He looked as though he hadn't gotten much rest, but at least he hadn't told her they'd never make love again. "Who was that?"

"Mike."

"What's going on?"

"Remember I asked him to get background information on the people in your office to see if we could get a lead on who might be the agent?" She nodded. "He's got the first batch of material. I added a couple of names including the two women you knew from headquarters."

"How much has he come up with?"

"Not a lot, but he's going to try to get the telephone bills you reminded me about," Ross said. "I told him I'd call him later."

"What time period did you tell him to cover on the bills?"

"The last six months. You received the message ten days ago. Assuming the plot was put in motion well before that, six months is the longest reasonable period to consider."

Emily nibbled on a finger. "You're probably right."

"Get dressed. I'll meet you in the lobby downstairs."

She threw on her clothes and was downstairs a few minutes later, adrenaline pumping through her veins. At least they were taking some action. Ross was surveying the lobby as she walked up to him. "I'm ready."

"Let's find a place to eat breakfast."

She preceded him out the doorway and they walked down the street. The air was cool and crisp, filled with the roar of traffic, brakes screeching, buses rumbling. New Yorkers walked swiftly along the sidewalks, their looks avoiding each other as they hurried to their destinations.

She wrapped her sweater more tightly around her. Early November weather in Manhattan varied widely and she usually wore a heavy jacket in the daytime, but she'd gotten accustomed to the warmer climate in Texas.

Ross opened the door of a restaurant and they walked in. They were seated a few minutes later at a booth in the corner. Emily picked up her napkin and began fidgeting with it. After a couple of minutes, it was in shreds.

After they ordered, he said, "Okay, out with it. You've been acting like you're about to explode. What is it?"

Emily sipped at the water from the glass the waitress left. "I want to go into my office today without you."

"Out of the question."

"Bait has to look like bait in order to work."

He ignored her. "I'm coming with you."

"You can't. It's a secure building and you'd have to identify yourself."

"Fine."

She sighed. "Besides that problem, you're not being realistic if you think I can walk into my office with a strange male in tow and not raise comments. As it is, I've been gone for several days without a word. People are going to want to know where I've been. I called in and reported sick the first day. Remember? Shall I say . . ."

"We were shacked up," he finished.

Her pulse thumped. "I know. And we slept together," she said evenly, "but no one's going to believe it."

"As I remember, sleep hasn't figured much lately in our lives." Why in the hell had he said that?

Even her forehead was hot. "But that doesn't mean . . ."

"You can get away with it," he said, not betraying the hunger that had caused him to stare at the curve of her hip, the shimmer of her skin as she slept, tucked against him. He'd awakened in the middle of the night, fully erect, even after making love earlier. Ross had barely restrained himself from waking her. The thought of a damp welcome had caused him to throb. "You could always say you lied about being sick."

"You're not being logical. There are all kinds of reasons for you to agree. And not a single good one for you to come with me."

"I still don't like it. There's no way to protect you if you're alone."

"The likelihood I'll be attacked in my own office is slim. You're just paranoid because of Harry and Bill. What I want to do is make the rounds and see how people react. The pressure has to be building by now."

"All right," he said reluctantly. "But be careful. I'll

be outside. If anything at all odd happens, get the hell out. I'm giving you one hour tops. Don't make me come in after you."

"Okay."

"I want you to tell people where you're staying."

"Why?"

"Give everyone who asks where you're staying the name of a different hotel. We'll keep track of what happens at each location. Remember those guys I told you about who were friends of mine and Mike's?"

"Yes."

"I thought about this last night. I think a couple of them would be glad to take a day or two off to help. I'm going to have them watch the hotels. Whoever shows up has to be in this up to his neck, since the only reason anyone would come to your hotel would be to make a snatch."

"Why can't we use someone from Walker's office?"

"Because that would defeat the whole purpose of the exercise. We still don't know who in his office is safe or if his telephone line is tapped. Maybe we can narrow the list down this way."

"Suppose they compare notes? They'll realize each one was told a different hotel."

He shrugged. "I don't have a better idea. Do you?"

She shook her head. He handed her a piece of paper on which he'd written the names of various hotels and she memorized it. They finished breakfast in silence.

Ross threw some change down on the table, and said, "Let's go. We might as well get this over with."

The taxi bumped over the rough streets and deposited them three blocks away from Emily's office. They walked the remaining distance until they were at the end of the street. Ross gripped her arm.

"I'm serious. You've got to be careful. Don't stay if something spooks you. When you've made the rounds, meet me at the Museum of Natural History on the West Side. I'll be following to see if anyone is tailing you."

"Which section?"

He thought for an instant. "Dinosaurs."

"Your best friends, no doubt." Emily flashed a brief grin.

"Not hardly."

"Late or early?"

"What the hell are you talking about? Be on time."

"Dinosaurs," she replied. "Late or early dinosaurs."

Ross rolled his eyes. "What difference does it make?"

"Several hundred feet and different rooms."

"Late. But you'd better not be."

"Don't worry. I'll be fine." She reached up and kissed him on the cheek, feeling his arm briefly encircle her before he released her. "I'll meet you at the museum," she said, then walked away.

Ross watched Emily as she disappeared into the building. His throat tightened with apprehension.

Bait, she'd called herself. She was right. And there was damned little he could do about it. He was reminded that the problem with bait is that it's usually eaten alive. But not this time, he promised himself.

Emily climbed the steps, punched in the security code that released the lock, and entered. Her surroundings were at once familiar and strange. The entrance hall was marble floored and the high ceilings soared above her head. She'd seen it thousands of times before. But now it had a cold, lifeless feel and Emily restrained a nervous shiver. There was a new receptionist and Emily had to present her identification.

Funny, she thought, as she moved to the elevator, how she'd never picked up on the atmosphere before. She glanced up and waved at the camera monitoring her movements. Teresa, George Rand's secretary, had a screen on her desk connected to the camera.

She exited the elevator to be met by Teresa's beaming smile. "Where on earth have you been? I'm so glad to see you. We all heard about your apartment on the news. I was worried sick."

Emily smiled back. "You shouldn't have. I took a few days extra leave to clean things up. I'm sorry I didn't call in."

"Everything all right now?"

"Yes. Fine."

"That's good," Teresa said.

"Tell George I'll be in to see him in a few minutes after I check my desk. I'll brief him."

"All right. He's been in and out the past couple of days with something new, but he's here now."

"See you in a few minutes."

The two women smiled again at each other and Emily slipped into her office. It looked exactly the same.

Desk, chair, bookshelf, computer with the dark screen. The office could have been anyone's. There was nothing to indicate she had used it continuously for years.

She walked slowly around her desk and sat down in the chair, her expression thoughtful. When this was all over, she was going to have to think about where she was going with her life. Judging from the barren state of her office, she hadn't been doing such a wonderful job thus far. She was on her feet, ready to see her boss when the door opened quickly and she stepped out of the way.

"Miss Brown."

Jody Donaldson's face was pale as he peered around the door. "I didn't know you were back until a couple of minutes ago. You . . . uh . . . you all right?" he stammered.

"I'm fine, Jody." Emily looked him over. The young man's face had regained some of its color but there were dark circles under his eyes. "You look terrible. Have you been sick?"

"Something like that," he mumbled. "It's been a pretty tough couple of days."

"Have you been able to go to school?"

At her words, his head shot up. "School?"

She looked puzzled. "Yes. Didn't you tell me you were taking some courses at night school?"

"Oh. That. Yes, I did. No, I haven't been the last couple of days with . . . uh . . . things the way they've been around here."

"Just how have things been around here, Jody?" she asked softly.

"Well," he began, "kind of crazy actually. Men from

Washington were in and out of here, very secretive, and I know they talked to Mr. Rand.''

''Oh?'' she prompted.

''Yes, and then . . .''

The door opening behind him interrupted his words. Emily bit her lip in frustration.

Paul Wilson stuck his head around the door. ''If I'd known you were coming in, I would have left you a surprise. You having a party?'' He grinned.

''Not exactly,'' she said wryly, ''although I was tempted to ask if we wanted to start a new fad to see how many people we can cram in this cubicle.''

She had the smallest office of the three cryptanalysts but with the best windows, a tradeoff she'd found acceptable until that moment.

''So you're back?''

''As you can see,'' she said. ''Jody and I were just talking about the excitement this week.''

Paul came all the way into the office. ''You mean the big shots from Washington? You missed the fireworks. George was in a tailspin over something. He went home early yesterday.'' Paul shrugged. ''No one ever tells me anything up on the third floor.''

She eyed him shrewdly. ''But you always manage to hear what's going on even up in your eyrie.''

He was nonchalant. ''It just takes talent.''

''I'll bet,'' she said, unimpressed. ''More like a bloodhound's nose. Perfect equipment for a spy.'' Paul didn't react.

''I've got to go, Miss Brown,'' Jody said, inching past her. ''Mr. Rand will kill me if I'm late putting out the mail.''

''Sure, Jody.'' She watched as he left.

''That kid was in a hurry, wasn't he? He's been jumpy as a cat all week.'' Paul shook his head.

''Perhaps George has been on his case. He doesn't take kindly to inefficiencies.''

''Probably. I also heard that he was having family problems.''

''Oh.''

Paul grunted in amusement. "You're usually quiet as a mouse in here. You wouldn't think anyone would know you were gone, but last week everyone noticed. It was amazing. Ernie and Hugh kept looking for you."

"I doubt I'd be amazed," she said dryly.

"Teresa told me George is expecting you . . . any minute."

She grimaced. "I'll bet."

"Better you than me." He laughed. "You'll get the Merry England speech."

"I think you mean the Better America version."

"Right. The one that suggests we've got to be slaves to our jobs for the greater glory of our country," he finished.

"That's the one," she agreed. "I'll be prepared."

"See you later," he said, as he walked to the door. "Good to have you back."

Emily stared after him. Ernie, Hugh, and Paul. Even Jody. They'd all shown a most surprising interest, even concern for her welfare. Very unexpected.

Walking towards her boss's office, Emily felt as though someone was staring at her, but when she turned, the hall was empty. She stopped and listened but heard nothing. Her brows pulled together, she continued down the corridor and found Teresa outside George's office.

"He's in there," she said, pointing behind her.

"Waiting impatiently, I bet."

"Afraid so."

George was sitting behind his desk which was piled high with printouts from computers, newspapers, and folders, all marked "Secret." He looked tired and drawn.

"Just the person I was hoping to see."

"Oh?" she said cautiously. "Why is that?"

"There's been an uproar around here during your absence." He looked momentarily put out. "Something about a security leak."

"Leak?"

He shot her a look. "Yes. And it has to do with you. I'm not sure exactly what, but that was the definite impression I received. A team of experts came down from Washington," he said. "They mumbled a bunch of jargon at me then left."

"How interesting," she said, and sat down. "And they didn't say anything else?"

"Nope. Where were you?"

"Texas," she answered calmly. She and Ross had decided she would tell George where she'd been, since he seemed the most likely candidate for the mole, but his behavior thus far hadn't given any direct indication of it.

"By the way, I was sorry to hear about your apartment. According to the news, a gas main had a leak. Is your apartment livable?"

"Not yet," she said.

"Where are you staying in the meantime?"

"A hotel near Grand Central," she said and named it.

"Will you be ready to go back to work on Monday?"

She nodded. "Yes. My personal problems will have sorted themselves out by then." That was her idea, to let everyone know she expected things to be resolved soon.

"Good," he said. "You've been missed."

Emily tried to watch him without appearing to while he brought her up to date on the office. After they'd finished and she'd started to leave, he called after her, "Take care of yourself."

She smiled. "I plan to."

The door shut behind her before she turned to look at Teresa.

"I heard you tell George about your apartment. Any idea when you can move back in?"

"Not yet. I've got to see about repairs, and so forth. I'm staying at a hotel near there." She named another hotel, finished chatting and went on. She needed to find Jody. Spotting him down the hall, she called to him. "Jody. Wait a minute."

He turned to face her, his brows gathered in a frown. "Yeah?"

His voice was surly and Emily looked at him sharply. He was normally even-tempered and calm, with a smile for everyone.

"In case I receive any messages, I need to tell you where I'm staying."

"Oh, sure."

She named a third hotel, remembering Ross's insistence they give different names to everyone in the office.

"Hope you have insurance."

"I do. See you later."

She walked off, conscious he was staring after her. Emily went to Ernie's and Hugh's offices, and on various pretexts, dropped the name of the hotel where she was supposedly staying. She called Paul on the intercom to tell him she wouldn't be back for a few days, and dropped in the name of the sixth hotel.

Checking her watch, she saw she'd been in the building over an hour and supposed Ross was chewing nails. She was walking towards the elevator, when Teresa called to her.

"I nearly forgot. A woman telephoned from headquarters the other day on the direct line. Wouldn't give her name. I said I had no idea when you'd be in, that you were out on sick leave." Teresa's expression was curious. "If she calls back, what do you want me to tell her?"

Emily thought rapidly. "Get her name and number. I'll check with you tomorrow."

"All right."

As Emily walked out of the building, a sense of reprieve gripped her. Nothing had happened. Yet. She headed towards the museum on an uptown bus per Ross's instructions.

Walking into the enormous museum, she headed directly for the elevators rather than the stairs. The sound of her footsteps echoed on the stone floors. She thought she heard something behind her but kept moving. Ross had told her to behave normally. When she'd told him that no one would believe she went to the museum for anything other than a clandestine meeting, he'd smiled.

"Exactly. So behave as you would for a clandestine meeting."

"How do I do that?" she'd asked sharply. "Slink around? Rent a cape and pull a hat over my eyes?"

"Don't be ridiculous. Be cautious but not paranoid."

She rolled her eyes at the pearl of wisdom. "You can give me a grade on my performance later."

So here she was, walking not skulking, her nerves stretched tight. Talking to everyone at work had been more demanding than she'd realized and she was tired. She slowly circled the huge room filled with dinosaurs. Bones of the great beasts had been reassembled and they stood in various poses. She looked upward at the largest, tipping her head back then screamed when a hand fell heavily on her shoulder.

"For God's sake, Emily," Ross said in exasperation, as she whipped around to face him, her eyes huge. "You were supposed to be on the lookout for me."

She put her hand to her throat. "I'm sorry. I guess I was daydreaming." She indicated the displays around her. "These are pretty fantastic."

"Yeah," he said, giving them a cursory glance. "How did it go?" He walked toward another exhibit. "Did you give out the names of the hotels?"

"Yes."

"Good." He steered her over to another door. "This place is an echo chamber. By the way, when I tell you an hour, I mean it."

"I was only a few minutes late."

"A few minutes could make a difference. Don't slip up again." He was clearly tense.

"Is everything all right?"

"As all right as it can be, given that we're guinea pigs mucking about in a dark room," he said sarcastically, holding her back from an outside exit. "Let me take a look around. I didn't see anyone following you, but it's better to be safe."

A few minutes later they were in a taxi heading south. Ross had given instructions to drive them to Lincoln Center. The huge performing arts complex, he told her, was a better place to determine if they were being followed.

He found a bench, motioned for her to sit and said, "What happened? And I want details."

"Ernie and Hugh both came by to see me."

"What did they want?"

"Just said they wanted to be sure I was all right. They'd heard about the fire. Hugh even said he'd missed me." She snorted. "At least he had the grace to admit what he really missed was my taking my share of the workload."

"And that was it?"

"Except that Hugh said he'd called my apartment."

"Is that usual?"

"No. Said he'd been worried because I hadn't checked in. I don't know. It was plausible, but . . ."

"Somehow it didn't seem right?"

She shrugged. "I can't really tell you why."

"Okay. Go on."

She continued with the descriptions of what had happened that morning. The conversation with George Rand produced a look of surprise.

"Was anything else said about the Washington team?" he asked a few minutes later.

"No," she answered. "Just that there had been a leak."

"Too bad we don't know who sent them."

"Can't you find out?"

"Probably, but it might involve Walker. I don't want to call him until we know how far the infection has spread. We're too close to the operations area."

She continued with her recitation and was interrupted when she repeated Teresa's last words.

"A woman called you? On the direct line?"

Emily nodded. "And it could only have been Virginia or Dana since that line is secure."

"That puts a different slant on things," Ross said, his expression bleak. "If this actually concerns someone from Fort Meade, we've got our work cut out for us."

"I don't know why you have to assume anything," Emily protested. "All Teresa said was that someone called. It's not ridiculous, you know," she said with irritation, "to believe that either Dana or Virginia might call me just to chat, or say they were coming to town. I think you're unnecessarily concerned."

"I might have been able to think that way once," he said quietly, "but not any more. Nor should you," he cautioned.

"I guess not," she said slowly, remembering Harry and Bill. They still hadn't learned how the two had discovered her whereabouts. "What about the telephone bills?" she asked. "If Mike can get those to us, maybe we can find a pattern."

He nodded. "He'll have them this afternoon. We may not do anything but give ourselves eyestrain, but we have to try. And of course, worry about the hotels."

By the time she'd finished describing each person, their exact words, the expressions on their faces, she was worn out. Ross hadn't let up. He made her go over it and over it again until she felt totally drained.

Finally, he stopped. "That's enough for now. Let's grab a quick bite to eat. I've arranged to meet Mike right after lunch."

He'd already called Mike, and they'd agreed to meet near Park Avenue. There were few shops and anyone having undue interest in them would be spotted.

Mike Reynolds was a tall man with graying hair and a pronounced limp.

"Hey, old buddy," Mike said, as he gripped Ross's hand in greeting. "You're looking remarkably hale and hearty for someone who's been in the center of so much action."

"I'm not sure I like the sound of that," Ross said dryly. "Mike, I'd like you to meet Emily Brown."

Mike grinned. "You've been busy, I gather."

Emily smiled back, liking the man immediately. He had a warm smile, and an easy, nonchalant style that contrasted to Ross's tightly wound state of mental alertness. But she suspected for all Mike's outward veneer, he could be a tough opponent. "I can't believe you let Ross rope you in," she said. Indicating Ross with her head, she asked, "What's he got on you?"

He laughed. "It's more like what I've got on him. He did me a favor once. I'm returning it." The two men exchanged looks.

"What happened to your leg," Ross asked, pointing down at Mike's foot which was in a loose-fitting shoe.

He stepped closer to the building behind them to let a

woman with a stroller pass. "You're not going to believe it but . . ." he began.

"You're probably right."

"It was really quite innocent. I was playing football in Central Park last weekend and turned to watch someone and tripped."

"Blonde or brunette?"

"Neither. A gorgeous redhead."

Ross laughed. "The same old Mike. One of these days you're going to quit looking."

"Never."

Emily marveled at the difference in Ross's manner. With Mike he smiled easily and seemed almost relaxed.

"The telephone bills?" Ross prodded. "Did you get them?"

"Yep." Mike reached into the briefcase he was carrying and pulled out a large manila envelope. "I took the names you gave me from the New York office and had duplicates run of all their home bills. The ones from Emily's office are proving to be harder to get since it's a secure installation, but I'm working on it."

Ross took the envelope. "Great. About the outgoing office calls, what about also getting records from the nearest phone booths?"

Mike smiled. "I already thought of it. There are three, excluding stores and shops, within a two block radius. I figured the guy we're after would probably be willing to risk a call from one of them, since he won't have known you were onto him until a week ago, and he wouldn't have called from a store where he could be overheard."

"What about the people in Maryland? The two women?" Ross asked, putting the envelope under his arm. "I guess they're not in here."

Mike shook his head. "Not yet. I hope to have it by later tonight or at worst, first thing in the morning."

"Fine. Emily and I will start with these right away, seeing what we can turn up. By the way, does anybody know you've done this?" Ross asked.

"Not a soul."

"Good."

ELEVEN

The traffic noise died briefly and in the silence Ross turned to Mike and asked, "Have you unearthed anything yet on the people in Emily's office?"

"Not much beyond the home telephone bills for the rest of the office staff," Mike replied. "I'm being discreet like you asked. Which means my search is circuitous. Unfortunately, it's taking longer than I'd like. I should be getting more information, probably this afternoon."

"Okay. I'll check with you later."

"Fine. Emily, nice to meet you." Mike smiled at her and then, after exchanging another quiet word with Ross, walked away from them.

Emily and Ross started on foot across town. After a moment, Ross peered down at her, noting her troubled expression. "What's wrong?"

"Not exactly wrong. I took a long hard look at my office this morning. What I saw was pretty depressing."

He took her arm as they crossed the next intersection. "Why? This morning you were ready for anything."

"Seeing the people wasn't what got to me. My office did."

Whatever he'd expected to hear, it wasn't something so mundane. "What on earth are you talking about?"

"I walked into my office this morning and stood there. Do you know what I saw?" He shook his head. "Four walls, bare of any pictures, a few books in a government-issue bookcase, my computer placed squarely in the middle of my desk. That was it."

"And that was depressing."

"Horribly," she agreed. "Because my office could have been anyone's office who was just moving in. But I'd been there for years. What the hell did I have to show

170

for it? Nothing. I might as well have inhabited a crater on the moon for the visible signs I left. The really weird part though was that everyone began dropping in to see me, and I was shocked.''

''Because they hadn't before?''

''No, and,'' she paused, ''I suspected everyone of dark motives because they did.'' She gave a small laugh underlain with bitterness.

''Of course, you don't know who to trust.''

''Yes. It hurt. And it was strange as well. I'd let my job consume me to the point where people were unimportant. Now they're not and it's too late.''

Ross said after a moment, ''I'm sorry.''

''No reason for you to be. None of this is your fault. Mine if anyone's.'' She put on a bright smile. ''Where to now?''

''You heard Mike. We're not going to get the rest of the materials for a while. We might as well return to the room.''

''We've got a variety to choose from,'' she said dryly. ''I'm on intimate terms with half the sleeping accommodations in New York.''

''The subterfuge was necessary,'' he said reasonably. ''Otherwise, we couldn't have given out different hotel names.''

''Yes, I know,'' she sighed, ''but I'll be glad when this is over.''

''Yeah.'' So would he. Emily was becoming more and more necessary to him and every hour spent with her made his own solitary future less bearable. Her words about her own life had hit home. Hard. But there wasn't any other choice. Was there?

He cursed silently. Why couldn't he keep his mind on his business instead of on her? He'd been staring at the tender joining of her neck to her shoulder while they were with Mike and looked up to catch Mike's gaze on him. Only the other man's raised eyebrow had indicated his thoughts. He cursed again, damning his inattentiveness. For someone who was supposed to be the epitome of professionalism in his chosen field, he'd stubbed his toe and fallen flat on his face because of a woman he knew he shouldn't have. God, he was tired. He rubbed his hand over his face, feeling about a hundred years old.

As they walked into their room, Ross threw his jacket onto the bed. "Let's check the hotels for calls."

"Suits me," she said, sinking gratefully onto the mattress and easing her feet out of her shoes.

The first four had none. When she reached the fifth, she froze. A woman had telephoned, without leaving her name.

"Which was it?" Ross asked as she hung up.

"The one I gave Teresa."

He nodded without comment. "Try the last one."

Emily felt her heartbeat accelerate when the operator said she had received several calls. But no one had left a name.

She looked at Ross. "We've got a problem."

"Not really. Four weren't even contacted. The sixth was the one you gave Jody wasn't it?"

"Yes."

"All right. We've narrowed it down to Jody and Teresa. That's a hell of a lot better than what we had this morning."

"I disagree. The other people might simply have decided not to do anything. No calls, no clues."

Ross grunted in agreement. "I hope you're wrong."

"I'd better try reaching Dana and Virginia next," Emily said with a faint sigh. "I can't exclude anyone."

He hated seeing the dispirited droop of her shoulders. She was taking the personal betrayal exactly the way he'd thought she would.

Hard.

The phone rang in Dana's office eight times and Emily was about to hang up, when a breathless voice answered. "Hello?"

It wasn't Dana. Emily hesitated. "This is Emily Brown in New York. I'm looking for Dana Phelps."

"She's on vacation for a couple of days."

"When will she be back?"

"I'm not really sure. I think by the end of this week. Want to leave a message?"

"Just tell her I called," Emily said. She repeated the conversation to Ross after hanging up. "Something's not right."

"Why?"

"Because Dana told me she was saving her vacation time for a trip to Paris this fall."

"Maybe she's visiting her family. An emergency might have come up."

"I don't know," she said. "She isn't close to her mother or her brother. I think her father's dead. Besides, I was told specifically she was on vacation. I'll try her at home." She held the receiver away from her ear a moment later. "No luck there either."

"See if you can reach Virginia."

The older woman answered at once.

"Virginia, it's me, Emily. How are you?"

There was a faint pause, then Virginia answered strongly, "Emily, good to hear from you. How are you?"

"I'm fine. Actually I called to see if you knew where Dana was."

"No. Why?"

"I need to talk to her. I was told she was on vacation."

"She probably is. She may have said something, but if she did I've forgotten." The older woman gave a small chuckle. "The older I get the more forgetful I am, so you can't count on me for anything."

"That's nonsense." Emily suppressed her irritation at the familiar refrain.

Virginia was Assistant to the Deputy Administrator but she downplayed her talents. At first Emily had thought Virginia simply felt inferior to the bright kids who poured through the agency. Now she wasn't sure that was sufficient explanation for Virginia's attitude.

"Are you in New York? I tried to call your office the other day and they told me you were out sick."

"It was just a cold," she lied.

"I also heard there had been a fire in your apartment. Are you staying there now?"

"No. Until it's repainted and cleaned up, I'm staying at . . ." she hesitated, then gave the hotel she'd already told Ernie she was staying in.

"Okay," said Virginia. "Gotta run. My boss is raving about something. Take care of yourself."

"You, too."

"Now we wait," Ross said.

"I'm not good at that," she admitted.

He smiled. "Your type never is."

"What does that mean?"

"When we were driving, you were giving orders and were impatient. Remember?"

She actually blushed, he saw with amusement.

"That was different. I was trying to get under your skin."

"I think we can both agree you did that quite successfully."

"Well, now I want to do something, make things happen."

He smiled wryly. "Don't worry, Emily. They will."

She grimaced. "You're probably right. Why don't we go through the file Mike gave us?"

"Fine," he agreed. "At least we'll have that out of the way by the time he brings us the rest of the material."

For two hours Emily and Ross pored over the stacks of telephone bills. They had agreed to divide them. Emily had those for George, Jody, and Paul Wilson. Ross had Ernie, Hugh, and Teresa's.

Emily worked intently, unconscious of Ross's gaze on her more than once, his expression somber.

He watched as she thrust her hand into her hair. He noted the thoughtful pursing of her lips as she flipped through the pages in front of her. He mentally recorded the clean line of her jaw, the soft curve of her chin, the arch of her neck. His fingertips tingled as he relived the previous night, the compelling warmth of her body.

Ross etched images of Emily in his brain, knowing as he did so, that memories would be all he'd have of her once they'd plugged the leak.

He shifted in the chair, and leaned back, trying to relieve the pressure in his groin.

"Found anything?" she asked, as his movements distracted her.

"Not yet."

Day edged into dusk as they worked in the silent room.

Sometime later, she raised her head and stretched wearily. "Would you rub my neck? I'm getting stiff sitting here." She needed him to touch her, to take away the pervasive sense of isolation. She shivered and rubbed her arms. The room wasn't cold.

But she was.

Emily saw Ross's fingers stop flipping pages, then resume their work. "All right."

After he turned the rest of the papers over on the table, he rose and moved behind her. She held her hair out of the way, acutely conscious of his body.

Ross's fingers kneaded the stiff muscles of her shoulders and neck. "That feels wonderful." She rotated her head, enjoying the sensuous pleasure of his hands. Dropping her head forward, she relaxed as he continued his massage.

He straightened up after a few minutes, and gave her a gentle push. "That's enough or you'll fall asleep on me."

She turned, her eyes heavy-lidded and slumbrous. "I just might at that. You were definitely giving me thoughts about going to bed."

Ross moved back to the table. "Later," he muttered.

"I hope that's a promise," she said, observing with interest the sudden flare of color in his cheekbones.

This time the silence was filled with statements that weren't spoken, but real nonetheless. Emily usually found intellectual tasks absorbing. Not now. She could barely keep her mind on the job. Instead, she found herself staring at his hands.

Remembering their tenderness. Feeling again the way they'd skimmed over her body in the night, as if he were learning her purely by touch.

She frowned sharply. There had been desperation as well in his touch, as though he were losing her. Her frown lessened.

She was going to hold him to his promise to take her to bed.

"I think I've found something interesting," she announced several moments later. "Here's a call from George to a telephone in Long Island." She flipped through the notes she'd been making. "It looks as though there's a pattern. Two calls back in July made late at night." She looked over at Ross, holding his attention. "They were very late. After midnight as though he didn't want his wife to know. Then two more in August, none in September. And four more in October."

"What about November?"

"Nothing. Which is rather odd."

"Perhaps," he said unconvinced. "Or it might be nothing."

"Can you find out whose number it is?"

"Yeah. Hang on." After a brief conversation, he turned and said, "It's listed to a Philippe Villiers."

"That doesn't sound good for George," she said. "Or at the very least a tremendous coincidence that he's been calling someone with a French name when we have a French separatist problem in Canada. You told me he didn't speak French."

"Let me find out more about this guy before we jump to any conclusions."

"Well?" she demanded, when he finished his inquiries.

"Seems Villiers is a college professor. Could be a cover but probably not. A lot of Canadians came south to the U.S. in the last twenty years. The East Coast is certainly a better location for a French-speaker than the southwest, say. Villiers is probably clean."

"I'd rather believe that than the alternative. What if I call? I could say I'm trying to find out if he tutors students privately in French. I don't think that would be too big of a tip off."

Ross nodded.

She dialed. Just as she was about to hang up, she heard a woman's voice. Her eyebrows rose.

"Who is this please?" Emily asked, hearing the heavily accented speech.

"Who are you calling?" was the swift reply.

"Professor Villiers."

"I am his sister. Do you wish to leave a message?"

"Yes. I'd like to study French. A friend of mine told me your brother gave private lessons."

"Oh? Who was it told you this?"

"George Rand." She'd taken a shot in the dark and hit a bullseye, she realized as she heard a sharp intake of breath.

"I'm sorry, but you'll have to call later."

Click.

Emily told Ross what happened.

"Maybe George is involved with the sister," was his only comment.

"Perhaps," she admitted. "But it was awfully abrupt. What would she have to hide?"

"He's married isn't he? Maybe he's the one with something to hide. This would fit with the late night calls. I'll dig a little deeper on Villiers' background and his sister's as well. If they're legitimate, George is out of consideration."

"I'd just as soon start narrowing the suspect list even further. Have you come up with anything yet from your stack?" Emily asked, rubbing her fingers against her throbbing temples. A headache had developed with sudden ferocity and she pressed harder.

"Lukas doesn't have a single long distance call on his phone bill. I find that odd. Either he never made any for the entire six month period or he went outside his home to place them. That's even stranger."

Emily considered his words. "I agree. What are we going to do?"

"Until we know more, Ernie stays on the hot list. I'll see what Mike can do about checking phones around Ernie's apartment. Nothing out of the ordinary showed up on either Hugh or Teresa." Ross stretched. He looked over at her, and frowned. "What's the matter? Headache?"

"Yes," she said, feeling the pounding behind her eyes intensify. "It's probably a reaction to no food."

"I'll get some sandwiches. Why don't you take a break? I'll be right back."

He left and Emily lay down on the bed, feeling her bones ache with fatigue. She shut her eyes and concentrated on relaxing. The headache slowly diminished, until finally she slept.

She was dreaming. Shadowy figures appeared on a blurry landscape, apparitions that were vaguely threatening. One moved forward from the group, a hand upraised. Fright gripped her, and she took a step back. Then another. The person seemed familiar but his face was blurred. An overwhelming sense of sorrow moved through her, and she cried out from a sense of betrayal.

When Ross returned, he stopped in the middle of the room at the sight of Emily asleep. Curled on her side, she looked defenseless, and her face was pale with exhaustion. Moving closer, he saw moisture on her cheeks.

He sat down beside her and gently kissed her dampened skin. He felt her rouse slightly and continued nibbling, and tasting the softness under his mouth. She woke slowly and focused on his face.

"Ummm," she mumbled approvingly. "What time is it?"

His thumb traced the contour of her cheek to the edge of her mouth and stopped. "Almost seven. You were crying in your sleep."

"It was just a dream. I'm fine now."

He knew she wasn't. She'd changed since he'd first met her. Her original insouciance had leached away, leaving strain in its stead. The stress of losing her personal sense of security was written on her, in the faint downcurve of her mouth, the lashes moistened by grief, the trace of pallor in her skin.

Betrayal had marked her.

He could feel himself being drawn closer, to offer comfort, bring surcease from her pain. An inner voice mocked his altruism while heat surged in his belly at the heavily weighted stillness of her body. Her eyes remained locked on his. For whatever reason, he had to be with her, in her, around her.

Ross couldn't help himself. His mouth pressed gently against her throat as he enclosed her in his arms.

Wordlessly, she turned to him. Without haste, a reverent tenderness in his touch, he removed her clothes, caressing her skin, cherishing the woman he loved. His hands and mouth spoke of tenderness, safety, and a refuge against the darkness that had threatened.

Comfort, a sensation of being truly cared for, a deep, devastating gentleness flowed across her as he stroked her heated skin, arousing her to a point of almost violent sensitivity to his touch. She trembled. She was lost.

When they came together at last, it was a powerful yet gentle explosion that left them both breathless.

"Thank you," she said after her heartrate slowed, nestling her head on his shoulder.

"For what?" He could hardly catch his breath.

She turned to look at him. "For caring." She reached up and placed her palm against his cheek.

"You'd been crying," was all he said. He couldn't tell her how the sight of her distress had affected him. Ross stroked the tumbled hair from her forehead.

"I haven't cried since I was a child," she said slowly.

"Why today?" He knew the answer, but hoped the process of explaining might diminish her pain.

"Having to objectively, even cold-bloodedly, analyze everyone in my office finally got to me. Because it means that someone I know and trust has no real feelings for me. That is a very personal sort of betrayal." She sighed. "And thinking about George somehow made it worse."

"You liked him," he judged.

"Yes. He was very kind when I arrived in the city. I was pretty green and he helped me find an apartment and generally learn my way around." She could hear his heart beating steadily under her ear and moved closer, comforted by the sound.

"Emily, in my world, betrayal is expected. Hell," he added, "it's an art with some people. I'm sorry about George, and the rest of the office. But that's life." He spoke bluntly. "And it's not the life for you, or for that matter, for any normal person."

Emily felt a chill at his words which she knew were directed at her.

"I can take care of myself. I always have," she replied. After a moment, she pulled away from him, holding herself tightly against the excruciating pain. The hints he'd dropped at the cabin about the kind of life he led and how unsuited she was to it had been broad enough. Now he'd emphasized it again. When this was over, he was leaving, because she didn't fit in. Any other dream she'd had had been just that. Biting back a moan of anguish, she blinked rapidly. It wasn't Ross's fault. From the very beginning he'd made his position clear. He was a man who traveled alone, refusing to allow anyone to come close enough to feel the warmth and tenderness he kept buried so deeply within. She'd been kidding herself until now.

No longer.

Somehow she'd survive without him.

After dressing, they ate their sandwiches hurriedly. Ross finished first, and cleared a space on the table. "I'll call Mike and see if he's ready with the information we're waiting for."

Emily turned back to the sheaf of papers in front of her. She had picked up the bills belonging to Jody. According to his address, he lived in an apartment in Brooklyn.

It turned out Jody made very few long distance calls. That seemed reasonable, given his age and probable financial status. Her face tightened when she came to the last bill.

Jody had called someone in Fort Meade, Maryland. The number wasn't familiar, although it had the same first three digits as that of the National Security Agency. The fact that the numbers shared the same prefix in and of itself was perhaps unimportant since he might have friends in the area. But it still worried her.

Ross interrupted her. "Do you want to come with me when I meet Mike? He's ready."

"I'll wait here and keep working," she said, her thoughts on what she'd just seen. "Ross, I've found something that may be important." Emily told him about Jody's calls.

"It could be the breakthrough we've been waiting for," he said thoughtfully. "The likelihood that he would be calling Fort Meade isn't high, given his status as a runner. And definitely not from his private home phone."

She nodded. "I know. I'm going to keep going through the rest of the bills. I've still got Virginia's to look at."

"Fine. I shouldn't be too long."

"I'll probably call each of the hotels one more time." She checked her watch. "It's been almost six hours. Anyone looking for me would assume I'm in at night."

"While I'm out, I'll see what else I can dig up on Professor Villiers."

After Ross left, Emily once again went through the list of hotels. The first hotel informed her that a woman named Virginia Harrison had called and left a number Emily didn't recognize. Perhaps Virginia's home? Emily was suddenly struck by the realization that she'd never known Virginia's home number. She made a note to verify it through information.

There were no new messages anywhere else.

The envelope with the remainder of the bills beckoned. Rising from the bed, she went back to the table and sat down to work.

An hour later, she heard the key in the lock. Ross walked in with a strange look on his face.

"Confirm something for me." He named a hotel on Manhattan's lower East Side. "To which person did you give that name?"

Emily felt a cold chill creep up her back and her palms grew clammy. "Jody."

"That's what I thought. Your self-bait plan worked."

"How?" Dread uncoiled in her stomach.

"The room you were assigned was bombed along with those on either side."

Shock held her still for an instant. "Was anyone hurt?"

His expression impassive, Ross looked away briefly before meeting her eyes. "A bellboy was bringing a young couple up to the floor when the blast occurred. They're in the hospital but not seriously injured."

"They could have been killed."

"Or you could have." He'd sweated bullets just at the thought.

Emily struggled to remain calm. "Whoever did it had no idea if I was even there."

"Seems like the superefficient operator told them you'd checked in and hadn't left. Remember, we slipped out by the stairs." He paced restlessly. "There's another problem. Jody has vanished from what Mike tells me. We've got to find him."

"Who knows about the accident? Did it make the news?"

"Yes, and Jody, or whoever is running him, is going to realize you're still alive. They won't give up."

She felt goosebumps on her arms. "Ross, I'm afraid."

"You ought to be. Whoever is behind this doesn't give a damn at this point about anything except shutting you up," Ross said. "And anyone else who might have seen the message."

"And," she said slowly, "the only way to do that is to eliminate the entire office staff."

"That's right."

"I thought we had more time," she said tiredly, massaging her temples. "And I still don't have the entire text of the message." She stood and picked up the bills she'd been working on, moving them out of her way. "I'd better take a look at it again right now. Maybe whatever we learn can be used to stop him."

"Or her," he added.

TWELVE

Emily settled in the straight-backed chair at the table, forcing herself to concentrate on the words in front of her, rather than on the fact that three people had been injured. She took in a deep breath.

"I want to see what we've missed. 'Ten-forty star two plus light crescent Rocket.' Then there's a gap, followed by the words 'Chimera dead.' "

"I've been wondering about something," Ross said. "You told me before you thought Chimera referred to the English-speaking Canadians. I finally remembered another interpretation for it. Not all Canadians, as you know, are happy to be considered an extension of the United States, and rightly so. The pro-French Quebec faction has been incensed for years because of the loss of the French language. I remember reading somewhere that one radical underground group used the term 'Chimera' to refer to the U.S."

"The United States? Why? This is all Canada's problem."

"Maybe so, but a Chimera is made up of many different animals, in much the same way the United States is composed of various peoples."

"If we use that interpretation, then we have something happening to Rocket that has the effect of killing the United States." She looked at him. "Why would they even want that to happen?"

"I can only assume that the struggle between the French and English speakers has become so bitter and divisive that it encompasses us as well. Let's not forget that we're the major trading partner for Canada. The French portion of the country accounts for about a quarter of the trade as well as the population of Canada. Suppose the event,

183

whatever it is, damaged relations between the two countries. That might create enough problems to distract Ottawa and let secession happen smoothly.''

"That's a big if," she said.

He nodded. "If we're looking at this message correctly, and there really is a plan to implicate the United States, we have to assume it's the work of a tiny cell." Ross got up and paced slowly across the room, looking out the window at the brightly lighted street below. "Which also means the precipitating event can't take place in Canada.''

"Because then the blame would be too squarely placed within that country and that's too risky," Emily finished, nodding in agreement. "Using the United States as a diversion might give the faction time to maneuver.''

"I'm afraid so. That's why the catastrophe has to take place here. Assume Rocket is the Canadian Prime Minister or at the very least, a highly placed individual who's a conservative, what about 'crescent?' We talked before about a Middle Eastern strike force.''

"I know but I don't buy it," she replied. "Why hire outsiders? They're right across our border and they blend in. It wouldn't make sense to go thousands of miles out of your way to hire a team.''

"Unless to provide indirection.''

"Possibly. On the other hand, maybe 'crescent' refers to a location in this country. Even New York.'' She stared into space, her brow furrowed in concentration. "That might explain why the message came here rather than to Washington.''

"Except we have no idea which official is coming to the United States any time soon. What's the time frame?''

She looked at the paper in front of her. "I would have guessed imminent judging from the attempts to kill me, except for one thing. The word 'star' may refer to Christmas.''

"I'd better get hold of Walker. He'll know if plans have been made for a state visit.''

"Do you need to route it through Mike?''

"I won't be on the phone long eoungh for a trace.'' He dialed and waited. "Walker? Ross. Have you heard any plans for a major Canadian figure to come to the United States in the next few weeks?'' His face tightened. "When? Are you sure? Listen, I think there's a plot to assassinate him." His fingers tightened on the receiver.

Emily could hear Walker's voice but was unable to distinguish the words.

"I'll have to get back to you as soon as possible. Right."

Ross disconnected and drummed his fingers on the small bedside table. "The Prime Minister and his wife are coming in early December."

"That's two weeks away which means the word 'star' doesn't refer to Christmas," Emily said. "So we still don't have a particular date, just a probable time."

"I feel better knowing we have a little leeway." He stood and stretched, his expression concerned. "We still haven't discovered who's behind the attempts on your life."

"Do you want to talk to George and see if we can strike him off the suspect list?"

"Might as well." He checked his wristwatch. "It's after ten now so he's bound to be home. We might as well head there now."

"Do you want to call first?"

"No. No point in giving him any advance notice. By the way, when we walk into his apartment, I want you to stand well away from me. Step back so he has to turn to look from one to the other. That way we'll make two targets. And if I tell you to drop, Emily, I mean at once."

"Of course." She stared unblinkingly at Ross. "I'm beginning to understand better what you've been telling me the last few days."

"What's that?" He looked warily at her.

"You've made the point that you can't ever know whom to trust. You and I don't really believe George is involved but we're having to go through a process of elimination, just to be sure. Makes it hard to have friends."

His mouth twisted. "It's the best reason I know of for keeping your guard up."

As he had, she thought silently; except for brief lapses when she suspected his control was worn paperthin. Her eyes narrowed as she looked at him in an expression that would have given him pause had he seen it.

Ross and Emily hurriedly left the hotel, grabbed a taxi and set off to the Upper East Side.

George and his wife lived in a typical East Side apartment building. Tall, built out of red brick, it projected an air of solidity.

Ross gave his name to the doorman, who then called upstairs.

"You can go up now," the doorman said. "Mr. Rand is on the tenth floor." They went to the back of the lobby where the elevator doors gleamed dully in the soft interior lighting.

When the apartment door opened, Emily braced herself for the coming confrontation. Her boss's face looked confused when he saw her with Ross.

"What on earth? Emily," he said, consulting his watch, "do you realize what time it is? It's a quarter of eleven."

"Excuse me, Mr. Rand, I apologize for the lateness of the hour," Ross said, "but Miss Brown and I need to ask you some questions. My name is Ross Harding. I'm here on a security matter. You were given my name last week." He handed George his identification card.

"Oh yes. Come in and tell me what this is about." He opened the door wider and stepped back, letting them precede him into the apartment. "You guys were all over the office the last couple of days."

The apartment was unexpectedly large and Emily's eyebrows rose. The cost of living in Manhattan was astronomical and this place, she realized, had to have cost in the hundreds of thousands of dollars.

Emily and Ross sat in chairs at either end of the sofa and George was forced to sit on the couch between them. He turned to Ross.

"How may I help you?"

Without any warning, Ross said, "Why have you been in contact with Professor Villiers?"

"How do you know I have?"

"Come on, Rand. You know as well as I do that information can be obtained if you know the right contacts."

There was a long silence while George stared first at Emily then at Ross. "Yes, I have called the Villiers residence to inquire about French lessons," he conceded slowly. "So what?"

Emily thought his phrasing a bit odd and shot a look at Ross to see if he'd caught it. A lifted eyebrow indicated he had.

Ross spoke quietly. "And it was necessary to call the professor's household at late night hours?"

George's face stiffened. "How do you know?"

"We've been over your telephone bills," Ross said matter-of-factly.

There was a heavy sigh as George said, almost with relief, "It started out innocently, frankly I never thought anyone would find out until it was all over."

"Find out what?" prodded Ross.

"Elise," George said simply.

"Elise?" Emily asked, bewildered. "Who is she?"

"The professor's sister. I was the only one in the office who didn't know French. I started lessons with him, then met his sister." He looked away from two pairs of eyes. "Then it turned into something else. My wife," he hesitated, "she knows. We're getting a divorce. But no one was supposed to find out yet."

"What steps did you take to ensure Elise and her brother are exactly what they seem? Surely it occurred to you that in your position as head of the New York office of N.S.A. you were vulnerable to any foreign national." Ross leaned back in his chair and waited for George to reply.

"Of course it did. I had a security check run on them," George said bluntly. "Before I started the lessons. Both were clean."

"So now what?" Ross asked.

"My wife and I are getting a divorce. And I'm leaving the agency. I'm getting tired of the constant stress. My wife relishes the excitement and my position. Elise doesn't."

"Who else knows about this?" Emily asked.

George turned to look at her. "I've told headquarters and my resignation has been approved."

"You've been careful," said Ross.

"Wouldn't you, in my position?" George demanded.

"Yes. Thank you for talking to us," Ross said as he stood.

"By the way, I forgot to even ask what this was all about—why you were going through my bills."

Emily glanced at Ross. "A security matter, that Ross asked me to help with."

George waited and when Emily didn't continue, shrugged. "I think I'd just as soon not know. Do you need anything else?"

"No. Come on, Emily." Ross turned and walked towards the front door, Emily following closely behind him.

Neither spoke until they were outside the apartment building.

"Do you believe him?" Emily asked.

"Yes. I never thought much of him as the mole anyway. We'll verify it with Walker."

"We have to go back to the fact that Jody was the one who knew the hotel where the blast occurred, although I can't see him as the mastermind."

"I suspect you're right although he's vanished. I need to see if Mike has checked in."

A call to Mike's office revealed he had left a message for Ross. He wanted to meet Ross at eleven o'clock at Grand Central Station. "We've barely got time to make it," Ross said as he flagged down a passing taxi.

Mike was waiting for them, carrying a briefcase, and he leaped into the cab when Ross opened the door. "Let's go to your hotel. I want to show you something."

"Are we getting anywhere?"

"You could say that," was all he would say.

When they got back to the room, Mike placed his briefcase on the nearest bed. He pulled out a small laptop computer and set it up, typing on the keyboard until he accessed a program. The screen lit up with numbers. "I was finally able to get the telephone bills from the two women in Washington and for the closest telephone booths to your office. Because the long distance calls from booths are third party calls, I found that Jody called a number in Brooklyn. Virginia Harrison called the same number.''

Emily said, ''Virginia called the same place Jody did?''

Ross moved over to sit behind Mike and focused on the computer screen. ''It seems as though Virginia called Jody at home.'' Then he turned to look at her. ''And you told me Jody called N.S.A. from one of the telephone booths.''

She got up from the chair and stood behind the two men. The telephone numbers were clearly visible. ''There's no good reason to use an outside phone,'' she said slowly. ''We can make personal calls from our desks within limits.''

''Have your guys found him yet?'' Ross asked Mike.

''He was spotted at LaGuardia catching the shuttle for Washington.''

''What's going to happen? Will he be arrested?'' Emily asked.

''No, he'll be watched to see where he goes.'' Mike checked his wristwatch. ''We should know something soon. The last flight left an hour ago, and from what the guys tell me, he's not trying too hard to throw anyone off.''

''I've got to go to Washington myself,'' Emily said suddenly, the tone of her voice bringing the two men's heads around. ''I want to confront her myself.''

''Stay out of it, Emily. You don't need to get in the middle of this.'' The explosion in the hotel had left his nerves feeling raw, exposed, as though his emotions were laid bare. How could he permit her to risk her life?

''The hell I don't,'' she said, anger coloring her voice. ''I know what you're worrying about,'' she said, referring to Marta, ''but I have a right to see this through. Just as you would.''

Ross knew he was handling it poorly but he had to make another attempt. ''Let Mike and me take care of it.''

''I took care of myself in Mexico,'' she said. ''I can

talk to Virginia. You and Mike can dream up every safe-
guard you want but I'm going. Remember what I told you
at the beginning?" She waited until she was sure she had
his attention. "My hide is on the line more than yours.
And," she added with delicate emphasis, "I'm not anyone
else."

Ross's face was taut and his eyes, normally a clear
gray, were turbulent. His jaw flexed. "All right. Mike,
where's the nearest field to rent a small plane so we can
get there directly without having to go through Washington?"

"I know a place," Mike responded, giving them the
name of a small airfield in New Jersey.

A telephone call before they took off revealed that Jody
had entered Virginia's house. He was still there.

"What's the plan?" Mike asked, looking to Ross for
guidance as they walked out of the air terminal after the
short flight.

"I want to get Jody out of the house first. Then we're
going after the woman."

Ross's tone was devoid of emphasis but Emily controlled a shiver. He hadn't looked at her since he'd agreed
to bring her and the coldness in the pit of her stomach felt
like a lump of lead. She'd known he would be angry.

"I could call Virginia and say that I've been thinking
about Dana's sudden absence," Emily suggested after a
pause. "I could say I want to come and see her."

"She's not going to believe you," Ross said.

"Who cares?" Emily replied. "She doesn't have to.
But she's going to be curious about my motives for the
trip. I think she'll jump at the chance to talk to me."

"I don't know," Mike said unconvinced. "It's pretty
shaky."

"Anyone got a better idea? If I say I'm taking the first
shuttle, Virginia will kick Jody out of the house rather
than risk me seeing him."

"And we pick him up," Ross said.

"So this accomplishes two goals. You get Jody out of
the house and I talk to Virginia," she added calmly.

"All right," Ross said finally, after exchanging a brief,

comprehensive glance with Mike. "When do you want to call her?"

"I thought if I tried about six in the morning, I could say I just wanted to reach her before she left for work."

"Why not wait until she's at the office?" asked Mike. "Won't she think it's strange if you call her at home?"

"Yes, and the excuse I'll give of trying to catch her before work is going to sound false. That may help to keep the pressure on. Look, at this point we're reduced to gambling that we can tip the scales with whatever we do."

"You're pretty gutsy," Mike said admiringly, earning a glare from Ross.

"Gutsy is another word for foolhardy," he muttered.

Emily just smiled. "No guts, no glory."

Ross shook his head despairingly. She was back to believing everything would come out all right. But telling her again about the risks would just make her mad. How to convey his dread without sounding overly emotional? Disasters in his business were always expected. But she cherished the notion of invincibility. There wasn't any such thing. He unknowingly clenched his fist then relaxed. After a brief hesitation, he turned to her.

"While we're waiting, tell us what you know about Virginia and Jody, whether or not you're aware of any prior contacts."

"Until we saw those telephone numbers, I wouldn't have thought there was any connection. I wasn't even aware they knew each other." She hesitated. "I'm sorry Virginia is the one but I guess I'm not really surprised in a way. When I talked to her earlier, she said something that struck me as odd."

"What was that?" Ross asked.

"Something to the effect that she had trouble keeping up with me and Dana. I remembered she always spoke as though she had an inferiority complex. But it used to bother me because I could never quite believe it. Now I know why. Virginia behaved as though she was in charge, and I should have picked up on the discrepancy."

"Why? You weren't even thinking about her in that

light," Ross said. He knew she was still struggling with the fact that people she knew, even liked, had targeted her for death.

"Did Virginia ever come to your office?" Mike asked.

"Once. A couple of years ago," Emily replied. "We normally met for lunch someplace in midtown."

"Was Jody working there then?" Ross probed.

Emily paused while she thought. "No. He would have been only about nineteen or twenty when she came to see me and we don't hire anyone under twenty-one."

"You said he went to college at night. Do you remember what he's studying?"

"Computer courses." She stopped, then gave a laugh. "I should have suspected then. Sometimes he would stand in the doorway of my office, trying to have a conversation, and he could have seen what I was doing on my monitor. If he knew enough about computers, he might have been able to figure something out."

"Don't blame yourself, Emily. You had no reason to suspect him, or anyone for that matter."

"I'd also like to know how he got past a security examination," Mike interjected.

"Virginia probably deleted his file," Ross suggested.

Emily nodded. "She must have nerves of steel to be able to do that."

"And may have had for years," Mike commented.

Emily walked across the room. "The scenario probably went like this. She made it a habit to get to know a few of the brightest students in any group of entrants. She would tell them she knew the ropes, and offer to help out with whatever little adjustment problems they were having. Just like with me. That way, when she continues to keep in touch, no one is surprised. Perfect for a spy," she said, bitterness edging her tone.

"Don't feel bad," Ross advised. "Anyone would have been taken in. You were a long way from home, and it would have been easy for her to make friends with you. What about Dana?"

"She and Virginia hit it off, too. Dana's from a small

town in Wyoming and felt as lost as I did. I'll bet she approached others in the class."

"And the better you did, the better for her."

"Wouldn't it have made a difference how well her proteges performed?" asked Mike.

"Not necessarily," Ross answered. "If she could also get someone to keep additional tabs on her proteges, maybe it would be enough just to know what they were working on. She may have used Jody for this in your case, Emily. The important thing is that Virginia was ideally placed as Assistant to the Deputy Administrator."

Cynically, Emily added, "She was probably doing a lot of other things there we don't know about yet. The kids were just so much gravy."

"Until this," added Ross. "And this is big time. Virginia must be desperate to find out what information you've passed on."

They continued talking, reviewing the message. Ross suggested that star might be a location.

"I don't think so," Mike said. "Star sounds like an individual."

"Suppose we're wrong about all of this," Emily asked, when silence fell, "and the bomb or whatever it is is already in place and can't be moved?"

"Travel plans can be changed," Ross said.

"As long as you know the target, time, and place," Emily said.

"I hope it's that simple." Mike's soft-voiced comment spoke for all of them.

"What kind of evidence does Walker need in order to wrap this up?" Emily changed the topic.

"That's not your problem," Ross said.

"Yes, it is." She looked straight at him. "We've been talking around the issue, Ross," she replied quietly. "We've assumed Virginia is the person we're looking for but we need proof. We also don't know if she works with anyone else. Walker told you that he was afraid there was another contact in your agency. That makes sense because too much was known about your trip to see me."

"She's escaped detection for years. Do you think she's

going to let some younger woman mess it up, destroy everything she's worked for? I think she'll brag about it first. If Virginia will talk, we can locate the source of danger that much faster.''

"You plan to goad her," said Mike shrewdly.

"Why not? We don't understand her motives at all. There's even a chance she's been blackmailed and is hoping someone will find her out. If she's not in this voluntarily, she could be ready to talk.''

"Fine. And she can—to me. If on the other hand, she's doing this because she wants to, then giving her a chance to spout off will give us the evidence we need to put pressure on her to reveal the rest of the network," Emily continued. "I'll call her, and set up a visit. You can wire me for sound and hang around outside," she said to Ross, feeling his eyes on her. "She won't be able to overpower me.''

"All right, but you'll have to follow orders." He felt like a drowning man, clutching at straws. She was hellbent on going ahead with it and short of sounding like a complete idiot, he had to let her. She was right, she was the best person to confront Virginia the first time.

No one spoke for a minute, until Mike broke the silence. "Emily, it's about time for you to make the call.''

She nodded, telling herself not to be nervous, that this was what she wanted to do. Turning to face the men in the back she said, a wry smile on her mouth, "Anyone have a quarter?''

"Sure." Mike produced the money between thumb and forefinger.

"Thanks.''

She stepped out of the car and Ross followed her.

"You can still back out. It isn't too late.''

"Yes, it is. You've made it clear we don't really have a future, Ross. Therefore, your concern for me doesn't have any bearing on what I'm going to do. Unless you're changing your mind about our relationship?''

There was a breathless silence and Ross eyed her with a mixture of admiration and distaste for her tactics. She had him squarely over a barrel. She'd implied that if he relented about a future together, she'd back down about seeing Virginia.

"I didn't mean to hurt you," he started.

"That's unimportant," she interrupted. "Just because I'm attracted to you doesn't mean I've lost my capacity for rational thought. Stop treating me like an idiot."

"I love you," he finally admitted, then added, "but it won't work."

"I know you think so," she said, the intensity of her blue gaze unnerving him.

"Damnit, Emily, don't make everything so hard." The minute the words were out of his mouth, he knew it was a mistake from her gently mocking smile.

"Why not?"

For reply, he pulled her to him, unmindful of Mike in the car behind him. Heat flared instantaneously between them as his lips touched hers, and he tunneled his hands through her hair, his fingers tightening on the narrow shape of her head, feeling her body pressed tightly to his.

He'd tried to forget her, and all he'd succeeded in doing was to build up more memories sure to haunt him in the dark nights ahead. At last, aware he was going to ache for hours, he pushed her away from him. "Go make your call."

THIRTEEN

Emily stared after Ross as he returned to the car, her thoughts whirling. He had the damnedest capacity, she decided with irritation, to turn her insides out, raise her blood pressure to medically unsafe heights, and then walk away. She felt like stomping her foot. Instead she went inside the small restaurant at the truck stop and found a telephone.

"Hello?" Virginia's voice was crisp.

"It's me, Emily. I've been lying awake most of the night worrying about Dana." She continued hurriedly before Virginia could speak. "I'm sure you haven't heard anything from her, but there are things going on here that concern you both. I wanted to call before you left for the office."

"You decided to call me at six?" She yawned loudly.

"I know it's early but I'm catching the first shuttle to Washington. In fact I'm at LaGuardia now for the early flight and had to talk to you. Can you meet me somewhere so we can talk?"

There was a long pause and the older woman said, her voice slightly different. "Of course. When will you arrive?"

"I should be in Maryland by about eight-thirty."

"Come to the house. I can be late to work this once. Have a good flight."

The trap was set, Emily thought with satisfaction, as she returned to the car.

"Did it go all right?" Mike asked as she took her place in the front seat.

"She's agreed," Emily said. "And she didn't even ask what the problem was. I find that interesting."

196

"That's not exactly the word I was looking for," Ross said from beside her. "More like a big alarm."

"This is what we wanted," she pointed out reasonably.

"Yeah, I guess." Ross started up the car.

"Where are we going now?" Emily inquired.

"We're picking up some sound equipment for you. We're going to have you wired." Ross indicated a radio Mike was holding that Emily hadn't seen before.

"Good," she replied.

He drove to a small house in one of the bedroom communities around Washington, and stopped in front.

"This is it?" she asked, peering out the window. "I'd expected we'd go to an office."

"This is out of channels, and safer," Ross answered, as he nodded to Mike.

Mike went inside and came out moments later, resuming his seat in the vehicle. He had a small, shiny object in his hand and a box.

"Here." Unceremoniously he handed her the device. It consisted of a silver disc with wires dangling from it. He pointed to a larger black box on the floor of the automobile. "This is a receiver that's on the same frequency. The disc is the transmitter. You're supposed to wear it under your clothing, so put it under your bra. With this, we'll be able to hear you from wherever you are. We'll get out of the car while you put it on."

The device fit snugly, and Emily moved it until she was comfortable. When she had it adjusted to her liking, she opened the door and stepped out.

"I'm ready."

"Let's give it a test," Ross suggested.

They had her walk fifty feet away and speak in a soft whisper. Ross whistled to her after a few moments.

"Heard you loud and clear."

"Good. And you don't think she'll check to see if I'm wearing one?"

Mike answered. "It's about fifty fifty. If she does, we'll hear and come in. If she doesn't, we'll know when to arrive anyway just from listening to the two of you. This is as safe as anything we could dream up."

Emily checked the watch on her wrist. "I'm not supposed to be here for another hour or so. Anyone for coffee?"

"Sure," Mike said.

Ross was notably silent while they waited for their order, only his fingers drumming on the formica surface of the table indicated his mood. Emily tried several times to engage him in conversation and finally gave up. Mike talked about his work and Emily was fascinated. She hadn't been aware of the advances in telecommunications that were outside her area of expertise.

Finally, Ross said, "Think it's about time to go. It's at least a twenty minute trip. You'd better drive, and let us off around the corner. We'll be in the neighborhood, close enough to rush in."

Emily nodded and started to slide out of the seat.

"Just a minute," Mike said. "I'd like to be sure Jody has already been picked up. No point in having surprises."

He strolled to a telephone in the corner and she could see him talking quietly. She felt Ross's eyes on her but didn't turn. She'd already decided there wasn't any use in talking to him until it was all over. Maybe then he'd see reason.

Mike came back. "Jody was picked up," Mike said. "He was terrified when he realized he'd been found out. In fact, he spilled all kinds of beans. He said Virginia was his aunt."

"Aunt?" Emily hadn't expected that.

"Yes. Seems Jody didn't know it for a long time. He's pretty upset that he's involved in something over his head. Says he had no idea what she was doing."

"If it weren't for the fact that Jody wouldn't lie now, I'd say it was fiction," Emily said. "N.S.A. prohibits nepotism."

"Either she managed to get around the regulations, or her file didn't show the connection. Maybe she'll say something to you. You might bring him up," Ross suggested.

"Of course," she agreed. "This at least helps explain his willingness to be involved."

Several minutes later, she dropped Mike and Ross off just at the end of Virginia's street and was pulling up in front of the house. The area where Virginia lived was a quiet, residential neighborhood. Houses were set a considerable distance from each other, and most had hedges and dense vegetation shielding their occupants from gazes of the curious. Virginia's was no exception.

Emily had seen Ross and Mike for a moment as they hurriedly made their way up the block, then they vanished. But she knew they were watching her from positions of safety. She rang the bell.

"Come in, Emily. I've been expecting you."

Virginia Harrison's face looked tired, and there were lines that hadn't been there when Emily had seen the older woman several months previously. She was smaller than Emily, bordering on stout, and dressed in a beige suit with a pale pink blouse. Unfortunately, Emily thought, the colors weren't flattering.

Virginia's gray hair was cut short, and it bristled around her face. "Let me take your jacket. I wouldn't want you being uncomfortable."

There was an odd undertone to her voice and Emily controlled a flinch when Virginia reached for her coat.

"Thanks for letting me come by," Emily replied, easing the fabric down her arms and handing the garment to Virginia. "I'm very concerned about Dana."

"I wouldn't have missed your visit for the world," Virginia replied smoothly. She indicated Emily should sit on the curved couch in front of the marble fireplace as she took a chair.

Emily surveyed the living room quickly, noticing the discreet elegance of the furniture. She'd never been in Virginia's house before and was surprised at what she saw. There was an intricately carved, antique cabinet in the corner. An Oriental rug in muted blues and scarlets was under her feet. Against a far wall stood what appeared to be an antique sideboard with a glazed pottery bowl on top. The room wasn't large, but it was beautifully decorated. Emily surmised there was a great deal of money in the furnishings and paintings.

Money that Virginia could hardly have earned at the National Security Agency as a secretary and then administrative assistant. For an instant, she thought she felt a brush of air across her face and frowned. She looked around for its source. The door to the kitchen was closed and the windows were shut. Virginia was watching her expressionlessly and Emily relaxed. Must have been her imagination.

Emily clasped her hands together in her lap, and said, "I suppose you're thinking it's a little odd for me to come by at . . ."

"Not really," came the cool reply. "You're going to tell me there's something odd going on at the New York office, and you're worried that Dana's absence has something to do with it. Except that I'm going to save you time." The smile on the older woman's face was mirthless. "By the way, Dana is away because her mother called her to come home . . . some kind of family emergency. So don't waste your breath on her. You're here because of me, aren't you?"

"Yes. And Jody."

Virginia's face changed slightly, a subtle hardening of the rounded features. "Jody?"

"He's involved in whatever is going on in New York."

"But you're not sure?" prompted the other woman.

Taking a chance, Emily said, "We know there's a plot to kill the Canadian Prime Minister in New York, but we're not sure about Jody's role in it." Emily saw a strange expression flicker briefly across Virginia's face at her words.

Across from her, Virginia crossed her legs and surveyed her visitor. "You don't honestly expect me to believe that's why you're here, do you?"

"What do you mean?"

"Don't take me for a fool." There was an undertone of spite in Virginia's voice. "I wondered at first when you called if you were really as naive as you sounded, but one look at your face tells me you think you can trap me in some kind of admission. It won't matter what you say in a minute," she said.

"Why is that?" You'd better be listening, Ross, she thought.

Virginia threw her a cool smile. "I can remember when you arrived at the agency, a green kid from the boon-docks," she said, without replying directly. Brown eyes surveyed Emily with disfavor. "You weren't as smart as you thought." She laughed. "You and Dana and others before and after you were simply targets, pawns to be used and discarded. Unfortunately, this time someone slipped up. But I'm digressing."

"You might as well. Jody's your nephew, isn't he?"

Virginia nodded. "Yes. I didn't even know I had a nephew until I was employed here."

Emily asked, "Why not?"

"I was adopted when I was young, and only had a faint recollection I had a brother."

"Did you try to locate him?"

"Yes. If you know where and how to look, it's not that hard to find someone. I learned a lot at N.S.A." She smiled. "Jody was delighted to learn he had an aunt. He was glad to help me."

"But it was your brains wasn't it? I mean, Jody is just a kid. I can't imagine him wanting to betray his country."

"Betrayal is such an emotional word. Really, Emily, even using it lessens my respect for you. The concept isn't relevant in this context. Besides, I like money and I'm paid well. It's simple." Her smile widened. "I need money and power, and working for both sides provides me with quite an acceptable income."

"And that was enough?" Not relevant? Betrayal?

"Most definitely." Virginia smiled with pleasure, and missed the flash of disgust on Emily's face. "In fact," she laughed, "it was remarkably easy. Americans have a totally ridiculous sense of privilege and arrogance. It's rewarding to see them taken down a peg or two. Anyway, dealing with Canada is hardly tantamount to selling out my country." She shrugged. "They're our allies. I'm just helping them resolve an internal conflict."

"That makes everything all right?" Emily felt like Alice

in Wonderland. Virginia had turned everything upside down.

"Well, they're not exactly our enemy, are they? Besides, they need to be taught a lesson as well."

"Is that the other reason you've done this, besides money?" Emily said. "To humble them and us both? What does the message I received have to do with this?"

"The first transmission, the one you received, was rather interesting. The target was the Prime Minister's wife. Imagine the impact if she were murdered by an American faction on her trip to the United States." She smiled. "Especially, if the group was known to be pro-unity. That would throw confusion into the entire separatist question. I think it will be rather amusing especially since the so-called Americans will really be Canadians."

The first one? What else had they planned? Emily hoped Ross was hearing everything. "There's been another message?"

"Of course," Virginia said smoothly. "Once we realized there was a problem at N.S.A., the plan was changed. The assassination takes place somewhere else."

"Why not here if you want the United States to take the blame?"

"We'll just have to plant evidence about the complicity of this country. It won't be too hard."

"Who would believe we'd do that? I can imagine a pro-secessionist organization being blamed, but not the other side."

Virginia smiled. "Let's suppose a radical anti-Quebec group feels the Ottawan government is giving away too much in the way of concessions. They could intend to kill the Prime Minister, and miss, hitting the wife."

"Except of course, the intent was to kill the wife anyway," Emily said. "The word 'star' in the message. Did that refer to her?"

Virginia's smile held triumph. "Yes. But you never figured that out did you?"

"No," Emily admitted. "What does killing his wife accomplish? Seems to me losing the Prime Minister would be more effective."

"Not really. If his wife is killed, the Prime Minister will be in a state of shock—but still functioning. That way, he won't be replaced by possibly someone even more conservative. The blame for her death will be placed on the unity movement which will ensure that they're perceived as unreasonable in denying the Quebec demands."

"Where was it supposed to happen in the United States?"

"In New York. The curved area in front of the U.N. was the 'crescent.' A small ceremony was scheduled for that spot, and the Premier's wife would have been an easy target."

"If you changed the plan, then why did those two men kidnap me?"

"I tried to pass the word, but obviously they didn't receive it." She looked unconcerned. "Those things happen," she added with chilling casualness. "Unfortunately, you wouldn't stay out of it. Honestly, Emily, you only have yourself to blame."

Emily controlled a shudder at the dead expression in Virginia's eyes. She brought her thoughts back with an effort.

If she could keep Virginia talking, perhaps she'd slip and provide a clue to the identity of the other double agent. "By the way, I was curious about something else. How was I found?"

"Once you didn't turn up at the office, I decided you'd try to be cute. And you were," Virginia said, half-admiringly. "I remembered you were from West Texas. We located every piece of property that your parents and grandparents had owned. After that, it was a process of elimination. We'd have found you the day before if those fools in the courthouse had just stayed open to let us check records."

"I didn't mean how you found me in Texas. Rather, how did you know that I was the one at the agency in New York who received the message? And why didn't anyone at headquarters in Maryland know about it?"

"I'm sorry to deflate your ego," Virginia said, "but Jody was able to access your computer through your password and learned you had been given the message. You were too trusting. He simply stood in the door of your office one morning and saw you type in the password. Anyway, once I'd learned that the message had been sent by error, I traced it to you in New York. It wasn't hard to block it at this end so headquarters didn't receive the text.''

"Who else knows about this?" Emily said, acutely conscious of the small transmitter she was carrying.

Virginia's face clouded with irritation. "You don't need to know," she said. "There's nothing you can do to stop it. I can't waste any more time."

The kitchen door opened soundlessly and a tall, gray-haired man with a hard face walked in. "You've already wasted enough time, Virginia, with your boasting." He had a French accent that was hard to place.

Emily had stiffened the instant she saw him and her hands clenched as she saw him produce a small, snub-nosed pistol from behind his back.

He turned to smile at Emily. "And you, you're simply of no interest to me any more."

He raised his hand to fire and Emily's breath stopped.

"Jean-Paul, not here for God's sake," Virginia protested.

The man's eyes turned to her, and Emily threw herself to the ground and rolled. Her sudden movement surprised him and she felt her back hit his legs. A table rocked and a lamp smashed on the floor.

Virginia yelled. "Stop, you're destroying my things." There was a note of panic in her voice.

Emily kicked out sharply with a leg, catching the man in the kneecap. He cursed and she saw his gun swing back in her direction.

The front door flew open with a crash, landing against the wall. Ross burst into the room, his eyes searching. A gun went off. Once. Then a louder boom as a second fired from behind her. Emily rose to her knees. The man called Jean-Paul was lying against the wall, his eyes closed, blood on his chest. Ross bent, and Emily saw Virginia reach for the gun the man had dropped.

Emily picked up a book end from the table beside her and threw it. It hit Virginia's hand and with an exclamation of pain she dropped the weapon.

Ross turned and his mouth tightened when he saw the gun fall from Virginia's grasp. "I owe you," he said to Emily. He rose in a swift movement and grabbed Virginia, pulling her arm behind her.

A look of hatred and rage crossed her face, and she tried to jerk away. Ross raised her arm higher and she subsided.

Mike appeared from the back of the house, his eyebrows rising as he surveyed the scene. "Looks like you've been busy."

"Yeah," Ross muttered. "I hadn't counted on our friend here on the floor." He indicated the man behind him who hadn't moved.

"Do we need an ambulance?" Mike asked.

"Unfortunately. I got him in the chest, missing the heart."

"You can't always be lucky," grinned Mike.

"He was going to shoot Emily."

Ross's voice was tight and Emily eyed him sharply.

"The house is clear," Mike said. "I'll make the call for a clean-up crew." He disappeared down the hall.

Emily got up slowly, her heart thudding as the reality of what had happened hit her. For one moment frozen in time, she'd expected to feel a bullet plow its way through her body. She took in a deep breath and willed her heart rate to slow.

Virginia panted as Ross held her squirming, twisting body. "You'll never get away with this. I want to know the meaning of this outrage."

Ross moved back, releasing her, and stood, holding a gun on her. "You can get up now."

He jammed her down into a chair and backed away out of kicking distance. "Don't move," he warned. "I'm not as nice as Emily."

Virginia glared at him.

"Emily, go ahead and tell her why we're here."

Emily said, "I've been wired. The entire conversation

has been taped and heard by several people. There's no way you can deny what you've said. Jody has talked, too.''

At the mention of her nephew's name, the older woman's face altered. "He did?"

Ross leaned against the couch. "Enough to implicate you and your associates. You have a choice. We'll leave your brother and his family alone if you tell us everything you know, or," he said, his voice hardening, "we'll see to it that your family spends years in jail. Along with you of course," he added, "and this guy on the floor once he gets out of the hospital."

There was silence in the room as Virginia Harrison took in Ross's words. "I . . . I can't . . ."

"Jody told us how you'd persuaded him to break into Emily's computer. He'll make a very effective witness at both your trial and his . . . if you don't cooperate. If you do, we'll drop the charges against him."

Emily was faintly surprised when Virginia agreed. "I want it in writing that you'll leave my brother and his family alone. Now."

Ross's head dipped in acknowledgment. "All right. Where's something to write on?"

Virginia indicated a desk in the corner of the living room.

Ross rose. Seating himself at the desk chair, he began to write. The room was silent while the women waited.

"Here." Ross thrust a piece of paper covered with writing in front of Virginia. Emily saw her read then sign it.

Virginia shot a baleful look at Emily. "If she hadn't been the one with the message, everything would have gone well. We tried to get the message routed to one of the other two cryptoanalysts but the random system was a problem. And I couldn't tell Jody too much." She swiveled her head in Ross's direction. "How much does he know about the actual plan?"

"Just that there was a plot to kill someone, but he doesn't know it included a bomb."

"I see." The energy that had sustained her earlier had

ebbed, and she looked drained, the power sucked out of her by her discovery.

"You told me earlier the location of the attempt has been changed. Where?" Emily asked.

"To Rome," Virginia said dully. "I don't know a lot more. Evidently the Prime Minister was planning on a trip there next week."

"So everything has been moved up in time." Ross swore under his breath. "I'll pass that on to Walker."

Mike returned. "A car is on its way as well as an ambulance. Jody is in Washington."

With that announcement, the last of the defiance in the older woman disappeared. "It's over, isn't it?"

"Almost," replied Emily evenly. "And the only way you have of being sure nothing else happens to Jody and his father is to give us the names of every contact you had within N.S.A."

There was a slow nod and in a quiet voice, Virginia gave the names of three other Americans as well as the contact in Washington that she knew were involved in the plot. "They were expatriates who had left this country during the Vietnam war, to avoid the draft. And," she looked over at the man lying on the floor, "that's Jean-Paul Tignant, a former OAS member who provided technical assistance."

"That makes sense," Emily said slowly. "The Algerian question kept France in an uproar for years. The OAS wanted Algeria to remain French. For Canada to be intensely pro-French fits."

"Yeah," Ross said, "and the OAS was known for not caring about how they achieved their goal. They could well have had Libyan contacts to keep a continuous cash flow."

"Did you call him?" Emily asked, gazing at Virginia.

"Yes. He arrived last night when I first got worried."

"Did you call anyone else?"

"No. We were kept isolated from each other for security reasons, but I had contacts in other agencies on occasion. That was how I knew you and this man were together. I almost got you, didn't I?'' There was a flicker of pride in Virginia's voice.

Emily repressed a shiver. She still found it hard to believe that the woman who had professed to be her good friend had coldbloodedly planned her murder. She had never met a sociopath, but suspected Virginia was one.

Ross rose and found the telephone in the kitchen and Emily could hear him making a call. When he returned, he said, "Things are moving. I've talked to Walker. He's going to pass on the information to the White House. The knowledge that a pro-secession faction is behind it will be conveyed to the Prime Minister at once and he's going to increase security. They'll also be looking for other OAS connections. Mike, I want you to stay here while I get Emily on a plane to New York.''

"What about you?'' Emily asked, her stomach dropping. He wasn't even giving her a chance to argue.

"I've got to clean up loose ends. You might as well get back and check on your apartment, see about salvaging things.''

Ross wouldn't look at her and she was uncomfortably aware of the compassion on Mike's face. Feeling as though she were fighting for her life, she said, keeping her voice level with difficulty, "But you don't know that the plot has been aborted.''

"The Canadians will take care of it,'' Ross said. "Of course we'll make Virginia and Jean-Paul available for questioning.''

The bravado and malice that had been so apparent in Virginia when Emily had first arrived had disappeared and the woman who sat quietly in the living room of her home had a shrunken look. She'd aged immeasurably in the last half hour.

"Come on, Emily. I'll take you to the airport. I'll see you later, Mike. By the way, I can't thank you enough,'' Ross said.

Mike grinned. "Any time you got any more excitement lined up, let me know. I get bored easily.''

"Boring is safe,'' said Ross dryly.

"Yeah, but who needs it?" retorted Mike unrepentantly, his eyes gleaming with amusement.

"You never know. One of these days we might decide to grow up."

"No way. Look at you. You're still going strong."

Strong? thought Ross as he stared impassively at Emily. I haven't been strong since I got involved in this mess.

"Just keep an eye on your charges," he said to Mike.

Emily stood and started out of the room, then stopped and turned. "I need to add my thanks to Ross's, Mike."

Mike laughed. "Not me." He nodded to Ross who was standing, waiting for Emily to leave. "He's the one."

"Well, thanks anyway."

Once inside the car, Emily said without preamble, "I don't want to say goodbye, Ross." She had already decided Ross wasn't going to help her at all. "And you don't either."

Without a word, Ross started the engine, and then drove smoothly away from the house. "You're shell-shocked from everything that has been happening to you in the last week. Having someone practically kill you didn't help. You're just disoriented. You'll feel differently once you get back to work and find a place to live. I'm going to be on the move for the next six months anyway and don't have any time for a . . . complication . . . right now." A muscle jumped in his jaw.

"Complication? Is that how you think I feel about you?"

"You don't have the faintest idea how you feel. Oh, right now, you may be experiencing a little hero worship," he said, ignoring an angry laugh from Emily, "but that'll pass."

"It never started," she said. "If you think this is hero worship, you're out of your mind. I thought we shared something while we were together, something important." She wasn't going to give up. "You told me you loved me. I know you're not a liar."

"What I feel isn't important," he protested. "I have no business asking anyone to share my life."

"You're a coward."

"What?" He looked thunderstruck.

"Yes. You say I deserve something better." She hitched sideways in the seat, and stared at him. "But that's not why you're dumping me. You can't hack it. Can't hack the responsibility, the possibility that something might go wrong."

Ross was furious. "If I'm a coward to want to preserve your skin intact, rather than making you open season for anyone who can get at me through you, then so be it. But that's the way it is."

Emily inhaled sharply at the realization he was still avoiding the real issue. Softening her voice, fighting the sting of tears in her eyes, she asked, "Was everything between us my imagination? Tell me that, at least."

"It meant something." He cleared his throat. "But not enough. Not in the long run."

Her head swam, and she felt lightheaded. The agony was so intense, she was afraid she was going to faint. Emily bit her lip hard, the physical pain briefly overriding the ache in her heart. Finally, when she could speak, she said, "That's clear enough. Sorry to have been so persistent." She produced a travesty of a smile. "If you'll drop me at the airport, I'll be on my way and out of your life."

Her voice had a dead quality and Ross winced. He'd been more effective than he'd dreamed, but this was the only answer. Cowardice was acceptable for the right reason, and he'd spoken the absolute truth when he said he could be manipulated through a threat to her. He couldn't expose her to that risk.

"Fine," he said.

Emily turned her head and quickly wiped at the tear that ran down her cheek. She was not going to make a fool out of herself.

The trees outside swam past her blurred vision, and she blinked rapidly. She hadn't thought Ross was cruel but he was. A deadly cruelty made all the worse by its face of kindness, of fairness. She promised herself she was going to walk away from him with her head up. With conscious effort, she managed to look at him as he stopped in front of the airport.

Ross sat braced against the driver's door as though for a blow and Emily smiled wanly. "Don't worry. I know when I'm licked. You're very good, Ross, at kicking people out of your life. Be sure you don't get too good at it. Someday you'll find someone you want. But, if you're not careful, you'll have lost the knack of connecting with people." She stuck out her hand, and didn't hear his sharp intake of breath.

"Goddamnit, Emily," Ross said harshly, jerking her to him without warning. He had to kiss her . . . just once more.

His mouth was hard against hers, and she tasted the flavor of panic, felt the rasping edge of his tongue as he probed her mouth for a devastatingly brief instant.

He raised his head, his breathing rapid. "Have a good flight."

The inanity of it made her close her eyes briefly. "That was a terrific one liner, Ross. You'll go far."

Emily opened the door and got out, then leaned back in through the open window. "One more thing. I hope I never see your face again."

She turned and walked away, not hearing the way Ross uttered her name behind her.

_____ FOURTEEN _____

Emily boarded her flight to New York, feeling numb. Ross had been stunningly clear in his rejection. Only a fool could ignore it—and she told herself she wasn't going to be a fool any longer. She hadn't lied when she said she didn't ever want to see him again. Masochism was for the birds.

A businessman in a rumpled gray suit sat next to her during the flight, attempting conversation, but her monosyllabic answers eventually shut off the flow.

As Emily walked up the long tunnel from the plane to the terminal, she was conscious of unutterable weariness. She'd read somewhere you weren't a woman until you'd had your first disastrous love affair. On that basis, she wasn't surprised she felt so grown up.

A man dressed in a tan jacket and darker parts approached her hesitantly as she turned towards the walkway leading to the luggage area. He had medium brown hair, medium brown eyes, and a medium face. Emily's eyes slid over him and then jerked back when he called to her.

"Miss Brown?"

Emily eyed him warily. "Yes?"

"Mr. Walker asked me to meet you and tell you about your new apartment."

Emily looked at him. She knew Walker was Ross's employer, but Ross's description of him hadn't made him sound exactly like Santa Claus.

"So?" Her tone was uncompromising.

The man looked uncomfortable. "Since your old one is no longer, uh, habitable, he thought you might like to go straight to a place he's found for you. I have the address here and the key."

"Give them to me. I'll think about it."

He smiled admiringly. "Walker said you'd be like this. By the way, it's a walk-up on West Seventy-fourth. Not too far from where you were before. About the same size." He handed her a brass key and a slip of paper with the address on it.

"Why?" She cocked her head at him. God knows it sounded wonderful but things didn't have a habit of landing in her lap. Not from Ross and company.

"Mr. Walker thought you'd been inconvenienced enough."

"Inconvenienced" covered a multitude of sins, she thought.

"All right. But I'm making no promises." She turned again to go towards the luggage carousel area, and the man started to accompany her. Emily stopped. "I don't need a babysitter any more."

Her sharp tone made her escort back off. He raised his hands, palms outward. "Fine. Fine. No problem."

After a brief look around the area, he walked away towards the main exit and Emily waited until he was out of sight before retrieving her luggage. She detoured towards a telephone booth, slung her suitcase under her feet and inserted a coin. When a man answered, she said abruptly, "Is this Walker?"

There was a second's pause then, "Yes. This must be Miss Brown."

Emily didn't think she liked the amusement she heard. "Is there really an apartment on West Seventy-fourth?"

"Yes."

Neither spoke for an instant, then Emily said shortly, "Thank you. Goodbye." She thought she heard him try to say something before she hung up. She'd talk to Mr. Walker later, she decided, when she was good and ready.

The apartment was better in every way than her old one had been except for one thing. It wasn't hers. Someone had made an effort to furnish it comfortably but that only made her more acutely aware that she was dislodged from her own environment.

Emily called her mother and chatted briefly, letting her

have the new address and phone number. She ignored the small voice in her head that said if Walker had the same information, Ross could get it also.

If he wanted to.

The next morning Emily returned to work, going into her small cubicle and shutting the door, looking around at the office she'd occupied for so long.

Everything was as she'd left it. It was still sterile and she nodded to herself in confirmation. She'd been right.

Emily walked slowly around the desk and sat down, knowing Ross had it backwards. He'd rejected her, believing his life offered nothing, that she was better off without him. He was wrong because she had nothing without him.

Her eyes burned and she blinked rapidly. But he didn't have anything without her either.

What a pair they were. For years she'd been rootless, without any strong ties to anyone. She'd maintained her self-imposed isolation, she now realized, by assuming she didn't fit anywhere. How did she know for sure, she wondered bleakly, as she contemplated the empty shell of her life. She'd made no efforts to do anything to change it.

She'd lived in New York for years, or perhaps more properly existed, and what did she have to show for it?

Not a damned thing, she thought, with a trace of anger.

No lover, husband, or children.

No real friends at her job.

Just emptiness.

How could she blame him for keeping people at arm's length? Wasn't that what she'd been doing for years? She fought a hollowness that threatened to overwhelm her.

She had a lot of thinking to do before taking the next step.

Two weeks later she wasn't any closer to making a decision. She drifted to work each morning and home in the evening, her mind only partly on the job. Her old apartment was being renovated, and the construction was taking longer than expected.

The relocation had another unexpected result.

One evening, Emily had detoured by the apartment, to search for an address. As she rooted through the debris, she'd found a card her brother had sent her from Texas. Homesickness stronger than any she'd experienced in years had swept over her. The poignancy of the emotional pull was powerful, and she'd stumbled out and down the steps, tears welling up in her eyes, the sensation of loss sharp. The nights were no better. Her dreams were troubled, and each morning, as she trudged wearily to work, she wondered if the pain would ever ease. Her telephone bills reflected her state of mind. Several times she called her mother just to chat, feeling her loneliness abate.

But Ross didn't call.

Three weeks after she'd returned to a normal existence, Ross still hadn't contacted her. Emily began to get mad, a slow anger building, simmering on its way to a full boil.

Perhaps it was time to take matters into her own hands. After all, she'd seen behind his harsh, rather aloof exterior, detecting warmth, tenderness, evidence of humor. There'd been evidence of caring, even love.

Emily couldn't, wouldn't give up.

When she'd left Ross at the airport, she'd been blinded by pain, too stunned to realize his attitude had been uncharacteristically cruel.

He'd been scared for her.

For the first time in weeks, she smiled.

What was life if not risk?

The next morning, she decided she'd waited long enough. The only person who could make her happy was on the run, and it was high time to start the chase.

When she dialed the Washington number for the second time, she recognized Walker's voice at once. "This is Emily Brown," she said without preface. "I want to see you."

Walker didn't sound surprised to hear from her, and Emily felt the first stirrings of unease when he said, "I'll be free tomorrow at ten A.M." She hung up, after accepting his instructions, and gave the telephone a thoughtful look. It was too easy.

By the time she landed at National Airport in Washington the following morning, she'd drunk three cups of coffee she didn't need and butterflies had taken up residence in her stomach.

When she walked into Walker's office, she stopped in surprise. She'd imagined Walker to be a lot of things, but not a middle-sized man smoking a pipe with a twinkle in his eye. Spymasters were supposed to be hard-eyed like bankers, faces free of emotion. This man looked like a misplaced cherub, a bit frayed around the edges, but nonetheless exuding good cheer.

He got up and walked around the desk toward her. They shook hands. "Won't you sit down?" He waited until she was seated then resumed his chair. "What can I help you with?" He puffed on his pipe and a cloud of smoke drifted up in a lazy swirl.

"First, where's Ross?" Emily said baldly.

"In Washington," he responded calmly, seemingly not at all put out by her bluntness. He tapped his pipe on the edge of a large, round glass ashtray in the middle of his desk, not looking at her directly. "He was on a trip and just got back two days ago. He's asked about you, by the way."

"He has?" she managed around throat muscles that had tightened.

"Yes. In fact, I saw him yesterday. We had quite a nice chat." He seemed mildly amused at the recollection, then sobered. "But enough of that. You must have had some reason for coming here to see me." He leaned back and surveyed her through a haze of purple smoke.

"I wondered if Ross had any new assignments planned that would take him out of the country. Far East, Europe, Middle East, wherever. And whether or not he would ever be based here."

Walker stared at her thoughtfully without speaking.

"I realize I'm probably interfering," she began.

"No, no, nothing like that," he replied, tapping the stem of his pipe against his teeth, the clacking noise drawing her gaze. "Just that I hadn't really considered it. I'm not sure what you had in mind."

"Well, maybe if he were going to be located more

permanently in this country, I could work for your agency, too," she finished on a little rush.

"Ah," he replied understandingly. "Two for the price of one?"

At least he hadn't made any snide remarks, she thought with faint bitterness. The decision to change jobs had surfaced in the middle of one night with stunning clarity.

Walker sucked contemplatively on his pipe, his expression faraway. "I could probably find you some kind of a job. Let me think about this. I'll get back to you in a couple of days."

"Thank you."

Walker's chair creaked as he sat and looked at her directly. For a moment, his eyes were unexpectedly sharp. Emily's wariness increased when the round face in front of her creased in a smile.

"That's all I wanted to know," she said finally, wanting to leave and figure out what the hell was going on. Her earlier misgivings returned in force. This was way too easy.

Disappointment was written on Walker's face as she rose. "That's all? Really? I probably shouldn't interfere but I suggest you look up Ross and tell him about your offer."

Emily managed a nod, her knees weak at the idea of seeing Ross.

"You'll need his address, won't you?" Walker said behind her.

Heat flushed her face and Emily stopped, then turned around. Walker handed her a piece of paper which she grasped tightly. A moment later she was out the door.

Emily felt her face tighten as she stood at the door to Ross's apartment. Her hand trembled as she raised it to the doorbell. She hesitated, then pressed the button.

The door opened and she couldn't move.

Ross stood before her, a towel around his waist, looking as though he'd just stepped out of the shower. He looked stunned for an instant then his expression went blank.

"May I come in?" She damned the obstruction in her throat and coughed.

He indicated the living room behind him and she walked past him, careful not to touch him.

"Give me a second to get changed."

She nodded. She had time to admire the long line of his back and powerful legs before he disappeared down the hallway. She remembered running her hands over that same body and her mouth dried.

A few moments later, he walked back into the room, dressed in slacks and a shirt, his feet in loafers.

She was sitting on the couch and he paused, then sat at the other end.

"You in Washington on business?" he asked.

Something was visible deep in his eyes which made her pulses thud crazily. "You could say that." She'd misread signs before, she thought with a trace of bitterness.

"I'm glad you came by," he said softly, his eyes on her face.

"Well," she said, the remaining huskiness in her voice infuriating her, "I just thought I'd drop in. Seeing as how I was here in Washington anyway."

"Oh? Why are you here?"

"I wanted to meet Walker. I've applied for a job. He told me he'd probably hire me as a spy," she said baldly.

He looked dumbfounded, then enraged.

"The hell he will," Ross roared. "I never heard a bigger bunch of garbage in my life. When I get through with him he'll wish he'd never been born." His face darkened with anger. "I'd never know if you were dead or alive. Damnit, Emily, didn't anything that happened to you make an impression?"

"Yes," she said simply.

"What the hell does that mean?"

She could tell he was still furious. "You asked me if anything made an impression. I said yes."

He forced himself to calm down. "Did Walker say anything else?"

"Just that I should tell you I'd applied."

The silence lengthened. "I see." And he did. Ross

felt a peculiar combination of rage and relief at Walker's interference. First the dossier, now this. "Well, Walker didn't mean it, about the job. Anyway, I won't let you."

"He seemed like such a nice man," she offered, watching with interest as his eyes flickered. She wasn't going to respond to his comment that he wouldn't permit her. She could do what she damned well pleased. "I don't think Walker would lie about the job."

"He'd lie to his own mother about the weather if he thought it served any useful purpose."

"Oh, that's too bad," she said in mock disappointment. His unguarded reaction had told her what she needed to know. A smile tugged at her lips.

He stood and paced across the room, wondering if Emily was deliberately trying to drive him mad. She couldn't have meant it, could she? Ross stared at her assessingly.

Emily rose and moved next to him, then hesitated near his desk.

He cursed fluently under his breath. There, in full view, was her dossier with her name on it in block printing.

"What's this?" Her voice was very quiet.

"Your file. Walker gave it to me yesterday."

Her dark blue eyes surveyed him. "I see. Did you ask for it?"

"I didn't have to."

"Why not?" she pressed.

"Because he knew I wanted it."

"Oh," she managed. "What does it say?" Her hand came out and touched the cover.

Ross drew in a deep breath, then let it out slowly. "More or less what I expected. You passed all the training exams with flying colors. You showed high intelligence, something of a temper, courage, and the ability to withstand stress. There was only one slight negative."

Her head cocked in mute inquiry. He was looking marginally more relaxed.

"Evidently you scared the driving instructor," he said smoothly.

"Hardly," she replied dryly. "He told me I was the best pupil he'd ever had."

"At terrorizing passengers?"

She waved a hand in airy dismissal. "Of course not. Anyway, I don't think I'll turn Walker down. Sounds like I'm an ideal candidate and so far I don't have a better offer."

She waited for him to follow that up. When he spoke, his words were direct.

"Why did you come here?"

Emily sighed. "To apologize. I was wrong to call you a coward, when I've been one myself all these years. I haven't reached out towards people. Instead, I've mentally accused them of rejecting me because of my intelligence. That hasn't been true. I've been the one pushing everyone away."

"You're apologizing?"

She could see the incredulity on his face. "Yes."

He was silent.

Emily felt like throwing something. She'd made every damned effort she could think of and he was motionless like one of those Easter Island statues. "I'm leaving," she said, pride coming to her rescue. The bastard deserved to be shot. She grabbed her purse and walked toward the door. His voice behind her jerked her to a halt.

"I surrender."

"To what?" she said, without turning.

"To you."

"Meaning?"

"I want you. I would have been on a plane this afternoon to New York. I just got back a couple of days ago. My temper has been vile, everyone has been telling me I'm not fit to be around. I need you to keep me sane."

Emily faced him and saw in his face what she'd been waiting for. "I don't know about that," she said, putting one hand on her hip, and staring boldly at him. "Convince me you mean it." With satisfaction, she saw two spots of color leap to his cheekbones.

"I'll convince you all right," he muttered, before reaching for her. "I love you, and you're going to marry me if I have to tie you up." He looked down. "Might not be a bad idea at that. You at my mercy."

"Sounds kinky," she agreed, turning into his arms. "What are we going to do about Walker?"

"We'll work out something. I've been thinking about a desk job for a while anyway. You could teach new recruits. That way we'd have enough time to take trips back to Texas. I saw how much you missed it. We'll both get claustrophobic on occasion up here if we don't get away once in a while."

"Are you sure?" She leaned back against his grasp. "I don't want to force you to do anything you don't want to."

"Of course not," he murmured mockingly. "You've only managed to drive me out of my mind for weeks. Why should a little coercion be a problem?"

"Coercion?" she asked, smiling.

"Yep. The Walker stunt was a good one. You sandbagged me like an expert."

"Oh. Well. You do what you gotta do."

"I couldn't agree more. By the way, I love you more than I imagined I could love anyone. So are you ready to accept my offer?"

The brilliance of her smile lit the room. "Yes."

"And?"

"And I believe I understood the terms," she said primly, her eyes dancing, "and have a few conditions of my own."

"Hurry up, you're running out of time."

His mouth was closer and she placed a hand on his chest, feeling the familiar tingle coursing straight to her heart.

"You have to tell me I'm wonderful at least five times a day, kiss me senseless more than that, and make love to me until we're exhausted. You've made me insatiable."

"Deal," he said, and then his mouth covered hers.

With a smooth, powerful movement he lifted her in his arms and walked toward the bedroom, pressing kisses on her uplifted face, stopping every few feet for another kiss.

He laid her gently on the bed. Clothes flew in a wild

tangle to land on the floor. Her shoes had fallen off enroute to the bedroom.

"At last," he said, his mouth moving over her.

The heat in the room intensified as Ross let his hands stroke the body of the woman he loved. Emily was panting, her eyes glazed when at last he slid into her welcoming warmth.

"I can't believe you made me wait three weeks," she got out as he thrust gently against her.

"It was necessary," he mumbled between kisses. "To make me smart enough to realize I deserved you."

"You're just a lucky guy," she said and he could feel her mouth and hands tormenting him, as he struggled for control.

"I know." Then he took them over the top.

SHARE THE FUN . . .
SHARE YOUR NEW-FOUND TREASURE!!

You don't want to let your new books out of your sight? That's okay. Your friends can get their own. Order below.

No. 17 OPENING ACT by Ann Patrick
The summer really heats up when big city playwright meets small town sheriff.

No. 18 RAINBOW WISHES by Jacqueline Case
Mason is looking for more from life. Evie may be his pot of gold!

No. 19 SUNDAY DRIVER by Valerie Kane
Carrie breaks through all Cam's defenses and shows him how to love.

No. 20 CHEATED HEARTS by Karen Lawton Barrett
T.C. and Lucas find their way back into each other's hearts.

No. 21 THAT JAMES BOY by Lois Faye Dyer
Jesse believes in love at first sight. Now he has to convince Sarah of this.

No. 22 NEVER LET GO by Laura Phillips
Ryan has a big dilemma and Kelly is the answer to *all* his prayers.

No. 23 A PERFECT MATCH by Susan Combs
Ross can keep Emily safe but can he save himself from Emily?

No. 24 REMEMBER MY LOVE by Pamela Macaluso
Will Max ever remember the special love he and Deanna shared?

Kismet Romances
Dept 1290, P. O. Box 41820, Philadelphia, PA 19101-9828

Please send me the books I've indicated below. Check or money order only—no cash, stamps or C.O.D.'s (PA residents, add 6% sales tax). I am enclosing $2.75 plus 75¢ handling fee for *each* book ordered.
Total Amount Enclosed: $_____.

____ No. 17 ____ No. 19 ____ No. 21 ____ No. 23
____ No. 18 ____ No. 20 ____ No. 22 ____ No. 24

Please Print:
Name_____
Address_____Apt. No._____
City/State_____ Zip_____

Allow four to six weeks for delivery. Quantities limited.